Swallowing
the Muskellunge

By Lawrence Patrick O'Brien

Mischief Makers
Swallowing the Muskellunge
Clochán

Swallowing
the Muskellunge

A Novel

LAWRENCE P. O'BRIEN

2025

Swallowing the Muskellunge
© 2025 by Lawrence P. O'Brien
www.lawrenceobrien.ca
LoonCE paperback edition 2025

LIBRARY AND ARCHIVES CANADA CATALOGUING IN PUBLICATION DATA

Swallowing the Muskellunge
O'Brien, Lawrence

ISBN 978-1-7778155-4-7 (hardcover)
ISBN 978-1-7778155-5-4 (paperback)
ISBN 978-1-7778155-6-1 (EPUB)
ISBN 978-1-7778155-7-8 (PDF)

I. United States—Canada—Black History—Immigration—Fantasy—Horror—1797-1801—Fiction
I. O'Brien, Lawrence II. Title

Swallowing the Muskellunge is a work of fiction. Any resemblance to actual events or persons, living or dead, is entirely coincidental. Although the Wrights, Oxford family and associates were historical characters, their journey north as written is purely fictional.

Cover design by Damonza.com
Published in Canada by LoonCE

Dedicated to my Grandmothers

My maternal great-great-grandmother Catherine St. John arrived at Montreal, which is an island in the St. Lawrence River, with none but her sister. Her sister got separated and was never seen again. Alone, she settled next to Devine Creek, which connects to the Bonnechere River which feeds the Grand River.

My maternal great-great-great-grandmother, Mary Johanna Kissane, who lost her husband came to the area with eight children. They settled near the Bonnechere River which feeds the Grand River.

My paternal great-great-grandmother, Margaret Dunne, left her husband, with a promise to meet him on the other side. She, unfortunately, died en route. Their daughter died at sea, she on an island across from Quebec City, and her husband in Ireland. The women died of cholera, and he likely of typhus. Three remaining children and an aunt settled in the township of Templeton, near to London Oxford's promised land. They settled next to the Blanche River that feeds the Grand River.

"....in the end nature does not belong to us, we belong to it."
Tales of an Empty Cabin
by Wa-Sha-Quon-Asin (Grey Owl)

"Disobedience is the true foundation of liberty.
The obedient must be slaves."
Aesthetic Papers
by Henry David Thoreau

PART 1: Pulling Roots

Missing

The blood-red eyes of the loon were captivated by shadowed wisps lit by the sunset's tangerine glare.

Maybe they're gone, he thought.

There hadn't been any lines of flying wings overhead for days. It was true enough that the nights were too long, breath steamed in the morning cold, and there was a fear he would be lost without them, but still, he hesitated.

Because they wouldn't be coming, he pouted.

But there was the taste of perch and crayfish from this special spot—easy pickings. And then there was a muskellunge to consider—wasn't there?

The loon fed in a small cove upriver from a cascading, cauldron-like waterfall. They had stopped here for several seasons. It was at the torrent of the river's edge where they lost her.

An outline of something near the surface caught his eye, so he dove for it. He returned to the surface and took a breath, enjoying the moment. He moved his head back to let his squirming catch slide slightly. As he bit down, he felt the small fish nervously pulsate.

Such an inviting taste—that long and slippery, he thought.

He plunged it into the water and drew down on it tight. Below the surface, he released his grip, and his meal twisted, trying to pull away.

With a wiggle and another bite, he swallowed it headfirst. Despite the fat belly and prickly barbs, he gulped it whole. Returning to the surface, he felt the small bass slither within his gorged neck. With a last, big gulp, he swallowed it away.

The loon raised his black head with the long, sharp beak, puffed out his white chest, and fluttered grey, white-spotted wings. His tongue savoured the lingering flavour of the smooth, fishy slime.

Alluring, he thought.

Reflecting on his next delectable preference, he wondered, *A little musky or maybe a long, wily pike. Either. Why not?*

A gentle kick enabled a turn. Not quite finished with his last course, though, he regurgitated, and a wiggly tail tickled his gullet. With a rise of his beak, he swallowed again.

The sheen across the water made him want to sing, so that's what he did.

He fixed on a spot to dive, but hesitated. A nearby island caught his attention. That's where he noticed the flutter of her wings. It was her place. It appealed to her because she believed it was safer and better. But he preferred where he and their chicks were. He liked to dive for what was in the deep and the weeds. She had ignored him for many sunrises.

That day when she fluttered, he remembered thinking, *Not right. She's nervous.*

He called her, but she continued to ignore him. Still, she flapped wildly.

He had been so distracted by this that the small eel he had in his beak managed to wiggle away. Without saying anything to him, she had flown away.

He saw some men-creatures behind tall shoreline grasses. Afraid she wasn't being careful, he reluctantly decided to follow and warn her. He called a predator warning to the chicks, telling them they needed to keep close.

He drove into the wind, racing his feet across the river and flapping his wings with all his might to catch up to her. Once in the air, he followed her arc east to follow the line of the river shore. Having a full belly meant he had to flap hard.

He watched men follow her flight path with raised sticks in their hands.

When she passed overhead, he heard a series of loud, repeating cracks.

Her flight twisted left, but she didn't glide out. She rolled, and the spinning continued into a fall. Shocked and stressed from flapping to reach her, he levelled his flight and watched her disappear into the river.

The men with smoking sticks standing onshore made crowing-like sounds. From one, he heard—"What?" It was like the echo of a raindrop into a shallow, stone-cupped pool. Above him, there was something even stranger.

Men high in broken trees flapped their arms, and there was a sound of . . . "all mine."

They walk. They don't do that, the loon thought. *They don't fly.*

"Thar," one of them said.

The figures continued to make babbling sounds.

"Damn you. He got it," said one.

"Mister Wright!" another yelled.

"Leave it," a tree walker croaked as he again motioned like he had a broken wing.

After circling, he caught sight of her motionless body being dragged by the steady-moving current to the end of the river. Flapping closer, he watched for ripples that a muskellunge makes before showing their teeth and terrible eyes. She looked so helpless.

When he passed across the cauldron waterfalls, he tasted the mist and felt the river's spirit echo across his body. He flapped back as he saw her pass over the river's edge. He flew round and round, but nothing came from the froth and the falling sound.

He was horrified and wanted to know where she had gone.

The loon called and called. He waited and waited. *Where was she?*

He remembered returning to the cove where his chicks were. From there, he called, called, and called. His distress song echoed long after the tree walkers left.

Now, the loon dunked his head in the water and blinked. Again, he pondered—*a little musky or maybe a long, wily pike?* Both were risky. He would have to swim among the weeds for a pike and into the black depths for a musky. The little ones he could have, but the big ones, without difficulty, would devour him.

The loon remembered witnessing another thing that haunted him. It was not many sunsets after he lost his mate.

It was at the same feeding place but on a different side of the cove. As ripples washed through the tall shore grasses, a swarm of shadow creatures emerged from the water. They appeared and moved like a flock of black ravens. They were tall, thin, two-legged, human-like, and screeched strangely.

He recalled witnessing his chicks rush back to him in a hurry. He had quickly tucked them under his wings and paddled back with them into deeper waters. When he gave a distress call to warn her to stay away, he had forgotten she was gone.

The shadow creatures hurried up the riverbank and attacked something. "Wìsakedjàk," the creatures repeated. It was a human they called to until he was taken down. When the victim's feet stopped moving, the attackers relaxed. The swarm of them drew close to the body. The loon licked his lips. The sight of uneaten food made him hungry. The oldest chick with light brown downy chest feathers managed to swim away from his protection.

A couple of beasts stumbled forward. The human, who was severely beaten, managed to get up, and again the shadows chattered loudly. They moved about quickly beyond the river shore's shrubs. When he rose, he stood taller than some shrubs. It had become something different and, judging by the others' wails, must have been monstrous. It began smashing the black things against rocks with their limbs twisting and cracking in ways they weren't supposed to. One was thrown and rolled back into the river. Others had holes punched into them.

The loon quickly paddled in front of his chick and hurriedly attempted to nudge it away from shore. When he turned around, he saw that all the remaining shadow creatures had fallen. The dreadful thing seemed to shrivel. When it squatted on the shore, it looked like a human being again. He remembered it staring at him.

He tightened his wings around the chicks and quickly paddled away from shore. When he turned, a fish in the air magically appeared. He was caught by surprise and let it go. He noticed that the creature had waded into the water and was bent down and staring into the water. The human—the Wìsakedjàk—threw him another small perch. He scooped it up before it wiggled away. When he looked back, the man had disappeared.

A day after seeing the shadow creatures, the loon witnessed what haunted him most. He saw the huge, sharp teeth first. His long, slender tongue licked the side of his beak. And then came its big eyes. The muskellunge took the little ones. The loon remembered attacking and defending. Without his mate to help protect them, it got all of them.

He called out again. He called. He called and called. To hear his echo over and over again was all he could do.

And now, in this new season, with darkness descending, he still recalled that sweet taste. The human being threw it to him, and he got it. Throughout the night, the loon dreamed of the Wìsakedjàk destroying what had taken his mate and imagined a day when he would swallow that muskellunge.

—❦—

From the blackness within Missa Wright's barn, London Oxford stared at the bright, vacant roadway beyond the property line.

"They's leaving," London whispered as he heard someone slam Missa Wright's entrance door.

The barn was behind Missa Thomas's house. The front door was on the other side.

The silhouette of London's son, Abner, stopped at the barn's entrance. "What's that, Poppa?" he asked.

"Nothing. I was just remembering something."

"Like what?"

"Just don't feel like myself," London said as he hung the horse's breast collar harness and bridle on the wall.

"Momma says you need to come in."

"I hear yah. Just finishing up is all."

Abner kept staring.

"I's all right. Just leave me with her. I'll be in when I'm done."

After his son left, he wiped the horse down. With the brush in hand he wiped sweat off his thick black eyebrows and woolly hair. With his forearms resting on the back of the horse, he stared at his dark forearms.

To get muscles to sling an axe and rip things out, that would be different, wouldn't it? he wondered. Telling folks and knowing things was right and good, but to stretch these arms for more and build them so he could hold on to what he had would be better. Just like them Wrights—to have a place of his own and sow what he could own. He wiped his scruffy beard with the back of his hand, and then his nose.

There was a hunger in him, and he desperately needed to get out of that house. It made him feel like he was going to starve.

He caressed the horse and then bent down to pull back a blanket. The horse's ear twitched. London grabbed some hidden carrots.

"Thought I forgot," he said, as he looked her in the eye and gave her some.

"If she's going to escape first, we'll have to fly off after her, won't we?" he asked as he grabbed another to munch on for himself.

Clatter

Thomas took another contented suck from his father's long clay pipe. He wore a buttoned brown frock coat with a black tie around his white linen collar. His woollen breeches and stockings that reached just below the knee were light-coloured. He was in his mid-thirties, which was a year older than his brother. His sister Elizabeth, being their father's favourite, of course, had two years up on him.

His wife, Mary, sat in a chair next to him. Her gown was light brown. The sleeves reached just below the elbows. A cotton kerchief with a mix of cream, red, and light brown streaks that was tucked in at the front of her gown gently draped around her neck, and she wore a ruffled linen cap. She impatiently waited for things to settle so that they could begin distributing the food.

It was early afternoon in the fall of 1796, and the Wright family was gathering together to discuss their father's will. Thomas Wright Senior had died the year before.

The Woburn family household was less than ten miles from Bunker Hill, which overlooked Boston Harbour. Only eight years had passed since Massachusetts joined the American Union and thirteen years since the American Revolutionary War ended, and the Wright boys were discussing leaving.

Thomas's sisters, Elizabeth and Eleanor, sat across from their brother on the living room sofa. Elizabeth wore a black gown, a silk bonnet, and laced boots that covered her ankles. Eleanor, who was the youngest by a couple of years, was dressed in dark green, along with a white linen cap that was similar to Mary's.

The group waited impatiently for their brother Philemon. He had returned from an exploratory excursion to the north country. Thomas Jr. laid out their father's will on a table next to his chair as his servant, London Oxford, escorted his brother and his wife from the front door.

In the kitchen, Jane Oxford eyed a cluttered counter and asked, "Where is that man? He'll be the death of us yet." She squeezed one-year-old Rachael as she removed freshly baked loaves from the fireplace. Lacking space on the counter, she put them on the kitchen table.

London, her husband, escorted Philemon and his wife past the kitchen toward the rest of the family. From the hallway, she overheard Missus Abigail ask, "London, have you talked to Jane about leaving?"

"Uh, no, Missus Wright. We're serving biscuits in the sitting room," he replied, and tried to rush them ahead.

Jane backed up and bumped her tea. The cup and plate spun off the counter and smashed into pieces on Missa Thomas Wright's kitchen floor.

Filled with a rant of curses but muffled by her daughter's inquiring stare, Jane was forced to take a deep, unsatisfactory breath. She set Rachael down against the wall so she could pick up the broken porcelain.

Annie, who sat at the kitchen table in the centre of the room, was stunned by the crash. She had her hands by her cheeks. Her mother put a finger to her lips, and Annie twisted to check the entrance to the hallway.

Jane knew her son, Abner, heard the crash, but he had pretended not to. Only the tail of his shirt and a bent leg in the door opening were visible. He was watching his father serve food to the Wrights down the hall. *Likely wondering if he'll sneak another biscuit,* she thought. *And if he can get more from him, too.*

She placed the broken pieces of the teacup on the counter and put a towel over it. After picking up her little girl, she took a tempting sniff of her fresh baking.

"Are we going to get it? Is Missa Thomas—" asked three-year-old Annie.

"You finish what's in front of you," her mother replied.

"Can I have some?" Annie asked as she stared at the fresh loaves placed in front of her.

"It's for the drawing room. It's for Missa Thomas, his brother, and sisters. Nothing else if you don't eat what's in front of you. You know that."

Jane sat back at the table and tried to feed Rachael another spoonful of mush. The daughter, like her mother, was distracted.

"Abner, you come here now and settle yourself down. Do you hear?" Jane ordered.

"In a minute," Abner replied. He was eight years old, with a mop of black hair, and had a boundless craving for testing limits.

Rachael grabbed porridge from the bowl and licked it off her hand.

"If you're going to have your supper—to the table, now!"

Jane looked down. Rachael stared up at her.

"Don't you make a happy face. No, no. No happy face," she taunted as she put the spoon down, grinned, and wiped Rachael's hand on the cloth draped across her shoulder.

Abner stepped back into the kitchen door frame. "Yeah," he said while unsuccessfully trying to pluck a bit of tree sap off his fingers.

"Don't," ordered Jane as Annie pivoted in her chair toward her brother. "He's coming."

Leaning his back against the kitchen doorway, Abner continued to stare down the hall. "No, he's not. I can see him. He's still setting the table," he said.

"Come on in here," ordered his mother.

"Missa Thomas is telling his brother and sisters something about a drunken cow," Abner said.

"It's his brother, Philemon," Jane said as she gave Rachael another spoonful of porridge.

"No, it's not. How do you know?"

"If it was Thomas, you'd hear the high-pitched voice of his sister Elizabeth. She's louder than anything. For the younger brother, not so much. She knows enough to mind."

"I can hear the hollering all the way from here," said Annie.

"Missa Philemon is having a fine time, isn't he?" their mother said. Looking at Rachael, she said, "And if it were you, I wouldn't put it past you," and laughed. "You'd love to tell everybody your mind."

Rachael turned her bowl to her mother to show that it was empty as she stared at the trays on the counter.

"Your father's coming for those. Bread and some nice apple jam is what I got. Like some?"

Rachael stared up at her mother, who, in turn, lightly flattened her nose and placed some bread in her bowl. With her hand, she beckoned Abner to come in.

The boy backed out into the hall, and his father, London, rushed past him into the kitchen.

"The tea and trays—just give me a minute," he said as he left out the back door.

"London, where are you going?" Jane said. "Abner, you get here this minute."

"It's the mare," London said, and the kitchen door quickly closed behind him.

"Abner, set yourself down," Jane ordered.

—❧⚬—

Thomas didn't get up when his brother and wife entered the living room. London took their gloves and Philemon's hat.

Philemon wore woollen grey breeches and an unbuttoned frock coat. Abigail wore a ruffled linen cap similar to the other women. Her linen gown was blue. The skirt reached above the ankles, revealing matching stockings and leather buckled shoes.

Thomas pointed to the sofa where their sisters were seated. Once the couple was settled, he asked, "Did you check the mine?"

"You know I just got back. Can't keep the girls waiting, can we?"

"Don't be presumptuous, Philemon," Elizabeth said.

"We could go out for a walk in the bush and take a look if you like," Philemon added.

"Boys, try to be civil, for once," said their sister, Eleanor. "Let's get on with this."

"Captain Symmes and my Job are with the children outside, in case you were wondering."

"It's the horses. They want the horses," Thomas said. Feeling Elizabeth's eyes drill into him, he added, "London's in the kitchen. Let's have some patience."

She anxiously looked toward the hallway, then asked the ladies, "How's the new deacon?"

At that point, Thomas watched his brother get up and start a walkabout.

After wiping her nose with the back of her porridge-spoon hand, Jane waved the spoon at Abner. "That's enough," she said. "I don't want to have to come over there. Come here and finish your breakfast."

Abner stepped through the kitchen doorway but got distracted by the screaming and hollering behind him. The commotion came from beyond the house's front door. As Abner stepped back, the front door slammed open, and a cacophony of twisting figures stormed in.

Philemon's children tried to tear past Missa Thomas's eight-year-old, Polly. A six-year-old smashed Abner against the wall. As she bounced away from him, her five-year-old sister squeezed her way between.

The six-year-old, with a green bow wrapping a ponytail, rushed until she crashed into the kitchen table, causing Abner's cup and dinner bowl to fall, break, and splatter across the floor.

Polly tried to hop over the mess but plowed into Annie's chair hard, slipped, landed on her butt, and cut her hand on broken porcelain. She leaped up and pushed her tall, thin older brother out of the way. Holding his jacket's lapels, the dazed boy took another breath and headed out.

Once Abner found his balance, he heard Missus Elizabeth Wright's nine-year-old, Betsy, groan, "Useless," and then, "Coon, out of my way," as she elbowed his head against the kitchen door frame. Cousin Abigail, who was in pursuit, laughed. Betsy avoided the mess on the floor but followed the ones ahead, yelling, "No chance." She reached for the tails of the boy's black wool jacket, but he pulled away.

Abner spun around, groaning. Standing in front of him, three-year-old Ruggles told him, "You're it." He laughed and chased after the others.

Abner was crying and holding his head when Missus Elizabeth Wright, who almost tripped on him, lifted her skirt as she pounded in.

"What in tarnation?" she said as she stared at the line of porridge on the floor. "What's wrong with you people? This looks like a barn. If my father were alive, no way would he put up with this."

Annie pushed away from the table and ran after the others.

Philemon Wright, who had followed his sister, stared at Abner, who had slunk to the floor and was grasping his knees.

"That's no way to handle this, Abner," Philemon said. "Go get some air. Ruggles. Yes, go take care of Ruggles. Make yourself useful."

"But—" he said.

"No. No, Abner. It's best. Your ma has things to deal with. Now go. Go before I find some real work for you." He waved him away and pointed to the kitchen door.

Jane Oxford looked on but was distracted by a bawling Rachael.

As Abner headed outside, wiping his tears, Missus Elizabeth asked, "Where are the other trays, girl? Really. I don't know why my brother keeps you people here."

Pointing, Jane said, "It's right there on the counter, and there's two trays of sorted meats and breads next to the tea set."

"A firmer hand is what's needed," Missus Elizabeth complained as she lifted one of the food trays. "And that London. No sense at all. Really."

After she left, Rachael's handful of mushy porridge splattered onto the shoulder of her dress. "Maybe I should get your father to do this," Jane said as she tried to feed her another teaspoon of porridge.

The kitchen door opened, and her husband came in. "What's Abner doing outside?" London asked.

Jane pointed the spoon with porridge at him like a weapon a couple of times. Her lips mouthed the words—**Don't you**.
When he stepped back, he found something mushy stuck to his foot.

"Don't get up. I'll get this." He hobbled toward the garbage bin and wiped his shoe. On his knees, London quickly grabbed some broken pieces and bits of apple bread.

She saw a reflection of the kitchen fire in his eyes as he mischievously gobbled a small piece of bread. "You've got to go. It's that Missus Elizabeth," Jane said.

London cut himself as he quickly picked up more pieces. He dropped what he collected into the garbage and sucked at his cut. He attempted to pick up a food tray and a tea set.

"Just a minute," Jane said. She pulled a cloth out from her décolletage. She wrapped some biscuits and pastries in it and handed the bundle to her husband.

He looked stunned. "But—"

"They're not all for you," she said, gently rocking Rachael. "Abner hasn't eaten."

"That's fine." He kissed Annie and told Jane, "I'd rather have a taste of where they're from, anyway," then smiled.

"Don't let them see," she ordered.

With a look down, he nodded. After wiping his cut with a piece of the cloth, he slipped the wrap into his shirt above his belt. He primly buttoned his jacket and subconsciously licked part of his lip.

Jane bobbed Annie on her knee as she watched him pick up the prepared trays again and march off again towards the Thomas Wright's drawing room.

—⁂—

What did I miss? London thought as he placed another tray and a tea set on the dining room table. *Jane was mighty riled. The boy not having something to eat; that's hard to imagine.*

As he sorted the plates and cutlery, he looked at the Wrights in the adjoining room. They were gathered in a modest drawing room. Small, pastoral oil paintings hung on the walls. Philemon and his wife sat on the couch under the windows. The window view overlooked the Wright's harvest.

Elizabeth shooed Eleanor out of their mother's chair. Eleanor reluctantly sat on the couch next to Philemon and his wife, Abigail. Thomas sat in his father's chair. His wife, Mary, sat in a chair at his left. Elizabeth's chair was on his other side but close to the couch. The three chairs angled away from the guests on the couch so they could face the lit fireplace on the far wall. A large, half-circle oak table was centred in the middle. Thomas tried to scratch something off the ankle of his boots.

"You're going to wear a hole in it," Elizabeth complained. "Put on some bootblack. Father wouldn't be amused."

"Elizabeth. Don't," Thomas replied.

London noticed Philemon eyeing something on the dining room table. *Cream or cheese. That's it. There's none. Any moment he's going to bite into me.*

"Why isn't Sarah here? Did you ask her?" asked Eleanor.

"Eleanor, Eleanor," complained Thomas.

"And?" she added. "Not interested, I suppose," Eleanor said. "Our half-sister, I'm sure, exchanged goodbyes at the funeral. She got what she wanted from the will. So now there's just the four of us. Isn't it time to move on?"

When London returned with another couple of food trays, Philemon was presenting a tray of assorted meats to his sister, Eleanor.

"Philemon, what are you doing?" asked Elizabeth. "Where's—"

"I'm right here, yessum," London replied as he placed an assortment of cheeses, preserves, and tarts on the dining room table. From there, he brought over a tray with an assortment of breads, fruit slices, chutneys, and jams to the guest's table. Next, he placed the teapot and tea settings on the table. He poured her some tea.

"That will be fine, London," she told him. "Take care of that young lad of yours, will you please?" and scooted him away with the back of her hand.

"Elizabeth, don't," said Thomas. "I'm sure Jane can take care of it."

Philemon grabbed the teapot and asked Eleanor, "A little more?"

She nodded.

"London, let Jane know you'll be out when you're done," said Thomas, and casually waved the back of his hand.

London brought some folded napkins to the table. As he was leaving, Philemon put the teapot down on the table.

"What was that about?" Thomas asked.

His wife got up out of her chair and poured him his tea.

"Philemon's children were rather rambunctious. One of them bumped into young Abner. Got a bad bash. Philemon made a mess of things, as usual."

"Elizabeth, you're being rude and definitely not fair," Philemon replied.

"For Lord's sake?" Thomas asked. "It's a lot of nothing. Leave it, please."

London, who stood in front of the entrance to the hall, tightened his fist and bit the side of his lip. "Damn," he softly muttered. He went back to the kitchen and, without saying a word or looking at his wife, returned to the sitting room with a tray of warm fruit pies.

After tasting another biscuit, Elizabeth added, "Well, boys, you're going to tell us about your investments, aren't you? Since Philemon got back, he's been pacing about like a proud peacock."

"Six hundred pounds sterling," Thomas said.

"Ahh, fresh pies," said Eleanor.

"Three waterfalls and more land than you can imagine," interjected Philemon. "We'll live like lords. We'll be masters of our own personal—"

"Kingdom?" asked Elizabeth.

"Fiefdom, maybe," said Philemon.

Eleanor pointed to her plate, inviting London to give her some pie.

"He told me, that he saw it from the trees," Thomas said.

"You're not one for climbing trees, Phil," Elizabeth said.

"I had my men cut some in half so we could walk up the angled tree fall. Quite safe, actually. The white pines in those parts are unbelievably huge. I was able to see above the trees on the other side, to the horizon. The land is on a powerful river not far from Montreal. It's a modern city, I'll have you know. I saw all of it, the falls, where we can build a town, and our pasture lands for miles and miles in many directions."

London served Eleanor and Philemon. He had to lean toward Philemon to serve his wife's plate. Philemon tripped him as he backed away. London stumbled and recovered, but the tray and the remaining pies fell to the floor.

"Terrible. Terrible. Eleanor, that almost landed on your dress," said Philemon.

"Now, Phil, that was just an accident," she replied.

London turned to look at Thomas.

"Get on with it, London," he ordered. "And have Jane heat up a couple more. Phil, what were you saying?"

As London scooped the mess off the floor, Eleanor said, "They're French, you know."

"I said it was near Montreal. Not in it," said Philemon. "Some speak French, but gentlemen speak English, and the crown rules, even there."

"So, it's somewhere cheap and in the middle of nowhere," said Elizabeth.

"It's on the Grand River," said Philemon. "It will be a powerful place, and it won't be nowhere. As long as we're willing to put shoulders to the plow, we'll make of it whatever we want."

"Here, here," demanded Thomas. "And it's an exaggeration to say that the place is in the middle of nowhere. Settlers from these parts have already built towns and villages along the St. Lawrence River. The land is less than a three-day march north."

"How do you know if it's safe? What about savages?" asked Eleanor.

"Eleanor, they're not the Iroquois, and it's not the Mohawk Valley," Thomas said.

"But don't tell me there aren't savages there."

"On any uncultivated land, there's going to be Injuns somewhere," Philemon replied.

"Frightful," Eleanor replied.

"We will be well-armed, and they won't bother us as long as we do God's work," said Philemon. "And there's enough fish, birds, and game for everyone. Besides, where we will be, no one else will care."

London returned to the kitchen with the remains of the splattered pies. To Jane, he said, "Philemon."

"What's that?" Jane replied.

"Three more," he said. "I need three more, and I've got to go."

"Fine," she said. "If Rachael settles down, I'll bring them in. Well, don't just stand there. Go. Get out," she ordered.

London returned to the drawing room. He topped up the teacups of Thomas and his wife and offered more apple bread and cheeses.

"I told you that my husband has more important things to do," said Elizabeth.

"If Captain Symmes persuades other men in arms to join us, wouldn't that alleviate some of your concerns, Eleanor?" asked Thomas.

"That's pretty presumptuous of you," said Elizabeth.

"Elizabeth, I meant nothing . . . I was—"

"My husband and I are satisfied where we are. I understand you want more land for the boys, but with a captain's pension and my inheritance, I don't see how it would be something we'd consider. And, if you buy up the land, how are you going to make a profit?"

"We'll get a percentage of what they grow and sell it," said Philemon.

"Will they pay rent?" Elizabeth asked.

Philemon fiddled with his watch. "We're working out the details."

"Personally, I am more confident when we manage our own investments," said Elizabeth.

"Elizabeth, don't look at me like that," said Eleanor. "Job and I just got married. Phil, it's foolish that you boys would expect us to go along with this frightful idea. No interest from other families, and you're asking us to just get up and go."

"What are you talking about? I—we . . . Eleanor, you don't know what you're talking about."

"Phil, don't be like that," said Elizabeth.

"Eleanor, he knows what he's doing," said Abigail. "He has it all planned out."

"Of course he does, Abigail," said Elizabeth, who took another bite of a biscuit.

"Thomas, are you going to bring the dogs?" Philemon asked.

"No. They won't be able to keep up," his brother replied.

"Are you going to leave the coloureds, too?"

"Phil, that is none of your concern," Thomas said. He gave his wife a quick look and then stared blankly toward the fireplace.

"Boys—" Elizabeth said.

"Where's that tea?" demanded Philemon, and got up and left the room.

As his wife got up to follow him, Eleanor waved the palms of her hands down and told her, "Leave him alone. He's out of sorts; that's all."

As London brought over more apple bread and cheeses, he heard the front door slam.

⟿⟬⟲

After the guests left, London placed a pile of trays on the counter and placed a hand on his wife's hip.

"Stop it," Jane protested. "Don't touch me."

London backed away.

An unfed kitchen fire was fading into cinders, and the candle on the table didn't light up much else. She ignored the cup of tea by her clenched fist. Rachael was asleep in the basket on the table next to the wall. Staring at the toddler, she said in a quieter voice, "He was going to go to bed without a bite. What was that about?"

"Well—"

"And you didn't give him the biscuits and cakes."

"But, Jane, I couldn't. They had me—"

"Didn't want to make them think you're getting fat?"

"But Jane—"

As he tried to touch her again, she told him, "And don't you **Jane** me."

"I'll bring it up—"

"He's asleep, and I took care of it already. And when you heard the holler'n, why weren't you there?"

"I didn't. I was outside. And they had guests. What was I gonna do?"

Jane went to take a sip of her tea, but gave a sour face. In a low voice, she said, "And those damn Wrights . . ."

Before she could finish, he said, "Jane," then looked both ways to see if they were overheard. "Girl—you keep that cussing to ya'self."

"Don't you tell me what I can and can't do. I know my own mind."

"That's the problem."

"That Philemon . . . The child smashed his head real bad. And what did they do? Sends him outside without even a bite or a good word. Not a bit of sense."

"Jane—"

"Don't you **Jane** me."

"I'll talk to him in the—"

"T'wasn't him. It was them. What are we going to do?"

"I got to talk to—"

"I mean they's going to leave," she interrupted. "What we gonna do?"

"What do ya mean?"

"Did they even tell you if we are going with them or even if they want us? Sure sounds like Missus Abigail wants us to leave."

"I just figured Missa Thomas is a good man."

"Philemon and his sister, they're something else."

"Jane, there's worse. We knows there's lots worse. I could ask Missa Thomas if he could ask another farmer if he needs help around here. Might not be able to do all we do around here."

"Where are they going?"

"I wonder if they know themselves. They bought someplace for a big heap of money. After buying it, only one of them looks at it. Their sisters are afraid of Injuns."

"Philemon," said Jane, "that one has no sense."

"There's work on the docks in Boston," London said, "but is it safe?"

She looked up at her husband and said, "Don't know. Sometimes you got a head like a block of wood. They might just knock it off, and that wouldn't be good for me."

"Maybe not." He scratched the back of his head. "But there'd be coloureds for the children."

"Not many like us on Sundays. Be different there. There's that," she said.

"So, if they take my head, y'all feel right 'cause you can pray on it. That right?"

"You go talk to Thomas. More I think on it, the more it's clear those boys have no sense. All those children. Think of that," said Jane.

"You're back to that Missus Elizabeth again? She's got eight."

"No. I mean, like, the oldest of those boys is Phil Junior, and he's only thirteen. Five children for Thomas and six for Philemon. That's a handful to bring to Injun country."

"You thinking of our children living with Injuns?"

"The Godforsaken? Of course not. But I have heard there are coloureds up there somewhere."

"Some folk say it's not like the South," London said.

"I do believe those Wright boys need us. Do we need them? That's the question."

"Are you coming?" asked London.

"Leave me to my tea. I have to clean up." She shooed him away.

Realizing he had just gotten out of having to help her clean up the kitchen, he quickly slipped away.

While taking a quiet sip, Jane mulled some more about how she was going to bury Missa Wright's broken dinnerware without getting caught. *For our broken kitchen dishes—no matter,* she thought. *But for their nice dinner dishes, Lord Almighty—there'll be hell to pay, and they'd be unforgiving.*

London followed the hallway to the children's bedroom. When he raised the lantern in hand, he saw the reflection of fiery red eyes on his dark face.

Missa Philemon is telling them all about how good the land is that he is promising to get them, thought London. *He knows as well as I do that he doesn't own any of it. The deed is worthless. So why is he trying to fool all these folks?*

In the children's bedroom, he saw that Abner and his sister were still but breathing gently. The moonlight emanated into the bare room from the sides of a thick blanket that covered the window. Sparse shadows stretched across small, scattered shoes, a floor mattress, and clothes hung on nails.

Their father crouched down. He was hesitant with guilt. London was supposed to say something, but couldn't or just didn't want to. He couldn't own whichever was true.

Wasn't right they was picking on him, he thought. *And her sending him out without having something to eat. Won't things ever change?*

Feeling the food in his pocket, he thought of putting it down beside the boy like she asked, but he knew the mice would get it there first. After passing his hand through Abner's hair, the boy rolled away, and his sister shifted slightly. London stood up, pushed his locks away from his forehead, and back stepped out of the room.

At the door, he pulled a cloth from his pocket. A dim light from the lamp shone on the remaining cake. He heard a run of tiny feet echo from inside the wall. As he took a bite, the scampering went up the wall and across the ceiling. Abner rolled back and away from his sister. London gulped the rest. He glanced back to the hallway before wiping his lips and putting the cloth back into his pocket.

Troubles

L
ondon Oxford was not a stranger to grief, b*ut just maybe the boy, like his momma, could get away from it,* he thought. *That's why we's going to town.* When asked how to get them from picking on him, he tried to help, but he knew he wasn't good at it. Jane told him so. She reminded him all the time. *Yes, she did.*

Abner and him were leaving at dusk to avoid anything that might cross them. *Not looking for trouble—no way,* he thought.

Jane's light in the kitchen shone through the open door into the barn. It lit up the traces. He made sure they were flat and not twisted. He aligned the reins for a straight trip to the bit and climbed up to his seat.

The door from the main house opened and smashed shut. He saw that the boy was wearing a wide-brim hat just like his pa. He had almost gotten away from her.

"Abner, open your arms wide," she ordered. "You'll need these. Some thick blankets to keep you warm." She filled his arms with blankets.

A big load for an eight-year-old, thought London.

When his son approached, London greeted him with, "What a strong feller you are." Looking up, the boy tried to stand taller as he raised his arms. His father put the blankets next to him. Looking his son in the eye, he said, "Abner, you're riding up front on Missa Wright's wagon with me," and then he lifted him up. He wiped the side of his nose as he checked to make sure she didn't hear.

After taking a secure hold of the reins and the whip, the horse's ears flicked back to listen.

"Missa Thomas needs some stuff in town. Abner, you ready?"

The boy nodded and pretended to flash a whip.

London drew the reins up so that there was a gentle, steady connection with the horse's mouth and tilted the whip slightly to the left over the horse's rear end.

London pulled the brim of his hat in acknowledgement. Sitting up straight, he gently braced his feet on the wagon floorboard, pulled slightly to the side, and gave a "Yaaah." As the wagon advanced, one of the other horses called out.

London could feel his back muscles work as the wagon shook. Keeping a grip on the reins with the first and third fingers, he raised his whip hand and blew Jane a kiss. He gave Abner a gentle nudge with his elbow. "Blow Momma a kiss. Make sure she hears."

Abner made it quick and wrapped a blanket around his shoulders.

This was their first trip together.

Boy's ignoring her, thought London. *Cause he's on a '**man's** trip'.* He smiled and gave the horse a light touch of the whip.

London was born a slave and wasn't free until the Wrights came and got him. 'As long as you're with us, you're free,' the Wrights had told him.

At the close of the Revolutionary War, the state made slavery for coloured and Injuns illegal. Massachusetts was the only state to make the rights effective immediately. A few other Northern states enabled similar freedoms gradually. Despite what white folk said, some landowners still kept slaves.

Even when you're free, no Massa would let coloureds leave, London thought. *Couldn't have no risk of damaging their property. No, sir. No way.*

Not many coloureds in these parts, though. Even less good ones, he thought. *Thank the Lord that Thomas is better to me than his father, and he knows he's done good in having fine Christian folk like me and my Jane.* London scratched his scraggly beard.

"Momma didn't want me to go with you," said Abner.

"It's not that she didn't want you to go," he said. "She just thought it might be too soon for me to take you along."

"But, Poppa, you need someone to help. I can help real good."

"I know you're right, Abner." He felt a nervous shudder come on.

Must be the cold, he thought. *It's just that to know what we can do, we have to do things. Well, maybe some prayin too; Jane does that best. She's full of prayin.*

The March wind from the east came cool and damp. It was just above the freezing point, but he expected to see more rain and maybe some snow.

Once the wagon came to a straight portion of the trail, London wrapped a blanket around himself to keep off the light rain. He made sure Abner's blanket covered his neck.

There weren't many farmhouses around the Wright's homestead, yet all the good properties were cleared and planted. They lived in a valley surrounded by gently rolling hills. The land was rocky in parts and covered with mixed forest.

"The Wright boys complain lots about how they can't get more good land," London said.

"Does that mean we have to move?" said Abner.

"They says there's too many people here."

"Any like me and Annie, where we're going?"

"Who says we're moving?"

Abner didn't reply.

"Probably not," said his father. "Your mother doesn't want to go. Don't think there are many coloureds up there." London pulled gently on a rein to guide the horse to the right to avoid a rough spot.

"But there's none like me here, neither," Abner said.

"That's something that your mother keeps telling me," London said. He scratched his beard and then asked, "How's the chickens doing?"

"That big Lady Red is really protective of her eggs. She's a scratcher."

His father laughed. "I think maybe she thinks she's too big for her rooster, and you're getting bit for it. Well, she is one big chunk of feathers."

They were quiet for a bit, listening as the rain pattered on.

"Abner, how is work in the kitchen?" London asked.

"Momma taught us to make chutney and pie."

"I'll bet it was some good."

Abner grinned. "Yes, it was. Abigail tried to have the pies thrown out because I touched them."

That's Philemon Wright's daughter all right, London thought. *She needs to have her way.*

"How was it handled?"

"Missus Mary gave her some chores to do."

That's Thomas's wife for you, London thought. *Philemon's going to be right put off by that. Have to watch these folks. More trouble coming.*

The sound of sleet falling on their wide-brimmed hats and shoulders was loud. As the horse pulled their wagon up the first hill, London gave close attention to anything that might be hiding behind rocks or trees.

They is a lot of men to manage, and he needs my help to run things, London thought.

Missa Thomas told him that if they go north, they'd have a small house and a plot of their own. 'More than a house,' he'd said. 'A whole town!' The way he talked, it was hard not to see the good of it.

And if his older sister Elizabeth and her Captain Symmes start giving orders, how will that be for us?

'Free to leave or stay,' he says. Thomas is not like his father. Soon he's going to sell, and there'll be nothing here.

When Abner looked up at him, London adjusted his son's collar to prevent water from running down the back of his neck.

"The old girl'd like something nice when we get there. There's carrots in the sack. We's almost there," London said.

After travelling about four miles northeast of the farm, a long, thin, and still lake showed itself on their left. It was called Horn Pond. A river from it flowed into town. The steep, forest-covered slopes behind were thick, dark, and green.

Two men on horseback lazily rode out from the trees. London brushed the left side of his hairy lip. *Keep going the other way is what I want,* he thought, and flicked the reins.

London passed two wagons leaving town. He tipped his hat to each, and they did in return.

Since it was early, there weren't many carriages or horses on the main street. When London hopped off the parked wagon, muck covered his boots up to his ankles. He lifted his son onto solid ground. When he reached the store counter, he said, "Hello, Missa Ainsworth. Missa Thomas Wright would like to buy these from you." He gave him the list of goods. "Apply it to his credit like usual. My boy is helping out today."

"Yes, sure, London," the store master said. His well-fed belly was bound by thick suspenders. His powerful hands swung a bag of flour up onto a shelf. "And you must be Abner," he said. "Your father is going to work you hard, I see. Are you ready?"

"Yes, sir," Abner replied.

"You're a good lad," he said. "I'll have Charlie bring them up to the front for you." He passed the list of his supplies to his assistant.

London double-checked the food items to confirm they were good quality. Abner took hold of a bag of sugar and started dragging it.

London stared at the storekeeper. "Mr. Ainsworth, do you have an axe or a pick?" he asked.

He gave a nod and came out with a couple of axes from the back storeroom.

London turned to his son, but he didn't see him.

"Abner, don't go out. You'll fall in the mud."

"We don't need none now. Missa Wright also wants to know if it be a problem to order us twenty thick winter blankets. How long would it take us to get some?"

"When does he want 'em."

"Sorry, don't know for sure."

"Next time you're in."

"Mighty obliged," London said.

He hauled two bags of flour. Abner's bag of flour lay in front of the door. London put his load down and yelled, "Abner." There was no call back.

From the open door, he saw a pair of strangers near his wagon, and Abner was sprawled under it. A hefty white man, with holes in his coat, was struggling to keep hold of one of Abner's boots. Abner was twisting in six inches of mud and shit. The other man, who was also solidly built, was holding the reins of a pair of horses.

London froze. "Missa Ainsworth. It's my boy! They's taking Abner. We need yah help. Missa Ainsworth, yah hear me?"

London wasn't a powerful labouring man, like some. He spent most days in the house and fixing the grounds. Come farming season, he and Thomas plowed and planted. He helped bring in the harvest, but he wasn't a mean fighting man, and he knew it. These two, as far as he could see, were used to making people suffer.

London marched toward the wagon and looked for a weapon. There were only two heavily soaked blankets and the bag of carrots behind his seat. He heard an "Ouch" and a splat. Abner must have kicked him.

"Want some help, Herv?" asked the man holding the horses.

The other man rolled out of the mud and brandished a long hunting knife. "Nah, I'll get the other one even if I have some cutting to do," he said.

London noticed that he had another knife sheathed at his belt.

"We'll get a good price for the boy," said Herv. "Maybe more if the other one comes along without too much trouble."

Abner was screaming and trying to roll away from the man's grasp.

London reached for a blanket, but Herv on the other side grabbed it first, threw it behind, and stomped it into the mud.

Mr. Ainsworth's teenage son came out with an axe at the ready. His father joined him with a metal bar and a large duelling pistol.

Abner managed to escape from under the wagon on the side across from the men. He tried to stand. Running didn't work, and the crying boy splashed flat on his back in the mud.

"Mr. Ainsworth, there will make sure you bleed out real nice tonight. You're not welcome here," said London. He helped his shaking son up and hugged him. The boy was covered with a thick mix of horseshit and mud.

"Herv?"

"What do you think, Bill?"

"I'd say the Negro goes down, but we're not going to reach the boy. Too much mud between them and us."

"Well—"

"London," yelled Mr. Ainsworth's son, and he tossed the axe to him.

It landed in the mud, where London picked it up.

Herv rushed back to join his partner.

The light rain turned into a downpour, and the vagrants rode away.

After watching the men leave, London carried his weeping and shaking son inside.

"Thank yah, Mr. Ainsworth," he said and squeezed Abner tight.

"Pa, what in the Lord's name were you gonna do with that piece of junk?" asked Mr. Ainsworth's son. "That probably didn't work when the British were here."

Mr. Ainsworth waved the pistol. "They didn't know that. Maybe time for something better." Before his son could reply, he ordered the boy to carry the supplies to London's wagon.

Once inside, Charlie brought London a couple of buckets of water and a rag so he could give his boy a quick wash-up. After the boy put on his boots, Mr. Ainsworth brought him a pair of blankets.

"Sure enough. Missa Wright will be good for that extra blanket, Mr. Ainsworth. Thank yeah kindly, sir."

"I should have his other nineteen next time you're by."

"If I lost him, I don't know what I'd have done," London said.

"I know how you feel, London," said Mr. Ainsworth. "There must be hard times out east for some. For some reason, we're seeing more bad types comin' through. There are good folk, and there are folk like them. Don't know what there's to do. Sorry, you've seen this."

London had him add more axes to the next order. When he carried his son back to the wagon, he dragged an axe through the mud.

Once out of town, London stopped the wagon and wiped his son's tears. He pulled him tight, and they rocked together. London kept telling him, "I'm sorry."

"But why? Why was they going to take us?"

"There's places that still pay money to get folk like us, that's why. And there's all sorts of bad people, but today, Mr. Ainsworth was a good man. In these times, it's difficult to tell where the monsters are." He readjusted his sobbing son's muddy hat and made sure the blankets covered his neck. "You're safe now. I don't expect to see those bad men again. Like Mr. Ainsworth said, it didn't look like they were from around these parts." Despite what he told his son, he didn't believe it. Before moving on, he carefully scanned the hills across the lake and the road ahead, looking for signs of trouble.

We got out of there only because they didn't have a gun and no resolve, he thought. *Law says I'm free, but I'm still not white. Do him harm, and no white folks would accept what I says over that white piece of shit. Damnation, a court could have locked us up in different jails. Could have sent us out of the state. Maybe sent us to different plantations. Momma and Mr. Wright might never have heard where we were,* he thought. *Mercy, we could have been lost forever.*

He gave the ground a spit and flashed the reins to move out. The lake looked dark and grim now. London, despite freezing hands, held his curled-up son close. The rain started to turn to sleet.

The horses' steps were strong and confident. The old girl doesn't seem to be put off much. Must have been the carrots. As long as she was given what she was promised. London considered biting into one, but after eyeing the forest, he would have preferred to kill something. When he checked the back of the wagon, he saw that the rain had washed off most of the mud, just leaving some streaks of shit. *Need to sharpen the axe when I get home,* he thought.

London tightened his grip on the reins and sat up. He stared at his son's muddy, shit-covered boots and said, "You make sure you take them off as soon as you get in and toast them by the kitchen fireplace. Your momma is going to help you with that. Maybe she's got some sweet bread. What do you think?"

Abner was staring down. "I don't know," he mumbled.

"You might be surprised to hear that something like this happened to my poppa. I've never told it to you before. The important thing is that if it hadn't happened, none of us would have been born." He stared into Abner's half-asleep eyes until the boy shook his head a couple of times. "I think I see a glimmer of life," London said and patted his son's back before putting a hand in his food pocket.

Drawing Circles

London dumped the kindling on the floor in front of the kitchen fireplace.

"I heard Missa Philemon say you's chopping too much wood," Jane said. "Way you's throwin' that axe, we'll have six cords in no time."

"Maybe he should go back to the Canadas," London said. "He could find himself something useful to do there. All I know is he likes talking and walking around and minding other people's business. You sayin' I should come in more?"

"You got to talk to Abner?"

"I'll try. I'll go see him. But the words don't come out." He bent down and neatly piled the firewood. "They're gone. Nothing I can do about it. Don't know what to say. I'm just no good at it."

"You need to try."

"Leave me alone."

Jane kept cutting carrots.

"You think Missa Thomas would treat his boy like that."

"Stop it."

"She's taking him to give him a piece of her mind," she said.

"Wha . . . what you talkin' about?"

"They's going on a walk. Saw them out the window.

"I'm not taking Abner to town again."

"I know," she says.

"Who you talking about?"

"When they have something they gotta say, they leave. Missa Thomas and his Mary."

"They'd be better to go to the crick on the other side of the hill then," said London.

"Then nothing would get done."

"What you mean? A lot would get done," said London. "Don't you remember?"

"London, teasing is all you do."

"I can think of a lot of ways a good man can help out," as he got off the floor.

"No. You finish that up. I got to finish this," she said. She put the carrots in a bowl, cleaned up and started folding a pile of rags. "Anyway, what's to become of the children when they're older?"

"Why you asking me that?"

"Missa Thomas's sister Elizabeth is giving him an earful, and she don't wanna listen. The boys, they got big plans. They's moving and no one else is crazy enough to go. All that money spent and no way to build everything, and it's Injun country. I'm sure his Missus Mary got lots to say."

"Still they's gonna move," London said. "You saying we should move to another state that has free Negroes like here?"

"We need to talk about what we're going to do," she replied.

"Then you talk to Missus Mary. Maybe they's not going." He got up and opened the door to go outside."

"Where you going?" she asked.

"To bring in some more wood," he said.

She didn't see him again until the next morning. He was on the floor and stunk of vomit and drink.

—◦◉◦—

Later that morning, Abner, along with some girls, was put to work crawling around in the dirt. He pulled up bigger root vegetables like squash, rutabaga, and cabbage and dropped them into baskets. Philemon's Maryanne, who was three years younger, and Thomas's Polly, who was his age, did the same with turnips, beets, and onions. The vegetable gardens were downhill from the main house and the barn.

"Why's they up there?" asked Abner. "They's supposed to be here."

"John and Bearie?" asked Polly. "Because they're being stupid."

Abner stared at the boys walking between the house and the barn on the hill. "They've got secrets, I'll bet," he said as he watched them whispering to each other.

The kitchen door flew open, and Abigail lifted her dark brown woollen skirt as she rushed down the slope toward them. She wore a long apron to protect her knees.

"Why does she have to come? I hate her," he said. With two hands, he pulled the remains of a plant and tossed them onto a pile.

After ripping out another plant and tossing it like Abner, Polly put her hands on her hips and asked, "So why do I have to be here with you?"

"Because the others don't like you, that's why," Abner replied. He rocked back on his heels as he pulled on another squash.

"You're going to get a licking; I know it," Polly said.

Abigail came over and knelt next to Abner.

"What are you doing?" he asked.

"Abner says he hates you," her sister Maryanne yelled to Abigail.

Abner looked at Abigail, hesitated, and then said, "That's not true."

"It is," said Polly.

"Well—" said Abner.

"Why don't you go?" Abigail asked. She, like her mother, had a hawk-like nose and wide-eyed stare that had a deliberate look that was fearsome when she got irritable.

"But—" said Abner.

Maryanne threw dirt at him, so Abigail did the same.

Abner grabbed a wad of squash leaves as he stood up and threw them at Abigail's head. They fell short.

Polly threw a handful of dirt and, like Abner, grabbed a wad of weeds. "Don't you dare," she said. Stop that right now, you hear?"

Abigail threw some beets, and they plopped off Abner's side.

Mrs. Oxford came running and yelled, "Stop it."

With a hand on Abigail's shoulder, she asked, "What's got into you both?"

"She started it," Abner yelled.

"No, I didn't," said Polly.

"He threw dirt. I saw him," said Maryanne.

"And is that what you're going to eat if nothing gets planted?" Mrs. Oxford said. "No sense. Get on with it. And those boys," she said as she eyed John and Bearie by the barn. "Think they're too good for this?" She waved them to come back as she marched back up the hill.

Abner moved to the next plot but faced the barn. He didn't hear what his mother said, but he could see her pointing in different directions. Whatever she said caused the boys to start running. John grabbed a wagon and hurried towards him.

Abner sat on the ground with his legs open and dirt in his hands.

"What are you doing?" Abigail scolded.

"Don't," replied Abner.

"Or what?" he said.

"Because," Abner said. He started digging in the dirt because he could see his mother following the boys back to the plot. When she got close, again she put a hand on Abigail's shoulder and said, "Abigail, you and Maryanne are going to do the next plot with Bearie. Abner, you work with Polly and her brother John here."

"But," said Maryanne.

"No way, Maryanne. If that's not done, there won't be anything to harvest. I'm telling you this is serious. Now get on with it. And you'll be more than glad if it's only me you'll have to talk to."

When Abner's mother was out of hearing distance, Abigail said, "I don't have to do what she says."

"I don't want to," whined Polly.

"Then you can go over there by yourself," John said.

"Lil Ab, do you think you can keep up?"

Abner just nodded and kept piling squash onto a pile. John piled the remaining parts of the plants into his wagon.

Polly reluctantly mimicked her brother.

⟶◉⟵

"You're looking better," Jane said.

"Your sweet potato pie," London managed to say before plowing in another bite at the kitchen table.

"I thought it was you outside, doing that chopping."

London spooned in another bite.

Rachael sat on the floor with a wooden spoon in hand. Annie stepped out toward the hallway.

"It was something terrible."

London pulled back his dish as if his wife was going to take it away. "Like what?"

Annie came back and kicked the wooden bowl next to her sister's foot to the wall.

"They found something," Jane said.

"Like?"

"Don't."

"Don't what?" as London looked around for some tea.

Jane shooed Annie away from her sister. She returned the bowl to Rachael.

"What?" asked London.

She stared at him and said, "The Wrights found something in the barn and—"

"So what is it?" London asked.

"I don't know. I heard Missa Thomas tell Missus Mary that Philemon's

Missus was awful distraught."

"'Cause why?" London asked.

"Didn't I tell you? I don't know."

"Did you ask her?"

"No. Did you hear about this?"

"Me. No." He stared at the last of his pie. Instead of asking for more, he carefully countered with, "So, they found something in the barn. Well, Missus Mary doesn't seem to know much. Bad calf, maybe?"

"Philemon's Missus is not going to give a torrent of tears for a calf."

"Well, Philemon might."

"Don't you go on. Don't. Just don't. You ask Missa Thomas. You let me know," Jane asked.

London quickly spooned the rest of his pie. "Could I have a spot of tea?" he asked.

Jane pointed to the wooden bowl that Annie was ignoring.

"You really can't let it go," said London. "I'm sure Missus Mary will be aching to tell you. Yeah, just—"

"It's something else, and it's terrible. I just know it."

"Well, if it's something else, that's dead, well, then, like what?"

Jane looked blankly at the table.

London looked at the pot of tea but figured it was too much trouble and said, "I gotta go. I gotta." He wasn't sure what he had to do, but he left before she asked him any more questions.

From within the darkness of Missa Wright's barn, Jane glared at her husband. "You never listen," she growled.

"Why is that?"

"But they's leaving," London said.

Jane left and headed back to the kitchen. London followed in pursuit.

Once inside, London asked, "So, how's moving to Boston better?"

"I know people," Jane said. There's a lady at church, and... Anyway, being with Negro folk is better. It's a lot better. And it doesn't have to be at the docks."

"You don't know that," London said.

"We'd still be free there," she replied as she moved plates on a shelf.

"I can get us some land to farm up there. I'll get me some cash money."

"Says who?"

"They've been making promises."

"Their word isn't worth spit."

"I'll talk to Missa Thomas. He hasn't been too bad to us," London said as he folded his arms.

"And that Philemon, do you trust him? He takes what he can get. And we's got our children."

"We'd still be free up there," London said and shuffled away from the kitchen door.

"What you know of that? It's not even this country."

"Maybe that's a good thing."

"Do you always believe what they tell you?" she asked as she grabbed a broom. "And you never listen to me."

"That's not true, girl. I listen to you a lot."

"Only when you want something. And what you're saying is not what I want. If I gotta take the girls, I will."

"I know we can get us work around here or there, but we's got to pay for a place to live. It's money we don't have. I'm sure going up there will be a lot better for us. Land is cheap, and there'll be lots of work. And those boys have been making a lot of promises."

"London Oxford, you haven't been listening to me."

The door London was leaning on started to shake. When London stepped out of the way, Tom Jr. stomped in. The boy looked down. He told London that his father needed to talk to him and that it was urgent. Jane knew then that someone or something had died.

—◦◉◦—

When London returned, Jane was busy rolling bread.

"So, out with it," she said after pounding the bread roll down on the counter.

"It's Abigail. Philemon's baby girl."

"What is it now?"

"She's dead," London said. "They's got me making a coffin for her. Say's she caught something."

"Lord Almighty," she said and stepped back. She wiped her hands on her apron.

"They found her in the barn."

"Was nothing wrong with her, when I's seen her," Jane said. "What was she doing in the barn?"

"I'd say she must have ate something, maybe poison, but they're all afraid of anyone touching her or seeing her even. And Missa Wright had her all wrapped up."

"There's something not right about this. Something bad. I can sense it. Maybe a sickness. Maybe a curse." She wound a finger in the air like she was sensing something.

"Who'd put a curse on a young girl?" London asked.

"You might be right. Maybe she was sick, is all, but one thing is sure."

"What's that?"

"London Oxford, there's no way I am going with those people." She tried to wipe the remaining dough off her hands again on her apron. "You hear me, London Oxford? I definitely am not going with those people. I don't trust them —no way, no how. I'm just not going," she repeated. "And you don't listen to me, why's that?"

He paused for an instant to consider standing his ground, but instead decided to slink away to search for Missa Thomas.

She waved him out the way he came in.

Rescued

L ondon steered the horse up through the forest behind the Wright's farm. He brought Abner along to help collect a wagon load of kindling. He noticed that the wildflowers were gone, oak leaves were turning, and the frogs weren't singing anymore. *Ducks got better places to be, I guess,* he thought.

"So why'd Abigail go get sick?" Abner asked. "Maybe it was because she was so mean."

"Abner, don't say that. Wasn't anyone's fault she died. Wasn't anyone's fault she got sick."

The steady clopping of the horse's hooves made Abner think of his mother. He remembered her touching Abigail's shoulder. She quieted right down. And then she did the same to John and Bearie, and they did too. She pointed, and they did just what she told them.

"It's not good for you to say that," said his father.

As the trees passed, Abner wondered if she put a spell on her. *Maybe it was Momma, and if they find out, we's gonna be in a heap of trouble,* he thought.

"Do you hear me, Abner?" London asked.

"Yes, Poppa."

Missa Philemon, Abner thought. *He'd be bad to Poppa. He can't know.*

London looked at him, not sure what the boy was thinking. "We'll start with that one," he said as he pointed to some broken birch branches on their right. He stopped alongside, circled, and lifted his son off the wagon. As the pair collected wood for the wagon, London said, "When my Poppa was alive, times weren't as good as we got here."

"What do you mean?" asked Abner.

London paused and thought, *It was hard, but he had us. Nothing was fair, easy, or just. Living may have been unbearable, but looking back, my Poppa caught on to something full, powerful, and special.* "Abner, I'm going to tell you how it was with my poppa," he said. "I'll even tell how he met my momma."

"Poppa's name was Coffey. A plantation owner in Oxford Town, near the southern border, got him when he was just a baby. He didn't know nothing, about his parents or where he was from. Only thing folks told him was that his parents gave him his first name. White folks told me that it wasn't true, but I knows it is because that's what he told me.

"Coffey's owner in Oxford gave him as a child to a minister as a present. Reverend John Swift lived in Framingham, which is in the southwest corner of this county. He was the first minister of the town's church.

"Respecting and honouring God was obvious, but he didn't like that reverend. What he said about religion, he liked even less. Being told that Negroes were slaves because God believed they were sinners didn't go far with him. He was born a slave and didn't believe what he did had anything to do with why the reverend and other owners treated them real bad. His owner didn't like what he believed, so he kept him locked up.

"Coffey told me that he got lonely because he didn't get to meet many other coloured people. The reverend taught him to read and write and forced him to read the Bible and do work for his church.

"When Poppa was all grown, the Reverend sold him to a plantation owner."

"Is Missa Wright going to sell us Poppa?"

"No. No. No. Missa Wright's not going to sell anyone. He's a good man. We's free. You, me, Momma, your sisters; we is all free. These times are different. Well, sort of … I mean, where we live in some ways is different."

He saw that Abner was still staring at him.

"Don't you think that. Don't you ever think that," his father repeated. "The man that tried to take you was going to take you to a bad place. There are still bad places men want to take people like us."

London grabbed the branch and said, "Help me pull it."

The two of them pulled a pair of fallen branches behind the wagon. London chopped the branches with an axe, and Abner piled the pieces for kindling.

"Wanta hear more about my poppa?"

"You said something happened to him, like me?" Abner said.

"So you was listening," London said with a laugh. "It's a story about hard times and how Coffey almost didn't marry my momma. His new owner's name was Colonel Joseph Buckmaster. He owned most of the land in and around Framingham town; was a judge, and a state politician. The colonel even had an army of his own. He was a powerful man. He had a big house and needed lots of servants. That's why he needed Coffey.

"He got Coffey because he could read and write, was smart, and was able to pick up and sign for supplies like I do today. He was even able to do some shopping at the market.

"One day, on an errand for his master, he came across the most opinionated and hot-tempered creature on this earth. He, of course, quickly fell in love with her."

London turned and looked at his son. Smiling, he said, "At least that is what he told me. He used to say, after taking a taste of his pipe, 'Oh-wee, when my Nelle Donnahue knows what she wants, Oh-wee, look out!'"

Abner gave a snickering laugh.

"She lived in Holliston, which was six and a half miles from Framingham. Coffey had ridden into town to confirm the status of a purchase of a herd of cattle. Fortunately, there were problems with the deal.

He returned a couple more times. He made follow-up visits on Sundays, and sure enough, he eventually proposed to her. 'Nelle,' he said, 'I want you more than anything. I never want to live without you,' he told her. 'She was special,' he used to tell me."

"Your momma?" Abner asked.

"Yes, she was," London said. He pointed to other sets of branches.

As they dragged them back to the wagon, London said, "You'd think that asking a woman to marry you and her being interested would be all that was needed to be done, right?"

Abner looked back and shrugged.

"Not by a long shot. You also had to get permission from both parents and both owners. Coffey went chasing after Colonel Buckmaster. He told his owner that he was thirty-eight years old and wanted to have children, and he found a woman who was willing to marry him. Another servant by the name of Luke, who was with the colonel, tried to shoo him away while he was talking.

"The colonel told him that he was real busy with some new properties. 'And don't you know that we're fighting a war with the French and their damn Injuns,' he said. 'My country is going to need my men soon, and we'll give the best we've got when it comes. I don't have time for this, Coffey. Give me a couple of months. You go speak to Luke first, you hear.' The colonel shooed both of them away."

"Why didn't Coffey say he just had to?" Abner asked.

"Coffey couldn't say anything more because if the colonel refused to give his permission, he and Nelle wouldn't be able to marry, and he would have made sure they never saw each other again. He understood that the colonel might put him off for years.

"When and if the colonel finally gave his permission, he'd have to convince Nelle's owner that he was a reliable and healthy man. If Nelle could get a better arrangement with someone else, of course, he'd be out of luck. Coffey felt helpless.

"Anyway, a couple of weeks later, Coffey drove the wagon to get some supplies at the store. When he got to the centre of town, he saw a grubby young man grabbing a young Black girl. She was hitting back and screaming for him to let her go.

"Coffey stopped the wagon and threatened the man with his whip and told him to let her go.

"The young man told him, 'You're not going to do anything; you're smarter than that.' The girl was now on his shoulder. He moved her legs to one side so that Coffey could see the gun that was stuck in his belt. The man was carrying her toward another man across the street that was holding the reins of two horses.

"Coffey asked him where he was taking her.

"'She's not yours; she's ours,' the young man said. 'We found her. She's a runaway, and we're returning her to her master, and there is nothing you can do about it.'

"Coffey didn't believe him.

"As the young man grabbed the girl tighter, the girl screamed for Coffey to stop him.

"Coffey froze. He looked around and saw some white folk, but they were beyond calling distance. He knew if a Black man hit a white man for any reason, he'd get thrown in jail and might even lose his life. It was unlikely anyone would stand by him when his word was compared to the likes of that trash.

"There were houses and shops along the street, so he screamed for help, but no one came. He was in a bad situation. Despite that, he dismounted the wagon.

"The young vagrant tied her hands and rode away with her, and the other one followed. In the middle of a turn, however, both men tumbled off their horses. When Coffey came close, he saw an Injun standing behind them. He had drawn a long knife from his belt. There was another Injun near him, and he was collecting their guns and putting them in his waist belt.

"The Injun with the knife raised it so the men on the ground could see it. He crossed his neck with it and used the knife to point to the other end of the street.

"That trash clearly understood the message, because they ran off right away. The Injun gave a mad, haunting yell while smacking the horse's haunches. Coffey told me that those horses were so scared they ran past their owners and didn't stop until they were on the other side of town.

"As the Injun with guns tucked in his belt untied the girl, Coffey noticed that there was another Injun behind him whose wrists were tied. The prisoner and the one who pulled the men off their horses wore clothes for a colder climate."

"What does that mean?" Abner asked.

"Other clothes? I don't know. I didn't ask, but Poppa told me that the other one wore a breech cloth and leggings above the moccasins like most Injuns. He also told me that the tied-up one had thick black stripes on his neck."

"Black stripes," repeated Abner.

"And when Coffey came over to the girl, he couldn't look her in the eyes," London said. He told her he was sorry, and he wished that he could've done more.

"Coffey turned to the Injun next to him and thanked him for helping."

"'It'd be a frightful time here if you didn't show up,' he said.

"The Injun from his side pouch took out some colourful flowers and gave them to her."

Abner looked up at his father with amazement. "What does it mean?"

"Maybe Injuns like picking flowers. Maybe they eat them," his father replied. "I don't know. Anyway, the other Injun joined them and said, 'Wìsakedjàk, if only it was as easy to get Wekatesk back'."

"What?" asked Abner.

"Wekatesk. My Pa told me it must have been his girl. He didn't tell me what happened to her—just that he missed her."

"Wekatesk?" repeated Abner.

"That's right. I asked my Poppa a couple of times. 'Wekatesk' is what he told me. Coffey told him his name and who his owner was.

"The Injun said that his name was Quinac and, with a chuckle, told him that you might call the other one Jack. The girl said that her name was Annie."

"So that's where—?"

"Yes, that's where I got your sister's name."

"Jack asked her why she was on the street by herself. She said that her Massa had sold her to a Massa Barnes. One of the neighbour's boys was supposed to bring her to him, but took the wagon to town and met some friends. They left her on a wagon waiting for hours while they were drinking. When they came out, those boys weren't in their right minds. They were talking bad, so she ran off.

"Coffey offered to take her back to the farm of the fella that sold her. He also offered the Injun a full tobacco pouch to help him load some supplies. They accepted, and Jack tossed their prisoner in the back as if he were a sack of feathers. The captive got his head smashed in the process, but they didn't seem to mind. Quinac told Coffey to stay away from him and that he was a lot worse than the trash that tried to kidnap the girl.

"After loading goods at the supply store, they took the girl back to her owner's farm, where she and Coffey told the story to the servants of the big house. Coffey told me that he didn't know what happened to her after that.

"Once he got the wagon back onto the main road, Coffey asked Quinac where he was from.

"He said that he was from Connecticut and that Jack convinced him that if he helped Injuns here, he'd be able to get some land for himself. He said he was here to remind those folks about the old ways. He said that a long time ago, when the foreigners first came to these parts, Wīsakedjàk and his brother warned brothers not to accept the white folk. 'If they listened, then perhaps we'd be better off,' he said. Coffey said that he looked at Jack, and they both laughed. My poppa told me that there was a joke there, but he didn't understand what it was that was so funny."

"Maybe the Wīsakedjàk was Jack's grandfather or something, maybe?" Abner asked.

"Don't know," London said. After finishing loading the rest of the kindling, they started the ride back.

"Quinac told Coffey that since Injuns didn't make good slaves, Negroes were brought in from the islands," London continued. "Coffey told him that he couldn't tell him much 'cause he didn't know nothing about his parents. 'But we's from Africa,' he said. Jack told him that it must have been hard not having a father. He had done good for standing by young Annie and he respected him for that. Quinac complained that those white folks don't know what they were doing. Jack told him to act smart. Quinac pointed a thumb at the prisoner and said to Jack, 'You too.' Jack told Coffey to ignore him, and the others laughed. I guess Jack messed up somehow," London said. "What do you think?"

Abner shrugged.

"Coffey told them that when they defended the girl, they were putting their lives on the line. Those white folks wouldn't have acted kindly on them beating up a white boy, even if 'twas natural enough that he deserved it. Quinac told him that they was on this land as free people, and to be truly free, a human being, when it matters, has to make a stand. It was hard for my poppa to hear someone say those biting words.

"Well, even for me now, even to repeat them, it's hard. Sometimes, I wonder if I should have been born an Injun," London said.

"You going to send us away?"

"Abner, why would you ever even think that? Of course not. We's your family. We's free and you and your sisters are all our children. That's never going to happen.

"Where'd that come from?"

Abner shrugged.

"You think we're going to join the injuns? No way. Now let's finish my story.

"Jack asked if his owner, Colonel Buckmaster, was sending his soldiers up north. Coffey told him that he got lots of soldiers in town, but as far as he knew, they hadn't gone nowhere. He asked if the Injuns were going to fight them. Jack told him that Quinac's people support Americans, but they were trying to delay settlers moving west of the Appalachian Mountains. He said that he was trying to keep them away from their hunting grounds and away from the Canadian Injun War. He also said that he got the impression that Coffey didn't like the colonel much. Coffey told him that they had a difference of mind. His Massa kept putting off his ask'n him if he could marry.

"'It looks like I have as good a chance of getting married to my Nelle as seeing it snow in June,' Coffey said.

"Quinac told him that he doubted that and that he'd seen stranger things happen.

"The conversation ended abruptly, and where they wanted to stop looked like no place special. They stopped next to the line of a forest.

"After Jack leapt off the back of the wagon, he told Coffey, 'It's a good thing to have a father. You listen to your children and believe in yourself.' Jack then picked something out of his belt and dropped it into his hand.

"'I'm sure she'd like it,' he said. Quinac gave the prisoner a quick shove, and they led him away.

"Coffey's eyes lit up. A really nice green stone lay in his hand. Before he could thank them, they had disappeared beyond the cover of a stand of trees.

"And you know what?" London asked Abner.

Abner looked up at him.

"I gave it to your momma, and she's still got it."

Abner's eyes were wide as saucers. "Oo-wee," he said. "What a great story for Momma. Wait til I tell her."

"Help me unload this, and then you can tell her," said London. *That'll give him something to bite his teeth on,* he thought. As he walked, he rubbed the calluses on his hand.

Can't wait for him to tell her, thought London. *With Momma Jane going on about leaving Missa Wright forever, young Abigail's death might give her another reason to leave; it would be good for her to hear something nice. But I think there's something more. She knows it, and damn it all—won't say. And, 'I never listen,' —what was that supposed to mean?"*

He felt like taking a bite of something, but his pockets were empty.

A Bad Turn

Abner moved his curls away from his eyebrow as he faced a line of Wrights on the other side of the grave. A drop of rain splashed on his hand.

From Thomas Wright's wife, Mary, he heard, "Terrible, terrible. So young. So full of life." She patted her tummy and said, "If this one is going to be a girl, we should call her Abigail. What do you think, Thomas?"

Her husband caressed her arm. To Abner, it looked like he was staring at the thick earthworms that were trying to wiggle out of the sides of the deep hole. The burial pit separated the Wright's side from the Oxfords' side.

Abner stood to the left of his father. Rachael was carried, and Annie held her father's right hand. The children's mother stood on the other side behind the Wright family. She was holding the hands of Philemon's two youngest children. Three-year-old Ruggles was at her left, and six-year-old Maryanne with a green bow in her hair was at her right. Missa Philemon's wife, Abigail, had a big tummy full of baby. Thomas Wright's wife, Mary, tried to console eight-year-old Polly's tears. A crowd of relatives and friends formed a half circle around the pit.

Missu Wright tried to grab Philemon's hand, but he stepped closer to fifteen-year-old Phil Junior and patted his back. His wife pulled out a kerchief to sneeze. After looking around, Philemon shuffled back and patted his wife's shoulder.

"Isn't she going to get cold?" asked Abner.

"What?" his father asked. "You mean young Abigail? She's gone to heaven already."

"But why are we here if she's already gone?"

"Cause we're paying our respects. She's gone, but we're here. There's more to life than just dying. Well, maybe she doesn't want to go yet."

"Why?"

Annie plopped down on her bum.

"Don't know," he said as he looked at her sitting there.

"Must be a good reason. Just don't know." He reached for Annie's hand, but she moved away.

"Oh," Abner replied.

London saw others looking at him. He beckoned Annie to come over to him.

"Maybe she's waiting to find out who did this," his son said.

London reached down and pulled Annie up by her hand. While patting her on the back, he said, "Abner, no one did this. Got sick. That's all."

Annie looked up at him.

London expected another question, but the boy didn't say anything. He stepped back and looked the other way.

"The minister is here, Abner. This way, please," his father said.

When Abner turned, he saw his mother scold young Ruggles. He was trying to get away. It reminded him of when she scolded his sister.

She deserved to be pushed back, he thought.

"Don't you dare, Abigail," he whispered and shook his finger at the ghost in the coffin.

Bad, bad, he thought.

Abner looked closer. His mother's hand was still on Ruggle's shoulders, just like she'd done after scolding Abigail. He wondered if she was giving him a curse.

Maryanne, who was being held with his mother's other hand, was crying. She looked grey and dried up. He thought that she might have what Abigail had, maybe. Abner's momma let go of her hand to caress her hair and then pulled her tight to her skirt.

Abner put his finger in his ear, took out some earwax, and turned around. He wiped it on his pants. He caught a set of eyes glaring at him. Abner looked down as he shuffled. Looking back, he saw a man who was talking to a bunch of strangers that were on the road. The man wore buckskin leggings, a leather vest, and a long black coat. The long coat wasn't something you'd expect an Injun to wear. He had dark, tattooed stripes on his neck. They looked like snakes. The squared black hat looked like it had a feather stuck in it.

Abner noticed that the men on each side of him didn't look like Injuns. The coat on one of them was the same colour as the man that tried to take him. They didn't look well. Their eyes were black, and all of them were slightly bent over.

The man with the long feather in his hat stared back. He had piercing, eagle-like eyes. His expression didn't change—just his eyes.

Abner quickly turned around and looked up at his father. London caught his glance but turned back and continued to watch the burial ceremony as he caressed the side of Abner's head.

The Injun scared Abner. *Why was he here?* he thought. *This is only for people that know Abigail. It's not right.*

Abner wrapped his arm around his father's leg. London let go of Annie and moved Rachael to his other arm so he could wrap an arm around his son.

Abner watched his mother caress young Maryanne's hair again. His father did the same to him. He looked up and saw his father looking at his mother.

The crawling sensation on the back of his neck was gone. Abner sensed that the man was gone. He froze where he was and didn't want to think of being anywhere else.

After the minister's prayers, a man shovelled dirt onto the coffin. Behind him, Abner watched the silhouette of the Injun who was now alone and walking away.

"Stop it," he heard someone yell. Beyond his father and five bunches of strangers, Abner saw a man swat a boy on the side of the head with his hat. The boy was trying to escape the man's grip. The man put his hat back on and, with both hands, pulled the boy back in front of him. "Don't you dare, or you'll get a beating like—"

The boy, who was just a couple of years older than Abner, stilled and didn't say another word.

"Who's that?" Abner asked.

"Joshua, Philemon's brother-in-law, is the one doing the hitting. He's a loose one. Father drinks his life away. He couldn't persuade his woman to put up with either of them. Best you listen to the minister, or I'll have to swat you myself, yah hear?"

To avoid his father's staring eyes, Abner focused on the ground and nodded.

A shower cut the ceremony short, causing everyone to scatter except the Wright's oldest boys—Tom Jr. and Phil Jr.

When it really started to pour, Abner looked back and saw that both of them were coated in mud. Tom was on his butt and looked like he almost slipped into the hole in the ground. The verge of a laugh was interrupted by a hard yank on his arm and a miserable, soaked look from his father. Remembering the Injun and Abigail's ghost, he pulled away from his father and ran past him and tried to reach his mother, who was far ahead of them.

Abigail's father, in the days ahead, would keep leaving for a colder place far away. In time, he would actually persuade the others to move away with him. Abner would see Joshua again in four years. Both would leave without their mothers.

PART 2: Preparations

Broken Pilgrimages

A traveller stared at a beckoning sunrise behind the old Cradock place. Standing by their barn, he found the rambunctious pigs distracting. "Don't like sleeping in," he reasoned.

He made his way to the kitchen door of the couple's house. Before marching up the steps, he removed his hat and examined the top for wear. Caressing the long feather in it, he said, "Maybe I should get rid of this. No reason to keep it, really, is there?" Well, it did have its uses—for writing, among other things. He knocked at the door and waited patiently. A plump, middle-aged woman with wild, frizzy, light brown hair answered.

With his hat over his heart, he asked, "Would you be Mrs. Marlene Cradock?"

Seeing a man all dressed in black scared her a bit, and she took steps backward. The long feather in his hat suggested that he was an Injun.

"Who are you, and who gave you my name?" she asked.

"Don't mean to bother you, Marlene. And don't worry, it's just me here."

"My husband should be here shortly. He's the one you should be talking to."

"Yes, of course. It is a nice place that you folks have got here. Lots of good grazing land. How's the sugar beets this year?"

"Right amount of rain for root crops," she said.

"And the feed for the chickens?"

"We got enough. Don't have to trade for much, besides milk and such."

"Marlene, Matthew is my name."

While staring beyond at the barn outside, she asked, "That husband, what's he doing?"

"I'm sure Merle will make an appearance when the time is right."

"What do you mean by that? How do you know our names?"

Actually, I'm here about church work. You're on the church council in Medford, aren't you? All that community service work, it must be an enormous burden."

"It's not like that. I mean, it's mostly good Christian folk we work with, and there's grace from doing God's work. We don't mind at all."

"That's nice to hear. I'm told that there's good Christian, coloured families here as well."

"They're all free here, where they belong. No migrants. You better get off this land if you're thinking of taking them." She looked around for a cross on the walls. The Bible, unfortunately, was in the next room.

"Nothing like that at all, Mrs. Cradock. I am a collector of stories. I am looking to meet those folks. They can give their stories, and maybe I can give some of mine. That's all. I am particularly interested in folk with connections to Framingham."

"I'm sure my husband would be more than glad to help you. In the meantime, we'll just have to be patient. If you don't mind, we'll wait until he comes round." She pulled on the handle to close the door. His boot stopped it from shutting.

"That's unfortunate, isn't it?" He put his hat on and let himself in.

After a profitable visit, Matthew led Mrs. Cradock outside. She had become very talkative and continued to spout gossip about the church, the neighbours, and pretty much everyone she knew.

"I'm sure that Merle will be ecstatic to see you, Marlene," Matthew said.

His arm was around her shoulder, which she didn't seem to mind. He led her into the pig barn. The pigs had already torn what was left of her husband apart. "Don't distress yourself, dear; this won't take long," the man in black said as he removed his hat. "I hope you don't find me too insincere when I say that I enjoyed our talks." He removed the feather from his hat and added, "But I also enjoy what I must do now, even more."

Matthew sat leaning against a tree across the street from Old North Church. It was in Boston near the docks. It was at the end of intersected, narrow, two-lane, muddy streets. The thin red chapel had a tall steeple that rose well above the surrounding three- and four-story buildings. The church and the surrounding buildings were dressed in light red stone.

Matthew attempted to levitate his feather in circles. It was a parlour trick that he'd mastered as a child. Before letting it go, he had to make sure he still had the skill. The woman he was waiting for was approaching. Before attaching it to his hat, he made the floating feather wave.

After a carriage and a rider passed, he hurried to intercept her as she started to cross the street.

Before she was able to cross, he asked, "Would you be Mrs. Ivy Walsh?"

"Sorry, but I am very much in a hurry. The pastor is waiting for me."

"He gives his condolences."

"What's that?"

"You know he's a busy man, with the Lord's work and all that. So much to do."

"That doesn't make sense. He sent someone to come fetch me. What are you not telling me?" She held a small handbag in front of her as protection.

"An emergency came up, and I'm not privileged to say what it was."

"Did he mention when we're supposed to meet?"

"No, but he told me that you are here to meet a coloured woman.

She's looking for a nanny. Did you find one?"

"And why is that your business, Mister—?" She moved towards the black iron gate in front of the church.

"Just call me Matthew. I am an acquaintance of your pastor. I am looking for folks with connections with Framingham. The woman I'm looking for is Jane Oxford."

"The coloureds in this parish, as far as I know, were all born near here. What's your interest in this?" Ivy asked.

"Just stories. We all got stories. Her husband likely has what I'm looking for."

"If you don't mind, I'd like to visit the church since I'm here," she said.

Matthew removed his hat and held it over his heart.

Yes, of course, Mrs. Walsh. He rushed around her and opened a small gate for her.

Matthew followed and closed the door behind him.

Once inside, Matthew reached for her shoulder.

"Don't you dare," she said and backed away towards a pew.

"Didn't mean to disturb," Matthew drawled.

She saw a pair of feet sprawled near the lectern. "Oh my God," she moaned.

Matthew again reached for her shoulder, and she yelled, "What kind of monster?"

"Where did I put my feather?" asked Matthew.

Jane Oxford accompanied Thomas Wright and his thirteen-year-old son, John, to an open market by the docks in Boston. She intended to meet a parishioner who could provide recommendations for a live-in nanny for the Wrights. It was prearranged that they would meet at a nearby church while the Wrights picked up some supplies.

"Jane, when you're finished, you'll find us here," Thomas said. "John, do you still have that list I gave you?"

The boy, unlike his father, was thin and had long hair that went over his ears and just over his collar.

"Yeah, I guess," he said, and almost got hit by a man on horseback.

"Well, Mister, I guess, I'll meet you in the feed store. And stay out of the dirt, or you can walk home."

He turned to Jane and said, "Two hours is more than enough time, so don't be late."

She had to lift her dress to keep it out of a thick layer of mud. It took a lot of concentration to avoid slipping.

For her protection, Jane avoided the port road and followed the next one from it. It was narrow and lined with tenement buildings and local folk. As she walked north, she found it was easier to avoid slipping, but the roads still stank like a latrine. Looking up at open windows, she wished she had an umbrella, like the ones that other women had. Horses tied up in front of stores on a narrow street didn't provide much allowance for wheeled or foot traffic. As she neared the church, pedestrian traffic thickened.

The Old North Church on Salem Street was a half dozen city blocks from the market. When she approached the church gate, a minister came out of the front door.

"Are you the pastor here?" she asked.

"Yes, I am. You must be Mrs. Jane Oxford."

Although the man had a white collar, the leather jacket and pants didn't match a regular minister's attire.

"I was supposed to meet someone here today," she said.

"That must be Mrs. Walsh. Something came up. Unfortunately, she is indisposed at the moment."

"We's looking for a nanny, and I's told that the parish might have some names for us."

"I do, but unfortunately, I have only one for you at the moment," he said. "Mimi Thompson is her name. You should be able to find her at Twelve Green Lane."

"By the way, who told you that I's coming?"

"Your pastor in Medford, of course."

"Thank you. We's appreciate this very much. Oh, and what did you say your name was?"

Giving a full-teeth smile, he replied with, "Pastor Michael Bradshaw, at your service."

Looking him over, she determined that the liar in front of her exuded the shiftiness of a snake oil salesman. Ivy Walsh in Medford had told her that the pastor of this church was old, fat, and not very coherent. The man in front of her was none of these. Ivy was also the one who told her to speak to Janice O'Shea and not this man. She was on the Old North Church council. Jane had gone into the church only with the intention of verifying Janice's address.

She left and headed back to the market.

"Jane," she heard the man say from behind her.

She looked back and saw him point with a feather.

"Twelve Green Lane is that way," he said.

"That's much appreciated, but I have some business to attend to first," she replied.

After walking a couple of blocks, she checked back and saw him walking after her. She meandered through some alleys to lose him, but caught a glimpse of him, first two blocks ahead, then one. He had ditched the priestly collar.

She headed west and noticed him cross the street and then look at her from the other side.

She realized that he was playing with her. He was steering her away from the Wrights and towards the Charles River Bridge, which led off the island.

"Dear Lord," she said. "Who on earth is this man? And why me?"

When she reached the bridge, she didn't see any sign of him. Other than the hills around Bunker Hill on her right, the land ahead was relatively flat and unencumbered for miles. She saw little cover to hide an escape. Medford, which was a few miles away, was a brisk two-hour march from where she was. On the other side of the bridge, she looked for help but didn't see anyone.

Stealing a boat sounded like a good idea. Stealing a boat and being Black was not.

She looked back at where she came from. There was still no sign of her pursuer, but there was a man driving a wagon that was heading to the bridge.

She stroked her hair with a hand, took a deep breath, and ran back across the bridge.

The man in the wagon was middle-aged and brawny.

"Missa, sorry to bother you this fine day, but I desperately need your help. There's an evil man that's chasing me, and I need to get to Medford."

"I's a fine Christian woman, and you won't have no complaints from me. My name is Jane Oxford, and I's got a family to get to and I got to get to them safe."

"Don't usually pander to strangers, but don't see the harm of getting you to town. Wasn't particularly going that far, but it won't be much out of my way, I guess." With hairy, well-muscled arms, he beckoned her to climb aboard.

When the wagon continued on toward the bridge, she checked back and still saw no sign of the man who was chasing her.

"David Cohen, at your service, ma'am. Do you know this man who is chasing you?"

"Never heard nor seen him before. I have no idea why he chose to follow me. I was going to join others who took me here, but I'm too scared of going back. He's a special kind of bad, and I know it."

"Well, Missus Oxford, you just relax. You can consider that I'm someone who can take care of himself, if you know what I mean. I fought in the Great War; you know it, and I'm still here to speak about it. Besides, I got my whip here, and I've even got a solid piece of wood behind me, should we run into that kind of trouble."

"Thank you, Missa Cohen; you don't know how much I appreciate this. Really didn't know what I was going to do."

"I know that you're not carrying anything, but did you finish what you intended to do in town?"

"Was looking for a nanny for the people we stay with."

"Did you find one?"

"I had the name of a woman, but didn't get to see her. There was a man dressed up as a priest. I mean, have you ever heard of such a thing?"

"He might have been a thief."

The wagon made its way to a trail lined with trees that followed the Mystic River toward Medford.

Although the Wrights lived close to Woburn, Medford was where the Wrights and the Oxfords went to church. It was where Jane and her husband were married. She hoped that if she could reach Medford, she might be able to find trustworthy people who could help.

The ride was calm and comfortable.

"We have the river onside, so not much farther," Mr. Cohen said.

The river thinned a great deal due to the peninsula they were approaching.

"I usually turn off here, but as I mentioned before, I'll take you where you need to be as long as you're safe. Where are we headed?"

"The church would be more than fine," Jane said.

"Good, I know exactly where that is."

From behind a tree, a man stepped out onto the trail ahead of them.

"Missa Cohen, that's him. That's the man.

"Dear Lord, how on earth did he get there so fast? It's not possible."

"Don't you worry, Missus—"

Before Mr. Cohen could raise his whip, the man in black threw his body against a tree, and something in it cracked. Jane grabbed the reins and snapped them to make the horse pick up speed.

She heard something behind her. The man had somehow managed to climb onto the wagon.

"Who are you and what do you want from me?" she asked him.

The man in the long black leather coat was stepping around Mr. Cohen's supplies. "You have something of mine, and I want it back."

"What are you talking about? I've never laid eyes on you in my life. You've got the wrong woman. Get away from me."

He kept coming closer. "There was a man named Coffey who took a stone from me. I want what's rightfully mine."

"What state was he from?"

"This one, he lived in Framingham."

"So why don't you ask him?"

"Because he died long ago. The plantation owner heard that one of the children got it."

"I don't know what you're talking about. Leave me alone!"

The man in black stopped and said, "Actually, I have good reason to believe him. And I have a way of finding what's important. You don't need to doubt me."

"I imagine that's so, but I'm not even related to those folks, so what's this got to do with me?"

"A little girl told me that there are coloured folk that go to the church in Medford and that they came from Framingham. And lo-and-behold, you folks go to that very church. Not many coloureds belong there."

He killed Abigail, she thought. "God Almighty, you're a monster—a devil. You killed a child for a stupid rock. May God damn your soul."

"So you know her," he said softly near her ear. He slipped back a bit. "It was just the name of the church I wanted. I had no idea you were there. Well, wasn't that a twist?"

"Folks talked about her at church. And more folks are looking for me, as we speak."

"I bet they are, but I don't expect this will take long," he said as he attempted to climb into the front seat.

She veered the wagon toward the water, which was about fifty feet away.

Matthew was thrown forward. Jane plunged a sharp kitchen knife deep into his stomach. He twisted and, with both hands, threw her off the wagon.

Jane bounced on the ground, smashing her thigh. She kept rolling until she collided with a small bush. Staggering to her feet, she saw that a sleeve was torn, and the forearm had a gaping wound. Her leg was sore, but she hurried ahead into the sparse cover of trees that followed the river's edge.

She heard the wagon spill into the river, but she hurried ahead. When she had to stop to catch her breath, she heard something climb out of the water. When she heard him say, "What a mean one," she kept still. She heard him groan when he pulled out the knife, and he added, "What a mean bite." That was followed by a small splash when the knife was tossed into the river.

He groaned and started pacing in circles. "And all that for this? Unbelievable, unbelievable. Well, I did leave the gates open for those poor creatures, didn't I? That must count for something."

When she saw the skin around the black marks along his neck move, she bit on her finger so as not to be heard.

"The scent of fear. I can feel it," he said. "She's still here."

She raced towards the Mystic River with everything she had. After hearing him say, "With the way this day has been going, this cut might never heal," the pace of his steps became so rapid that it was obvious that she had no chance of reaching the water.

At the next Sunday service in Medford, two stories got connected—a missing coloured parishioner who disappeared in Boston and a body found floating in the Mystic River. Thomas Wright was at a complete loss as to how to explain how a woman under his care had been found dead in a river outside of town. *Bodies don't float upriver,* he thought. *And why didn't she return to them as planned?*

The self-blame became an itch on his arm that he couldn't get rid of. Scraping at it just made the rash worse. *But it was a good plan for both of us, wasn't it?* he reasoned. *What the hell is going on?* He wanted to scream.

He hesitated to tell his wife about it for a whole day. In the meantime, she and her boys were left to describe the unspeakable. Their children's nanny had died the same way as his brother's young, cherished daughter. And her being found floating upriver suggested she'd been killed. *And Abigail? How was she connected?*

Or is it something we're all going to get? he wondered as he stared at the rash on his forearm.

Autumn Leaves

In the year following Abigail's death, each of the Wright brothers' wives gave birth to daughters in her name. It was in October of that year that Jane Oxford went missing. London, after spending two days searching for her, returned home.

In the morning, Abner and the girls sat at the kitchen table staring at the burned pot in their father's hand. London sloppily plopped spoonfuls of hash into bowls on the counter.

"Where is she?" Abner asked.

"Yes, where's Momma?" Annie repeated.

"I'm going out again. You'll be alright with Missus Mary while I'm gone. Don't know where, but we's looking."

"But. . ."

London put the pot on a stool and threw his apron on the table. "I gotta go. I don't wanna hear there's no trouble, you hear. You all wait while I goes and gets her."

"But—"

"I said no."

When Missus Mary Wright returned through the front door,

their father immediately left through the back door. London didn't return until late. The children had fallen asleep. They didn't see him the next evening, nor the one after that.

On the fourth day, before supper, Mr. Thomas Wright and his sons entered the house through the back. Hearing his father's name, Abner ran into the kitchen. When Missa Thomas's oldest son, Tom Jr., passed by, he respectfully nodded and kept looking at the floor. Abner had never seen him do that.

Abner's father looked tired and angry.

"Where is she?" Abner asked.

"It's time for bed," London said.

"No, it's not. It's still light."

"Don't argue with me. Get to bed. Take the girls with you. Abner. Now! Take care of them."

It was then that Abner realized that the girls were his responsibility. He hurried because he didn't want to get hit.

—⚬⚮⚬—

Abner was woken up by Tom Jr. the next morning. He led his sisters to the kitchen table, where his Missus Mary was doing the cooking.

"Where's Momma?"

"Annie, don't," said Abner.

"I understand …" Missus Mary said. "You should talk with your father. Best you eat up before it gets cold. Tom, Polly will mind the girls today. Abner will work with John in the fields. Your father's got chores lined up for you."

Tom Jr. reached for the pot of porridge that was hanging on the fireplace.

"Hold on. Get back," his mother said as she took his bowl, filled it for him, and brushed him away to the table.

When Polly came into the kitchen, Missus Wright nudged Tom Jr. out of the kitchen as he tried to guzzle what was left of his porridge.

Abner quickly finished and chased after him outside. He grabbed his hand. "Where's my momma?"

"I ... I can't say. You heard ma'am," said Tom as he buttoned up his black wool jacket.

"Someone took my momma."

"Well, no."

"Someone hurt her."

"I see John," he said as a distraction. His brother was two fields away. He wasn't close.

"Why did someone hurt my mother?"

"Abner. Abner."

"Where's my Poppa?"

"I don't know. Haven't you seen him?"

"Of course not," Tom Jr. replied.

"Well, if you had, he'd tell you," Abner said.

"No one hurt her."

"Then why isn't she here?" Abner asked as he let go of Tom's hand.

"She's in heaven," thirteen-year-old Tom Jr. said. "Oh, my Lord. I didn't mean that. And look what you made me do. My pa is going to kick my ass."

"What are you saying?" Abner asked as he stepped back and folded his arms.

"She must have got Abigail's disease. All grey and old-looking, real quick."

"She's not old-looking," he said as he pounded a foot. "You're just stupid. You don't know anything."

"My father said that she looked just like Abigail, and he wouldn't let anyone touch her, not even your pa. They was scared we'd all catch it. They didn't move her until they got the coffin. We lifted her into it on a blanket, and then we made a fire and burnt everything remaining in the barn.

"Don't tell anyone. Let your pa tell you. You hear? You tell anyone, I'll beat you up real bad. You hear me, Abner? Do you? I'll smash you so bad you won't be able to get up. Do you hear me?"

Abner stared at the ground and nodded.

"Well, say it. I want to hear you swear it."

"I's gonna have my poppa tell me."

"And. . ."

"And I swears; I'll not tell."

"Spit."

Tom Jr. put out his hand, but Abner spit on the ground and stepped on it.

"You's better not tell your sisters. I mean, your pa's going to tell them anyways, right?"

"But Momma wasn't sick."

"I don't know nothing about that," Tom Jr. said. "I only knows what I saw. Come on, I's got to go see my dad. Hurry it up before John leaves. Come on. Let's get." Tom pulled on Abner's shoulder, and the two of them ran.

At the end of the day, Abner checked the pot ,and there was nothing in it. The three Oxford children waited around the table for supper. Polly kept peeking in to make sure no one went near the fireplace.

Tom Jr. came in prepared and served them some really soggy porridge. After noticing someone at the back door, he left in a hurry.

It was their father who was at the door. Abner glared at him.

Annie got up and told him, "I want Momma."

"Finish up," London replied.

"Momma," she repeated and pushed his leg.

Her father pushed her back, and she fell backwards onto the floor.

"No," screamed Abner.

Annie got up and backed away from her father and the table. Rachael started crying.

"I, I—Get ready for bed! All of you," he said, and went outside again.

"Momma?" Rachael repeated.

Abner got up and asked Annie if she was hurt.

"Go away," she said, and she stepped away from him.

No one came to help clean up, so the bowls were left on the table.

Abner blew the lantern out, and they followed in line through the dark hallway. Rachael slipped in between Annie and Abner after they plopped onto the mattress that lay on the floor.

"It's something bad," said Annie.

"Poppa?" asked Rachael.

"He's outside," Abner said.

"Maybe Momma's gone away," Annie said.

Abner rolled away from them because he knew she was asking him.

"Well, is she?" she asked.

"Leave me alone," said Abner.

"Where's Momma?" Rachael asked as she crawled up over his shoulder.

"No," he said as he tried to push her away. "Just leave me alone." He rolled away onto the floor. "I don't want to talk about it." He grabbed his shoes and pants and said, "Just go to sleep." He left the room and went outside in the dark to be by himself.

Outside, he sat leaning against the barn, with his arms hugging his legs. He felt stupid for not bringing his coat. Thick clouds blocked out portions of the moon and stars. "Momma," he said. "Why did you leave me?"

She didn't hesitate when she told Tom and Phil to get to work, he thought. *Did they do something 'cause Abigail died?*

He remembered his mother hugging him. And there was that pain in his arm when Maryanne smashed him against the wall in the kitchen. Then Missa Wright kicked him out. And just like that, she's gone. *Poppa, how could that happen? It's not fair.*

Clouds blocked the lights in the sky. When the last light in the house went out, it got very dark.

"And now there's just me," Abner said.

When he couldn't stand the cold no more, he returned to bed. Rachael had taken over most of his spot, so he shifted to the bottom part of the mattress. Her feet were by the back of his head. Abner was cold, and once snuggled under the covers, he fell asleep quickly.

A smash and shaking of something next to him forced him to wake up. When he rolled over, he found his father sprawled across the floor. He moaned and threw up. Abner rolled away. It was smelly, but he realized that this was where they needed to be.

In the morning when Abner got to the table, he heard Rachael say, "Me too." Polly filled up bowls from the pot that hung over the chimney fire. London gave the children the bowls but left a stack of kindling that had spilled across the floor. He grabbed one for himself and sat next to Abner.

"Where's Momma?" asked Annie.

"Eat up," her father ordered.

"When is she—"

"Annie, I said that's enough."

"She makes it better," said Rachael.

"Rachael," said Abner.

"I want Momma," said Annie.

"She's not here," her father said. He smashed the bowl he was eating from, and it shattered into pieces. A piece cut Abner's arm. "Ouch," he cried.

The children were stunned and stared at their father.

"She's gone away. We'll talk about it later."

"When is she coming back?" asked Rachael.

Abner really wanted to say something. He looked around to see if someone in the hallway was listening. His father looked like he was only half awake.

"Maybe you should take your bowls outside for now," said Polly. "It's a nice day. Now hurry. Take your bowls with you. I'll come and get them in a few minutes. Let's go. Hurry up."

When they got outside, it was cold, and they didn't have jackets. None of the three wanted to go back inside.

"Where is she?" Annie asked Abner.

Abner didn't see anyone else around. "Ask Poppa. He knows."

"But . . ."

Abner hadn't finished eating, but he left his bowl on the ground and ran away from the girls, hoping to find someone, anyone else to talk to, but he didn't.

—◦◉◦—

Missus Wright made supper for them that night. The girls stared at her.

She patted Rachael's hand. "She drowned. That's all. It happened so fast. Only God knows why. Let me take your bowls, and I'll get Polly to help you settle in."

The girls stared at Abner.

"Why you looking at me? They was going to beat me up. Ask Pah. He knows."

"Momma's gone. So why didn't you say?" She pounded the table with her little fist. Two-year-old Rachael did the same with her hand.

"She's dead like Abigail, and there is nothing I can do. We got to ask Poppa."

—◦◉◦—

London, on his return from the lake in the forest, found Abner sitting on the ground resting against the barn. It was cool; stars were out, and a bright moon made it difficult to hide in the dark. "You should be in bed, shouldn't you?"

"Why didn't you tell us?" Abner asked.

"Couldn't believe it. I don't really know why she left. Dear Lord, I'm still trying to figure why she would have done such a thing without me."

"But that's not true," Abner said.

"All I know is she went to see people I never knew, and then the Wrights told me that she was gone. I don't know what to tell you. Looks like she got lost on her way back. Maybe if I'd been with her, she'd still be with us."

"What are we gonna do? What about Annie and Rachael?"

"What ya mean? You've got me."

"Wrights don't think so."

"Never you mind. Just get yourself to bed. For them folk, it's up to me to worry about. Get to bed. The girls need looking after. Now go on."

As Abner returned to the house, his father remained staring into the forest. He didn't tell him that he was haunted by something when Jane went missing. He couldn't reach her, but he felt her slip away. Eyes belonging to a hunter stared back from the black. He kept taking sips from a flask to still his shaking.

After serving his children breakfast, London gave the girls a kiss and a hug and joined them at the table.

London looked the girls in the eyes and then focused on the table. "Some things are hard to talk about. And I'm not especially good at saying things." His voice cracked. "I know I don't tell you how much I love and am proud of all of you." He kept scratching the back of his hand anxiously. "Other folk have told you how Momma passed."

"How come?" asked Annie.

"As I told Abner last night, I don't rightly know. Missa Wright told me that they was told that she drowned. In a couple of days, we will be saying goodbye to her like we did to young Miss Abigail."

"But couldn't Momma swim?" asked Annie.

He leaned back in his chair. "In her own fashion, I'd say yes. They think maybe she hit her head and fell in. I only knows what they told me. They's taking us to church Sunday so we can have a few words said. We'll let God know how much we really miss her."

"But what about before I go to sleep?" asked Annie.

"Yes, siree. Momma, the angels, and all the spirits will listen in then. Just that there's more folks, all at the same time at the church, wanting to give their say. She might like that."

He said some prayers then, more that night, and took them to church on Sunday. But inside, he cursed everyone, including himself, for the unimaginable—that his Jane was gone.

⟿◎⟿

At the funeral, Thomas Wright told Abner not to get too close to the grave. Some nails in the coffin didn't go in all the way and were smashed and bent. It wasn't smoothly cut and shaved to make a fine corner. A side plank stuck out past the end. The wood wasn't as good as Abigail's coffin, either.

Tom Junior's cousin, Phil Junior, helped him lower the casket into the hole by loosening the ropes. The front rope got loose, and it tipped, almost smashing the front against the dirt. John Wright managed to stop it by hauling up his end of the rope.

"Good Lord," Philemon's wife said.

"Mercy," her sister Lavina gasped.

Abner stepped back and bumped into Annie. Rachael stood next to her father, but he wasn't holding her hand. He stood oblivious and lifeless. As Abner stood back, he grabbed Rachael's hand. Annie grabbed the other.

Rachael tried to go to the hole like her brother had done, but he pulled her back. She tried to pull away and started crying. Annie came around and grabbed her other hand.

Abner looked behind. If the Injun was there, somewhere, he didn't see him.

The crowd around the hole in the ground was small. There were the families of Missa Thomas, Philemon, and their sisters, but there was no one like him. *Poor Momma,* Abner thought. In his pocket, he held tightly to his mother's necklace. The tears came again. He kicked dirt into the pit. Again, he asked himself, *Why'd Poppa lie—why she's gone?*

Blethering

Three weeks after Jane was buried, he took another trip by himself. He had heard that Philemon had convinced one of his sisters-in-law to go north with him. Her husband was a capable young man, and she wanted to talk to him about what he thought about going to another country.

When London was led away from Colonel Buckmaster's plantation, he was told that he was going to be free. Philemon asked him if he knew what that meant. London just shook his head. Philemon told him that he didn't have to stay where he was, and could do what he wanted. 'That's what a freeman can do,' he said.

He was asked to move again. He knew what it meant to be free where he was, but he wasn't sure what it meant in those Canadas.

Will I ever *own land and feed myself respectable-like? And can I ever get what other folks got, is the question? London wondered.*

As a free man, I'd ask for more, but that's the least that I want. He had been munching on some chewing tobacco and spat the gob out.

London found Samuel raking out his barn. He was clean-shaven, and his hair was kept close-trimmed. He had an oblong face, a long, thin nose, and big ears. He was tall and wiry.

Although it was chilly on this late November morning, his vest and coat were left draped over a fence. Steam rose from what he was clearing.

The Choates were a new family. They had two young ones, and Margaret, who was Abigail Wright's sister, was carrying another. Although only in his late twenties, Samuel was educated and well-respected.

"Hello, London," he said and kept raking. "Was wondering when I'd see you."

"Missa Thomas didn't say you would be expecting."

"Perhaps you could give me a hand," Samuel replied as he stared at a pitchfork that leaned against the wall.

After the cleanup, Samuel had London examine one of his cows. It had a fever, was losing weight, and was suffering from diarrhea. London confirmed that it wasn't going to get better. "If it were me, I'd butcher it," he said.

Samuel gave him a dour look but didn't say anything. Instead, he put on his vest and coat and led him outside. He escorted London to his livestock in the pastures behind the barn. After closing a fence, he started complaining about how cold it was without a hat and mitts. He then slipped his hands into his vest pockets.

"Missa Thomas is considering selling some of his stock," London said.

"When I talked to him last, he sounded a bit skittish," Samuel replied.

"Leaving everything and going to a new place is a big risk," London said.

He'll get a better price in Boston, than in Woburn or Medford. Have you been to Boston, London?"

"A few times. That's where I met my Jane Ammon."

"Deepest sympathies. News of it came on so suddenly, didn't it?"

London nodded.

"Have you decided to move on? What's your plan?" Samuel asked.

"I'm considering it."

"I heard that Thomas was having second thoughts."

"He likes to test the waters," London said. "Like his brother, he likes folks to think he has loads of options. I know for sure that he definitely is not going to stay. Not unless you offer him your farm for a good price, that is." London held his vest and laughed.

"Not in the range that those boys would want, I'm afraid," said Samuel.

"How about your livestock? Are you going to sell them at the market?" asked London.

"What? Me? Yes, I guess I am."

Samuel stopped, held his vest, and looked at the trees behind the barn.

"So you're not thinking of moving to Boston," Samuel said.

"No. Why would I?"

"There's work at the docks—the market even."

"It costs too much to live, and it's not safe. I know Missu Thomas is going to need help getting the livestock to market, but getting to know folks and making arrangements for me and my girls to live is going to take more time than I got. Nobody's been asking me to go, but I believe I got as good a right to go up north as any of you's.

"You're leaving. Why?"

"Good question. It's not just the land they're promising, and they're promising a good amount. It's the opportunity."

"Missa Elizabeth says that it's just land covered by trees, in the middle of nowhere, and probably filled with Injuns and wild animals."

"Contractors are going to clear the land for us and a great deal more. The Wrights are going to survey more than a hundred thousand acres. That's more land than anyone could want. They're going to need to get lots of folks to move in. I've heard him say that he's going to invite the woodsmen to stay if they want."

"So if they stay, they'd get land and be able to build and farm on it?"

"That's my understanding," London said. "The way I see it, that's what it means to be free, isn't it? I mean to own something and farm it?"

"I suppose," said Samuel.

"You got a nice house here. Is your missus willing to live in a tent?"

"I'm told that the Wrights are bringing along workmen to not only clear the land but also build some homes out of timber. They'll build a couple in the first year and more in the next. I admit that it's stepping down, but it'll work out for us in the end. What's more, they're planning on establishing a respectable-sized town, not just a few farms. Building things is what interests me. They'll need a new church, town hall, bridges, ferry services, and more. I've got my eye on creating a gristmill and a sawmill. Thomas seems to be focused on selling their foodstuffs to Montreal and Quebec. The more settlers there are, the more he can sell."

"What's it like for Negroes up there?"

"I am not an expert by any means, but from what I've read, it's now illegal to buy slaves in Lower Canada. Shouldn't be a problem in the place where we're going."

"If the Wrights have been promising the woodsmen land, then I don't see that I'm any different," said London. "I'm a free man. A promise to them then is a promise to me, and from what I've heard, he's paying them cash money. Yes, siree. Sounds like it wouldn't be a bad thing for me to do.

"Samuel, you know me. If you need me to look in on your animals, you let me know," said London. "I'm sure Missu Thomas wouldn't mind me taking the wagon out. That reminds me, before I go, I'd like to get something from you, if you don't mind."

After finding his hat and gloves in the house, Samuel returned with some carrots from his root cellar for the horse.

⤚◎⟋

Abner sat on the cold ground with his back against the barn. His hands were on his cheeks, and his elbows rested on his knees. *I shouldn't have pushed her away,* he thought. *We both pushed Rachael away. Both of us. How could that have happened?*

Couldn't tell Rachael—that's Tom's fault, but if Poppa told her ... Damn. Damn. He watched Ruggles screaming at his cousins. The girls were ignoring him.

Abner kept throwing rocks at a tree. He missed most of the time.

Momma wasn't sick, but they says she was. How does someone get sick and die right away? Why did Missus Wright say she drowned? And falling in the water doesn't make people old-looking, does it? And Abigail wasn't in the water? Missu and Missus Wright, Tom, and my Poppa—they're all lying. It makes no sense. Momma, why'd you leave me?

He dropped the stones and drooped toward his knees.

Ruggles sauntered over. "You look sad," he said.

"Leave me alone."

"No one will play with me."

Abner was quiet.

"Why you here?" Ruggles asked.

"Cause."

"Cause you're supposed to be playing with me."

"I am."

"No, you're not."

"I am a monster bear, and I'm going to eat you."

"No, you're not. I'm an Injun, and I'm going to shoot you dead with all my arrows."

Abner got up. "Injuns don't kill monster bears because we're terrible and really mean. We eat all kinds of Injuns, and I'm going to tear you apart." He raised his arms and made a ferocious growl.

Ruggles staggered away. "No, you don't," he yelled. "I'm of the Woburn tribe, and I'm going to kill you dead."

"Blang, blang," Ruggles said as he shot invisible arrows.

Abner continued to howl and roar as the two jumped around and around.

"I got you," Ruggles hollered.

"No, you didn't."

"Injuns always win."

"No, they don't. You can't kill me. Some of us can't die because we're special." He roared and howled again as he chased him.

"Arrows don't work against the monster bear."

"What?"

"We'll eat anything, including you," growled Abner as he reached for the sky. Ruggles tried to bowl over his cousins, and Abner followed. "There's only one thing that stops a monster bear from eating Injuns," he yelled as Ruggles headed back toward the house.

Just before the kitchen door slammed behind the little boy, Abner said, "Something better—kitchen treats."

Looking up and reaching up to the sky with claws again, he let out another loud, prolonged AWRRRG and followed it with some long howls. He was interrupted by the sound of one of the girls crying.

"Whoa," yelled Thomas. He pulled back on the reins of the oxen's yoke. "Year after year, more rocks appear; the devil's work," he muttered as he unstrapped the plow from the ox.

His brother marched across the field to meet him.

"I heard you swearing. You'll need this," Philemon told him, and he gave him a sack.

"Wasn't cussing, and I see you only brought one."

"It could take a couple of rounds until you get that rock out."

"Always doing the easy thing."

"Tom, I was just . . . Why do you have to be such an arse?"

"Just no reason for all these rocks, is all. Get over it."

"The cheese is in the bag. The milk is in the kitchen. My Abigail said she heard you might have some asparagus left. She has a liking for asparagus soup."

"Getting a little late for that, but Mary's the one to ask."

"What about Elizabeth and Eleanor?" asked Philemon.

"You mean about moving? No, neither is going. Not much interest from Captain Symmes's associates, at least not the kind of interest I'd like. But I can't blame them."

"Abigail's sisters, Lavina Allen and Margaret Choate, are committed," Philemon said. "Maybe her brother Joseph."

"That'll suit you, won't it?"

"What's that supposed to mean?"

"It's their Irish, unquestioning—"

"No, they're not. They're fine, hardworking, pious people from this state."

"So of your Missus's relations, Lydia and Joshua aren't going?" Thomas asked.

"What are you going to do about London? You did enough for him. You don't owe his brother anything."

"That's my concern. Stay out of it."

"He's not keeping up. Why keep him? I'm sure you could find a younger couple. Someone more pious and without a drinking problem."

"Philemon, you're avoiding what really matters. You're telling everyone we're leaving, and we don't have anywhere to go to."

"The Grand River. Thomas, what are you talking about?"

He put a hand in front of him and said, "It's not worth shit. The crown revoked the land grant. The title isn't worth wiping my ass. Hell will freeze over before you get money back from that huckster. You filed in the Vermont court last fall. What happened?"

"Oh, you mean Jonathan Fassett," said Philemon. He removed his hat and waved it around while saying, "Thomas, you're blowing things out of proportion. You know, we filed with the crown last spring, notifying them of our intentions. How can they refute the hardworking industriousness of religious, god-fearing white folk like ourselves?"

"They've said no, and they can say it again."

"Nobody is on that land. Governments change. Add a few pounds in the hands of the right bureaucrat, and we'll be their first. We still have the title. We'll work it out."

"Thought so," said Thomas as he wiped the sweat from his brow. "And not a cent from Fassett. Philemon, there's no way I'm selling my property."

"So you'll wait until after I've invested my stake in it, and when we get to the first setback, you renege. You're a scoundrel, Thomas."

"I'm not exactly saying I'm out," he replied as he put his hands on his hips.

"What does 'exactly' mean?"

"So why are a bunch of landowners going to give up all that they have to farm in some unknown place where they don't own their land?"

"I'm working on it."

"You're not going to tell them, are you?"

"I told you, I'm working on it. You know what we're working with. There's more land available than you can imagine. Tom, you're thirty-nine. A chance like this only comes once in a lifetime, and you know it. It's not just your chance. Think of your three boys. Hell, and what if there's more coming? And there are dowries for your four girls."

"I'll probably go, but like I said, I'm not ready to sell. If it fails, I need a fallback."

"And London?"

"He'll go to Boston, I'd expect. I've had Samuel have a word with him."

"You could barter him for something."

"I'll have you know, I follow the laws of the state."

"I didn't say sell; I said barter."

"How's there a difference?"

"I'm just trying to help."

"You could have put more work into researching the land grants."

"I've dug this rock out. So don't just stand there. Help me roll it out. Are you going to help me, or do I need to get my boys?"

A month after Jane died, London Oxford and his son went on another trip to town. He steered Missa Wright's carriage horse to the left of the path. They were going across some rough patches. London could see ahead that fallen branches blocked the trail.

London stopped the wagon, got off, and told the boy to stay where he was. After securing the reins, he gently patted the horse.

"But Poppa," his son whined.

"You keep bundled up in that blanket. You'll help plenty when we get to town."

London looked around and noticed that it wasn't particularly windy. He quickly cleared the path by throwing the branches aside. When the wagon started rolling again, he said, "Sometimes when branches get broken in a storm, they just hold on in the trees. Over time, gentle winds can shake them loose. You never know what will bring it down or when."

The broken branches reminded Abner of his mother's hidden green stone. When asking her to show it to him, he learned that she had stored it behind a baseboard in the bedroom. The necklace was wrapped in a nice piece of cloth. When he asked his mother why she wasn't wearing it, she told him that she didn't because she didn't want anyone to steal it. If they saw it, they'd steal it or throw her in jail. They'd do that even if they knew it was hers. She made him swear not to tell anyone about it.

London looked down at Abner, noticing a dreary look on his son's face. "What you thinking?" he asked.

"So Grandpa thought he had no chance of marrying Nelle," said Abner. "He must have felt pretty bad. Even if the Injun gave him that nice stone."

"I guess it's time you heard the rest of the story. If a horse kicks me in the head, or I get sick like your momma, there'd be nobody to tell it, would there?" London snapped the reins, and the wagon continued on to town.

He brushed his nose and said, "Yes, siree, my poppa must have wondered if he would keep being right in the head. I mean, without his Nell and all." He spat on the ground.

"Anyways, two weeks after your grandpa Coffey got rescued by the Injuns, he was approached by one of the other servants. It was Monday, and he was organizing a cleanup in the big house. The servant said she was supposed to tell him to go see William, who was his master's second-oldest boy.

"Later that morning, Coffey went to the stable and prepared a horse for riding. The mare was old, but so far she had proved herself reliable. To keep good relations with the old girl, he brought along a couple of carrots.

"At Missa William Buckmaster's house, Coffey dismounted and tied the horse to the hitching post by the stables. He walked around to the front door and knocked. A servant answered. He asked her to tell her master that Coffey had arrived, that he wanted to see him, and that it was real important. A few minutes later, another servant led him to Massa William's sitting room. His son was sitting in his father's chair."

"'I have summoned you here for an important matter,' he said. 'I'm told that you want to get married. If you are serious about the affair, I strongly recommend that you bring the matter up again with my father tomorrow morning. If you delay beyond that, I'm afraid you'll have lost your chance. I know my father, and he can get set in his ways, if you get my meaning.'

"Coffey asked him how he had come by that opportunity.

"'Not rightly sure,' William said. My father was in a dour mood about property matters, and someone he met gave him something new to chew on.'

"'Something he et?' asked Coffey.

"'Ideas, dear boy. It was ideas,' William said. 'My father told me that he had the fortunate opportunity of talking with a young man of great intelligence and clear mind,' said William. 'Right sort and tied to the right family, apparently. My father told me that they talked about the Injun wars we're having.'

"'He doesn't believe the government should pay folks to move out west,' said Coffey.

"'Well, well, Coffey, amazing, you're very perceptive for a Negro. How did you pick that up?'

"'It was just something I heard in passing, sir, and I don't know anything more than that,' he said.

"'Well, Coffey, I wouldn't mention that anywhere else. We're at war, you know. We don't want to lose our scalp here. Anyway, the young man offered some ideas for winning the war and was very persuasive. More to the point, he gave Father some ideas about acquiring advantages after the war. My father is absolutely convinced the war is going to be won, and he's preparing for what comes next. He needs to develop his assets. More wealth and resources mean a good property manager needs more support staff. Coffey, that's where you fit in. You need your woman to make lots of babies while you have time. I don't think you'd complain about that part. That's why I've asked you here. Get on with it.'

"Coffey was absolutely speechless. He felt like he'd been hit by a bolt of lightning."

London, pretending he was William, gave a sneer and a flippant wave.

Abner gave his father a quizzical look, but he was focused on the road ahead.

"Maybe William was trying to manipulate his father," London said. "Wealthy people like to lead people on."

"It was Nelle," Abner said. "He knew it was just right."

London laughed and playfully socked Abner's shoulder. "Or maybe it was Coffey's sad brown puppy dog eyes. If you met him, I'm sure you'd think so too.

"Anyway, Poppa told me that he remembered the Injun named Quinac telling him that he had 'seen stranger things in his day.' I'm sure it was nothing stranger than what he was seeing right there."

London looked at his son and asked, "What do you think?"

Abner shrugged.

London stretched on his seat.

"Coffey returned to the waiting room and was kept waiting for another hour. The servant that led him there asked, 'He hasn't got back to you yet?'"

"'No,' said Coffey."

"He took him outside, and they went looking for him. They found the colonel looking at flowers in the garden.

"'Hello, Coffey, is that you?' he asked.

"'Yes, Massa, it's me.'

"'Coffey, what brings you to me?'

"''Massa, I had told you about a fine Nelle Donahue. She wants me. She is a right, smart, good gal, good health and can help make lots of healthy, bright chil'n. Maybe, Massa, you might consider to consent that me and she, might be married.'

"Colonel Buckmaster walked away and ignored him for a bit. He came back and said, 'Coffey, you're quite demanding these days, aren't you?'

"'What's that, Massa?'

"The colonel checked out the state of the shrubs and made notes. 'Lots of things to be done before our guests arrive,' he said. 'What's Nelle's owner's name?'"

Coffey told him, 'They live in Holliston, sir.'

"'I'm familiar with him. Acceptable, I suppose. I'll ponder on it. Come back in a week.'"

"Coffey, without much of a smile, repeatedly thanked him and was escorted out."

"On Sunday afternoon, Coffey managed to borrow the buggy in order to propose to Nelle. Folks at the plantation were rooting for him. It took about two hours of travelling by buggy to get to her."

London stopped the story there and took a deep breath. "You know, after all this, she could always have said no."

"But—"

"Yeah, and you know how that part ends. But anyway, Coffey finds her, and he takes her near the river, bends his knee, and asks her."

"And she—"

"Well, Coffey told me that her mouth stayed open, and it froze him solid. He thought he was going to die. From his pocket, he took out the green stone he got from the Injun and gave it to her. She was caught up about how nice it was and all. She let him unload his pack of stories until she gave him an answer."

"She said yes?" asked Abner.

"No, she actually said she wanted to think about it. As Coffey started walking away, she yelled, 'Of course I will.' And you'd think that was that, wouldn't you?"

Abner shrugged.

"Well, it wasn't. After that, Coffey had to get permission from Nelle's parents. He met with them that night. He told me that he remembered Nelle's mother complaining that he wasn't a free man, but she did say he was a kindly man.

"'Good church-going man, Momma,' Nelle told her.

"'If he was an Injun, you'd be free,' her father said.

"'Poppa,' she whined.

"'Just teasing you, Eleanor,' he told her.

"Her father called her that, but everyone else called her Nelle. Before Coffey left, they gave their blessings. Coffey told me that they were fine folk. He didn't get to know them much."

"Why?" Abner asked.

"Nelle's father got sold because he was getting old, and Nelle's momma died less than a year after they took him."

"So what do you think happened next?" asked London.

"They got married?" asked Abner.

"No, he had to ask her massa. On Monday, Coffey arranged to take the wagon out for another supply run. Coffey was escorted to Nelle's massa's sitting room.

"'Hello, Coffey, is that you?' he asked.

"'Yes, Massa, it's me.'

"'Coffey, what message did your master send by you?'

"'Didn't send no message, sir, I comed myself.'

"'What you mean to say is that you have run away, Coffey?'

"'No sar, Massa told me as how I might come and see you, is all.'

"'Well, Coffey, what is it? Does your master intend to hire you out next year, and you want me to hire you?'

"'No sar, he wants me hisself. But I comed to see you, Massa, cause I think that your gal Nelle is a right smart, right proper, good gal.'

"'That so, Coffey?'

"'And I thought that perhaps, maybe, that seeing as you and Massa Buckmaster was good friends, and being as I want to be no bad Negro at all, that maybe, possibly, you might consider to consent, so we might be married.'

"Nelle's massa looked Coffey over. He asked him if he had any bad habits."

"'No, siree. I'd be right good for Miss Nelle.'

"He checked him for any visible defects. 'Well, Coffey, I like your looks, and I will think it over. You come and see me next week, and I will tell you.'

"Coffey asked him if he could see Nell. 'Yes, Coffey, you can see her when she finishes her chores. I would expect that she will be free in about three hours. Come back then.'

"He couldn't afford much time with her because he had to return to Framingham again to do his chores. On the next evening, he got an audience with his own Massa.

"'Hello Coffey. You here again? What do you want this time?'

"'Well, Massa, I comed to see as to what you thought about me and Nelle getting married.'

"'Get out, boy. Out of here. I don't want to be disturbed.'

"'But Massa told Coffey to come.'

"'How's that, Coffey?'

"'Massa Buckmaster told Coffey to come in one week, and then Massa tell Coffey as how he can marry Nelle or not.'

"'Oh yes, I remember now. Well, Coffey, after church, I discussed it with Nelle's mistress. She doesn't see a problem. Her owner and I had some details to work out. We've decided that you'll marry Nelle. He's going to build a cabin, and Nelle can live there.'

"Coffey thanked him and was escorted out. Later on Friday afternoon, Coffey borrowed the old mare and visited Nelle's massa again.

"'Coffey, your owner, Colonel Joseph Buckmaster, has, as you probably already know, given his permission for you to marry Nelle,' her Massa told him. 'You'll be married on the Lord's day, so it won't affect either of your work. We agreed that it should happen near Christmas.'

"Colonel Buckmaster's oldest son, who was an ordained minister, found out about it and persuaded people to have the marriage done in Waltham, which is near Woburn. So Nelle, Coffey, and all the guests walked there on Sunday. The time for the wedding came and passed. Hours after the wedding was supposed to have happened, a boy showed up and told them that the reverend apologized, but he wasn't able to make it. To make up for the inconvenience, it was arranged that the marriage would happen on the following Tuesday. None of the rest of the family and friends, with the exception of their parents, were able to take the day off. Coffey, fortunately, was able to borrow the wagon to make the ten-mile trip to Waltham. So Nelle and Coffey finally got married on Tuesday, December 12, 1758. Afterword, Nelle and the children continued to live in a cottage on her massa's property. Coffey was permitted to visit Wednesday evenings and Sundays."

London looked at Abner, who was huddled up, tightly holding the blanket wrapped at his neck.

"Mighty quiet. What are you thinking?"

"Was that what it was like with you and Momma?"

"No, but it could have been." In a reflex, London pulled the brim of his hat down to protect his eyes from the bright sun. It hadn't come out from beyond the clouds, but it might, was the thing.

"Not the same in this state, but it's like that in most places in this world."

When he reached into an empty pocket, he dreamed of the taste of Jane's delicious apple bread.

They—all of them: keep telling me what's not true, he thought. The Wrights—thems just like the Colonel. Drowning is what they say. They knows something else. One thing, for sure—them white folks might not give me the land I'm owed, but somehow, I am going to learn why in God's name, she left us. He yearned to dive into the black waters and destroy what had taken his Jane. He took another drink from his pocket flask, whipped the reins, and the horse pulled on.

Reservations

Thomas took another bite of apple cake bread that he'd stored in his pocket as he and his wife hiked through the woods behind their property to the river. It was a warm spring afternoon, almost half a year after London's wife had passed.

"You didn't offer me any?" his wife, Mary said.

He offered her what he was eating.

"No, no—no," she huffed.

He offered her a wrap of cloth from his pocket. From it she removed a couple of slices of fruit and handed him back the rest.

"Only the best for my Mary," he said.

"Only the best when I catch you," she said.

"What did London say?"

"Well, as you know, he's been working hard in the fields with the boys."

"He's supposed to be doing housework and chores. We've got five under twelve, and there's three of his. Work outside isn't helping me."

"When we move, he can make himself a place of his own."

"Are you really considering bringing them along? I've heard you boys talking. Putting ours and Philemon's all under one roof, and his too. Really, Thomas, you aren't thinking this through."

"He's working hard."

"And drinking his life away at night. Maybe you don't see it, but I do."

"Without Jane, it's been hard," said Thomas.

"I pray for them folk. And you know they are better off here. There's no place better for Negroes than here. And he can go to Boston like we talked about. There's more coloured folk there. I heard them talk about it when Jane was alive."

"He's not prepared for change. I'm afraid of what leaving us would do to those children."

"They're not ours, Thomas."

"I know that. This has come up a couple of times, but I just couldn't find a way to get my words out."

"Thomas, I'll pray on it, but get it done." She stopped and went into a crouch.

"What are you staring at?" asked Thomas.

"Just a cute turtle hiding in its shell."

"Better leave it. I hear they bite." He grabbed her hand. "There are better things to see at the pond. Come on."

—⟡—

Abner and his sisters walked down the hill away from the kitchen entrance. Polly marched up to meet them.

"And what do you think you're doing?" she asked.

"Your ma'am sent us here."

Rubbing a scar on her hand, she yelled, "You stay away. Not going to get what you got. No way. You go over there. That's where coloureds belong." She was pointing at the barn. She huffed off to complain to her brother, John.

"What we got?" asked Annie.

"Maybe we should spit so she gets whatever she thinks she's going to get.

Serve her right."

"I'm gonna tell," said Annie.

"What?"

"Missa Wright said we're supposed to do that," replied Annie."

John, seeing the commotion, marched over from a wagon he'd parked. He pointed to a field that had already been picked. "Yeah gotta pile what's left. It's gonna be for the cows."

"How come we're not going with the others?"

"Because. Just because."

Annie spat. It was more a sound of one than a gobbed kind.

"What's that? She sick?" asked John.

"Maybe you'll get what we got," Abner said.

"Do the one beside it, when you're done. Yahs got enough work there to take you all day. Now go on."

When they got close to the plot, Annie asked, "Are we gonna get sick? Do we have what got Momma?"

"They don't know nothing." He stared at both of them. "Do you feel sick?"

"I'm hungry," Annie said.

"That sounds right to me," Abner said.

When he reached the plot, he kicked the dirt and then gave it a spit. Annie and Rachael laughed and did the same thing.

Three days later, Abner accompanied his father to deliver a load of cheeses to Philemon Wright's. "How come we haven't heard about other people that got what Abigail got?" Abner asked.

"I don't know. I don't even know what it was that she had. Why don't you talk about something else?"

"The girls are picking on Annie," Abner said.

"Are they picking on you?" his father asked.

"Why don't we go somewhere else?"

"When it's time, I hope to go north with these folks. I wanna get us some land and a place of our own," London said. "I think you'd like that."

"What do you think happened to that Injun?"

"Who?"

"The one in your story."

"Don't know."

"And the one that they had tied up?"

"Maybe some of it wasn't true. Coffey told me it over and over, and each time he would add more stuff. Maybe—"

"Why would you wanna tell me something that wasn't true?"

"Didn't say that. It's just that he loved to talk. And life is hard and..." London lost his train of thought. "What's important is I don't want you talking to Missa Philemon. He'll cause trouble."

"And when are they leaving?"

"Just don't complain to them. Let's just make this drop quick."

"But—"

"Don't talk back, or I'll let you off here. Now keep quiet. We're almost there." He gave a slap of the whip.

Abner pulled the blanket tighter to keep out the cold.

In late November, Philemon joined his brother, Thomas in the barn.

"I thought you were going to help me with work in the mine," Philemon asked.

"What does it look like I am doing?"

"You're taking the wagon apart."

"We need the wagon, but the wheel needs fixing. It's the spokes."

"The small axe?" asked Philemon.

Thomas pointed to the wall.

"I'll think more on it," said Thomas.

"You mean the coloured?" asked Philemon.

"We need help minding the children. A female is what we need. Could get a female to help after we settle in."

"See your point. You can't just kick them out, though. I mean, I know he's a mess, but he's not always like that."

"You like to be contrary. You're just going on with this to spite me."

"I did bring him here, and we did owe them."

"That was a long time ago."

"What I was trying to say is that if he doesn't want to go, he could be of use," said Philemon. "I mean, we're hiring lots of workmen, and he can handle a sleigh. He's good with livestock. He can read and write, and he would cost almost nothing. He's worked in the fields with us, and you know him. You can't say the same for the woodsmen. And he could always move on to Montreal once we're settled."

"And what about Abigail's brother?" Thomas asked.

"And you just make sure his boy shows his worth. Don't need more layabouts like your Tom and John," his brother said.

"You love to try to set me off, don't you?" said Thomas. "I can take you down just like I used to—so don't."

"You're—"

Thomas interrupted with a wave. "Don't have time for that," Thomas said. This wagon wheel won't fix itself."

-๑-๏

A snowstorm blew over the farm a couple of weeks after London was informed that he and his family would be part of the expedition to the north country. Late at night, while the storm pounded, London made his way into the woods at the back of the property. Hiding behind a tree, he swallowed his hidden stash of shine. It was his only solace. The days were long, and it was hard to get away from the children. The harsh cold, tempered with that raw taste, kept him awake. It was terribly raw, but it was his.

A fresh field of soft, deep snow and thickening clouds shrouding a fading moon wouldn't stop him. He hadn't walked to the crick beyond the forest in weeks. It's where he talked to Jane. Today, he really didn't want to listen to what she'd tell him. It would be about leaving, and he just couldn't bear it.

His fingers and thumbs were freezing because the old mitts didn't cover them. Each swig was painful, and when he attempted to put his hand under his armpit, sometimes the shine would splash on his jacket.

There had been nights when he'd lost the jar. Those nights he'd fallen on the way back and wrestled with thoughts of letting sleep take him in the snow. But he had a rule: he had to check on his daughters before he went to sleep, so somehow. So far, he always made it back.

He toasted the invisible animals around him. He didn't see any tracks. *They must all be asleep. They're probably smarter than me,* he thought. He took another sip.

Going closer to the shore scared him, where he and Jane used to sit. "Damn that Philemon. And all those others. Treat us like their dogs. And nowhere to go. Them bastards," London said, and then took a piss. His bottle slipped and disappeared somewhere in the snow. "Damnation," he muttered.

Losing his balance, he fell back, missed the tree, and plopped into the snow. As the frigid, numbing night soothed him to sleep, he wondered if he was going to get up this time.

"My Jane, she's here somewheres," he said. "We know it."

In January of the next year, Abner helped his father with milking cows. He fed them and helped his father carry buckets of milk. It was cold in the barn. Steam came from their breath, the cows, and the fresh piles of shit.

"How is that Missa Thomas decided to take us along?" Abner asked. "And what about Missa Philemon?"

"They need someone to drive the oxen across the snow, and they don't trust the new men with the supplies. They told me that if there's somewhere we want to go after this, we can go. We is free, they says."

"What? So where we gonna go?" asked Abner.

"Don't you worry 'bout that. Just mind your sisters. And Philemon's nephew, Joshua, is going. His family doesn't want him, so he's with us."

His father picked up his pace and marched back towards the kitchen. Milk was sloshing out of his buckets.

I thought that the only reason we were moving was to get a place to live, thought Abner. *Poppa, what are you doing?*

Heading North

After church on the first Sunday in February of 1800, five families climbed aboard winter sleighs. They were the Wright boys, the Oxfords, and two families of Philemon Wright's wife's siblings, not including young Joshua, who came without his father. Agnes Wright's sister Lydia wasn't going because she was going to give birth. She was Lavina's twin, and the family was ready to go, but the caravan couldn't wait. Unfortunately, before the caravan reached the border, she'd be dead. Her son's birth would kill her. It would be another year before the sisters were told.

London's family accompanied four couples with young families. Nineteen children were twelve years or younger. The three oldest children were younger than eighteen.

Each sleigh was pulled by an ox. Thomas Wright's sleigh at the front had a pair, which would clear a path for the rest.

Of the fourteen horses, two were ridden by the oldest Wright boys. Each of the families, including Thomas and his brother, drove their own sleighs. Where the trail was well travelled, the horsemen rode ahead.

Although London's sleigh was the last of the family sleighs, it was followed by another couple, which carried tools, provisions, and building supplies. More than two dozen single men carrying axes walked behind.

Enough seed and food were brought to last beyond the next harvest. There was enough scheduled time for men to hunt for fresh game and do some fishing.

While his father checked the straps on the oxen, Abner wrapped blankets around his sisters, who were curled in a space behind the sleigh's front seat. They were surrounded by the sleigh's heavy load.

Abner was shivering. "Poppa, why are we leaving now? Why, when it's so cold?"

"We have five weeks to get there. To make the quickest trip, the sleighs will be pulled across snow and frozen rivers. We have so much stuff, we'd never be able to carry it all.

"What if it takes longer?"

"The ice will melt, and the sleighs will sink to the bottom, but we won't let that happen. Now, while I'm helping the others, I want you to help your sisters make a nook under the canvas behind me. You'll be like Injuns with your own tepee."

When London got back, he heard yelling under the tarp. "Annie kicked her back," Abner cried.

London pointed to the kids.

Abner, in turn, pointed to his pocket.

"Lord have mercy," London replied as he reluctantly handed off a roll of bread.

Before squeezing in the back, he broke a piece for himself.

Phil Jr., who was seventeen, rode on horseback toward the Oxford's sleigh. A boy about Abner's age followed.

When young Phil Jr. came alongside, Abner stood up in the back.

"Are you lost yet, Abner?" the boy asked.

"No, sir," he replied.

"London," he said. "I've got another passenger here for you. This here is Joshua."

Abner remembered him from Abigail's funeral. He was standing next to the horse.

"I'm not going with them. No way," yelled Joshua.

"Good. We don't want you either. More room for us," Abner said.

"Why are you holding us up?" Phil Jr. asked.

"I told you, I ain't goin' with no coloureds," Joshua replied.

"I wouldn't give you the time of day if you weren't family, but my mother has a soft spot for her layabout brother," Phil Jr. said. "London, I don't want you to indulge this scoundrel. Where we're going is a place for a new start. That goes for coloureds and bastards." He pointed to the sleigh. "Now, get in or get the hell out of here."

"Auntie Abigail," Joshua yelled.

"Oh, I'll definitely let my mom know."

"How come he gets to ride a horse?" Joshua asked.

Phil Jr. rode ahead. He must have overheard him because he pretended to tip his hat.

London climbed up to his seat and grabbed the reins and whip. "Boy, I want no trouble from you. If you's coming then—" and he beckoned him to come up.

Joshua looked up at London's stern face. "Yes, sir." He jumped up on the seat and threw his pack at Abner's back.

"Ouch," yelled Abner.

Joshua was the same age as Abner. His face was square, his nose pudgy, he had a scar on the side of his forehead, and his dark, brown, wavy hair was short and poorly cut. He was of a stockier build than Abner and had big hands for a twelve-year-old.

"Watch what you're doing!" Abner groaned as he dragged the bag to the back under the canvas.

"You don't look like you're dressed for winter," London said. "No gloves and nothing on your ears. Where do you think we're going?"

"To a land of promise, wherever that is."

"Sure, that will do, but if you don't want to lose hands or those looks, you'll need something warmer. Abner, go fetch the boy something. Wouldn't be good for white folks to find one of their own dead back here, would it?"

Abner climbed up and sat between the two. "If he falls in a snowbank, maybe they wouldn't find him." He brought some thick blankets and elbowed Joshua in the side before giving him one of them.

The caravan headed out after the men folk prayed and everyone took last-minute latrine breaks.

"Don't pay mind to Missa Philemon; he likes to blow smoke out of his ass."

"Joshua, you watch your mouth," London said.

"But you ..."

"You best quote the Bible, than getting us in trouble." London stared at the boys and laughed. "He does have a way, doesn't he?" and laughed again. "You best take in the view. Remember it, 'cause ya will probably never see it again."

The caravan rode all day and stopped only for a couple of short toilet breaks. The rolling pasture fields gradually were replaced with thick, uncultivated stands of mixed woodlands.

The next morning, the caravan moved out shortly after sunrise. The weather was mild, the snow a mushy powder, and the clouds wispy. Some of the contractors walking behind had their jackets unbuttoned and their scarves dangling loose.

As they headed northward, Philemon rode up alongside London. "It's time you got these. You need a new pair." From his saddle, Philemon tossed him a bag and then hurried back to the front of the caravan.

"What's that?" asked Abner.

His father was quiet while he looked inside the bag.

"He loves to talk, and he said almost nothing. What was that about?" Abner asked.

When London took a boot out, Joshua said, "Ya got new boots. Looks like they've never been worn. Isn't that something?"

"Mind yourself. I don't need them," he said as he put the boot back. He started to swing the bag in an attempt to throw it away when Abner yelled, "Don't you dare."

"What?" his father asked mid-swing.

"Your boots are torn," said Abner. You can't even walk properly in them. Where's you gonna get another pair from?"

His father crossed his legs away from him.

"If you's gonna throw that away, I'll take it," said Joshua.

"You'll never be big enough," said London.

"Then I'll sell them."

"Boy, you'll do no such thing."

"And how's you gonna walk in the snow?" Abner asked.

"He knows nothing," London replied.

"But Poppa, we're gonna need you. I need you. You's not thinking right."

"Leave me alone," London said.
Seeing Abner's sullen face, he took a breath and pushed back on his seat. "Have the girls find me a good pair of socks."

Annie popped up behind him. "We're getting 'em," she said before disappearing again.

Under the tarp, things tumbled, and there were sounds of ripping.

"That's yours, I hope," London said to Abner.

"No, I think it's Joshua's."

"You, stupid coon," Joshua groaned.

"She's no coon. She's a fox, and she'll tear the life out of a no-good like you."

Young Rachael popped up and put a sock on her father's shoulder.

"Where's the other one?" London asked.

"I took it," Annie said, and gave it to her father. "And if he comes near me, tell him I'll bite," she said as she and her sister disappeared under the tarp.

"Stay covered and keep the cold air out." London adjusted his scarf to cover more of his neck. After putting the new boots on, he squeezed the old boots between himself and his son. Seeing Joshua staring at them, he said,

"You can't have them. They're mine."

Joshua took them and threw them away.

"And why'd you do that?" asked Abner.

"You know he wouldn't keep the new pair unless I done that. The sole was coming off, and the leather was really bad."

"You know that makes no sense," Abner replied. His father pulled his brim to the side and took another swig.

"And there's a storm coming," he repeated. "Settle down, boys, or I'll let you off here. Will Wrights go back for you's? No, siree. No way. No how."

On the second day out, Abner was getting bored. Joshua told him he saw a deer, but 'cause Abner didn't see anything, he thought Joshua was lying.

"Where are we gonna stop?" Abner asked.

"You'll see when we get there," his father said. "Let me drive."

"Has it got a name?" Joshua asked.

"Near Lunenburg," London said. "Why don't both of you get in the back?"

"Ain't enough room," Abner said. "That place has something to do with the moon. I heard Missa Thomas say," said Abner.

London ate some dried apple from his pocket and took another swig.

Before entering the town, Abner saw that Missa Thomas and Philemon had stopped to talk to someone near the treeline.

So now their boys are steering the sleighs. That's not good, he thought.

The men had dismounted. They were holding their horses' reins, but the horses were trying to pull away. They were acting skittish.

When their sleigh moved closer, Abner recognized the tall hat of one of the men. It was an Injun. It was that Injun that he saw at the cemetery. He had his hand on Missa Thomas Wright's shoulder. They were all smiling. When their sleigh passed, Abner froze. The Injun had a steady glare on him. When Abner looked back, he was still staring. He looked like a ravenous animal that wanted to eat him. Abner wanted the next stop to be a long way away. Unfortunately, the clouds were thick, and a disappearing sun wasn't providing consolation.

PART 3: Moving Along

Bone Chilling Cold

When he bit down on his lip, he wondered if he was still alive. The frigid cold wouldn't allow him to feel pain. The harrowing wind was constant and unyielding. Snow had turned to ice on his shaggy eyebrows and beard. London couldn't see anything beyond his arms, and the accumulating snow on his body made him feel like a ghost; with the snow blindness, he felt like he was disappearing. Raising a forearm to protect against the howling wind and blinding white glare didn't help much. It took him back to when he was younger than his boy, to Buckmaster's, when the colonel still owned him, and when he was more afraid than he could ever have imagined. The constant lines of grey-green trees along the winding trail reminded him of when he was taken from the surface and entombed. Sod covered the boards. It was as dark as death.

And there was that single pipe for air. I sucked on it like a calf on a mother's teat. It's what kept him alive.

"Throw'd into the ground for no reason," London moaned. He grabbed the reins firmly with both mitts. *"Just meanness. To spite Poppa? Maybe. Who knows?"* he thought.

He remembered those foul days when they told him they was gonna plug it, and they did. Five minutes, they said it was all it was. Don't know, London thought. It was his poppa's tears that woke him. He was looking down at him.

It was awful. They threw him in two more times after that. He remembered Poppa telling him, again and again, *'Don't you dare close them eyes. Don't you dare. You won't come home if you do.'*

"No," London said.

In the dark, he just wanted to go to sleep, but he didn't want to die. He was scared. Real scared.

"No, siree," he said and then took another drink from his flask before opening his mouth to the clouds.

No one shitted in the same place down there. You didn't need to know where people dumped because there was lots of shit everywhere. Grabbed me handfuls of dead leaves before they locked me in. I fooled them, London thought as he leaned further forward.

"Wasn't getting much light in from the pipe 'cause I had to suck'n on it. Oh," he groaned. *And my back and my knees hurt real bad, he thought. Pipe being so low, couldn't kneel proper-like. Couldn't make a mound of dirt to lean on—too much wet shit, and something rock hard below the dirt.*

"*Dear Lord, maybe someone was b*uried under there," he muttered. "Wouldn't that have been something?"

"And no food," he said. *Well, suppose with all the throwing up and shitting, what would have been the point?* he thought.

He let the ice land on his tongue and swallowed it.

He remembered trying to breathe in the dark. It was usually dry, but when the wind blew, it was like a tiny crick of sweet air that drained into his mouth, but his lips and nose remained chapped as ever. When the air was warm it didn't seem to have the same life to it. There were times when it had different flower tastes. Sometimes different grasses. Once, he thought he recognized a sweet apple taste. Wasn't sure how 'cause he hadn't seen no apples on any of Buckmaster's fields. The wetness in the air kept him awake. It reminded him of Poppa's tears. He was sure if he could stay awake, that someday he was going to feel better, and somehow, he and Poppa was going to have breakfast. London bit on his lip again.

"They's not going to make me sleep," London said. "No way. No how." He loosened the scarf under his chin. "Gotta do what my poppa told me." For a moment, he could see streaks of brown on the ox's hide in front of him. This also reminded him of being underground.

He was told that when ol' Coffey was put into the ground, with none of his family, the colonel had Reverend John Swift say words over him. And Poppa told him that he hated that man.

When the Oxford plantation got my poppa as a baby, they didn't even pay. Church got a slave as a present. 'Sold him for good money though,' he told me. When they lowered my poppa into another hole in the ground, the reverend went on about how Negroes was owned 'cause God believed they was sinners. Dear Lord. The terrible and unholy things they did to us. I heard my poppa once say he'd like nothing better than to see that same Reverend dead and him piss on him on the way down.

"Ooh Wee," London said as he bundled the reins in a loop and squeezed his mitts around it as he leaned forward again into the blizzard.

That would be something to see, wouldn't it? he thought and took another sip.

London's father told him that the Reverend sold him to Mister Buckmaster because he wasn't holy enough. Got to be with lots of coloureds then, but there was lots of whippings too.

London gnawed on his mitt for no reason and stared blankly at the snow coming in.

We need to be free, and there needs to be lots more folk like me, he thought.

He got a tapping on his shoulder. Annie stood behind him. "Cold," Annie said.

Her hat was coming off.

"Long ways to go," London said. "That hat, pull it down." He wrapped her scarf around her ears and mouth as he held the ends of the reins between his knees. "Need to be together with others under the blankets. Way too cold up here to be with us, Annie."

As expressive and determined as her mother, isn't she? London thought. The hat that was coming off revealed the floral ribbon that secured the bun in the back for her wavy hair. It was Rachael, however, who had Jane's feral eyes and loose black curls. Ponytails on each side tried to tie down her wild hair.

Although Rachael might keep her powder dry before letting go, Annie, like her mother, wasn't usually one to hold things in.

"Ooh-wee?" Annie asked.

"Thinking of my poppa — that's all," he replied. "Been a long time." From his pocket stash, he gave her some of his bannock. "Your momma would want me to give you some." After a quick reach for it and a blink, she tore off a piece and handed it back to him. She disappeared under the canvas. He pulled his hat down and tightened the scarf around the raised greatcoat collar to cover his freezing ears and mouth.

"Cute as a button, aren't you?" he said. "Just like your ma."

He rode thoughtless and unmoving for a long time, as blasts of snow pellets continued to assail his face.

Why did you leave me, Jane? he wondered. *Why did she leave without talking to me? She wouldn't be in the ground. She'd be here with me.*

He felt her breath against his neck. He saw the look of her hips when she left in a sulk. He remembered her silence meant he was wrong, and she wasn't going to let it go.

London took off a mitt to have another drink from a flask, but it was so, so cold.

"Jane Ammon, don't," he said. "Don't. I know it's not Boston, but it's all we got." No message came back from her through the steady blowing snow.

The snow came in worse, and when he wiggled his fingers, he felt the bone chill.

The snow got so bad he couldn't see the evergreens anymore. *Have to stay awake,* he thought. He remembered the glaring predator that stared back at him from the dark waters that took her. The cold immunized him from the chill of its taunt.

Cause the girls gotta get to the promised land. He took another small drink. *Hopefully, the food will last. Hope they have a lot of ducks in the*

Canadas. The way she used to cook them was mighty fine.

He went to brush away a tear, but it had crystallized, and the snowstorm was getting worse. London couldn't find his way. He couldn't see nothing. Could barely see the ox's ears. Eventually, he couldn't tell if the sleigh was moving or stopped. It—just felt like he was continuing to disappear.

The white was relentless. Couldn't see anything. London was tired and numb. He felt like he was asleep.

Maybe this is what it's like to be dead.

Jane liked to walk to that crick, didn't she? And that time she found that dead wolf. Stay away from it, I said. You're . . .

And what does she show me? It was that damned pup. Goodness Almighty. It was latched onto her dead mother's teat. Not much there. Must have been Thomas. He kept shooting it. Never much of one to clean up. 'Get us some milk for it,' she said. 'Don't just stand there.' She wasn't much for cussin, but she did then. Jane Ammon—she was always determined.

London howled into the white—JaaayEEEEEEEEnnnn. Three times he howled, but the storm quenched most of the sound.

Didn't tell the wee ones until it was grown and able and gone. They called her the wolf momma, and that she was. She was the wolf momma. And for a time, I thought she was ours.

No tears came out. They froze before they could fall.

He took a tear of chewing tobacco and searched for the back of the ox ahead of him. After spitting, he flapped the reins. He felt the snow part when he whipped the air, revealing some brown fur. London Oxford wasn't going to fade away yet. There was too much cursing time left.

Joshua crawled out from under the canvas.

"Thought you's falling asleep," he said. "Whoa. Can't see nothing out here." He adjusted a cloth on his face.

"Her ears will tell," London said, nodding to the ox.

"Are we in Canada?" asked Joshua.

"We left Massachusetts, but this definitely ain't Canada. Get there sometime next month. Still a long ways."

In the afternoon, Abner stepped up and pushed Joshua away from his father.

"Couldn't sleep?" asked London.

"Not enough room and snow was getting in." He pushed Joshua again and got punched back.

"I could throw you boys out. Think the men back there will find you? Wouldn't bet on it." London's voice was shaking with cold.

"Pah we gotta stop soon. And we gotta get a fire going."

"Is it going to be cold like this—all the way?" Joshua asked. "Are we going to die out here?" Joshua's arms were crossed as he leaned into the wind.

"S-some might, but y-you w-won't, 'cause you gotta d-dig a shitter," London said and laughed. "I's sure Missa Thomas is g-going ta stop s-soon. Five young ones and his missus have much to say. Don't expect his two b-boys back there with the horses are doing fine neither."

Hope the crew chief's got someone to start the fires, London thought. *So darn cold, don't know if I'll be able to get up and walk.*

The chill stilled the conversation for a long time. Abner, like Joshua, hugged himself as he again bowed into the lashing wind. His weighing need to give in to sleep was disturbed by what he thought was something racing past him.

Looked like Joshua was falling asleep, so Abner elbowed him.

"Stop it," yelled Joshua, and he pushed back.

"Well, what are you waiting for?" London asked.

"What?" asked Abner.

"Tell us when it's done."

Abner just stared at him.

Outlines of something raced past again.

"Th-they're coming for you. G-guess who's c-clearing snow for the sh-shitter?"

⚬

The snowstorm continued to rage as the drivers parked at a bend in the road. A single blazing bonfire was made. The woodsmen built lean-tos for the families close to the fire. The ones for the settlers leaned against the sleighs, and the rest were freestanding and meant for the workmen. The frames and ground covering were thickly covered with cedar and pine boughs. The lean-tos circled questionably close to the blaze. Three-quarters of the space around the flames was taken up by frozen woodsmen.

As dawn faded, the freezing blasts blew with savage disregard. Everything except the fire was slowly being buried under snowdrifts. While woodsmen attempted to keep parts of the camp dug out, Abner and Joshua brought the settlers hot grub.

An insular peace was interrupted by loud yelling. Lavina Allen was shouting, "He's gone! Where is he? I can't find him!"

"Who?" asked Philemon.

"Young Christopher, of course," she said.

"Oh, the two-year-old," he muttered.

Dozens of woodsmen quickly formed a radial search for a body. Eventually, all of them disappeared into the forest. Inexplicably, they left Abner and the other twelve-year-olds—Joshua, Polly, and Bearie—to care for the dozen younger children who were left running and crawling around the fire. Polly convinced some toddlers to huddle together. Joshua and Abner chased after the belligerent rest.

Abner, after checking on Samuel's ox that was supposedly going limp —it wasn't, took a sip of tea. Despite all of the commotion, he noticed that not all the Wright boys were up and about. Philemon's son, Tiberius, was still sleeping. Everyone called him Bearie, except his father. London kicked the boy next to him and asked, "What were you doing?"

"I had to pee," the boy said.

"Christopher, your momma thinks you wandered off. Bearie, you better get up and tell them. They all thought that it was the end of the world. Better git."

Once things settled down, more tea was served, and the ladies persuaded folks to give some time to prayers.

When the first of the tea was poured, Philemon began to say something, but Thomas quickly stood up. "Phil, that's fine," Thomas said with a downward motion with his hand. "I'll take it from here." He took his wife's hand and patted it. "We'll start with an offering of grace."

She withdrew her hands because they were cold. The air continued to bite. Some would go on to say they heard a howl. Others said it was a scream.

Woodcutters Lament

With the worst of last night's storm dissipating, bright patches of blue sky cracked through the cloud cover. People came out like flowers unfurling. The settlers, after digging themselves out of snow dunes, were keen to get back to the open road.

When the crew chief asked Thomas Wright why the camp wasn't packing up, he let folks know that they had to wait for a couple of days. "More men coming," he said. "Don't worry yourselves. It's part of the plan," is what was heard.

"Devil finds work for idle hands," Margaret said, but no one was paying attention. The camp was set too close to the thick, overbearing evergreen forest. The settlers were edgy and absorbed in their own concerns. Similarly, the children were looking for an excuse to fabricate an escape.

Phil Jr., at seventeen, was the oldest. Cousin Phil Jr. was a year younger. Polly and Bearie at twelve were the same age as London and Joshua. All of them reported directly to their fathers except Joshua, who was supposed to be under Philemon's thumb. In Joshua's mind, however, it was his aunt Abigail who administered the law.

The Wright's other seven children, along with Lavina's, and Margaret's and London's other nine, ran untamed in a free-running, risk-laden menagerie. Abner, Joshua, and Polly, in practice, felt like they were expected to act like herding dogs for a trip of stubborn goats.

When word got out that some boys were escaping, any child capable of running—pushed, kicked and raced to get away. Rambunctiously, they attacked each other as they rolled, slid, and stumbled across waves of snowdrifts, crossing the wagon trail as they moved away from camp and the turn in the road. The Wright boys, like Pied Pipers, led the children beyond to a hidden, unmarked place. Unmonitored, the bunch felt free to become wild, noisy, and fearless.

Abner arrived late. Camp cleanup chores delayed his arrival. The children collected along a creek that fed into a small frozen lake. Animal tracks crossed the lake, wound along to where the young ones were, and then on into the forest.

Abner's sister, Annie, stood behind Polly and Joshua. She was staring at widening cracks in the ice as Ruggles stamped. Abner hurriedly slid down a slope to get to them.

Bearie tromped across the creek to the other side with his sisters. From the other shore, they lobbed snowballs at the others.

"Bearie, we's supposed to be where they can see us," Abner said.

Bearie tossed snowballs at him. "Go away," he yelled.

"Rabbits," Polly said to her sister.

"Lots of rabbits," repeated Polly's younger sister, who was standing next to John.

From the other side of the creek, John threw another snowball at Abner's head once he was in range. "Abner, you heard him, go," he said.

"And I think those are baby rabbits," a child said.

"And we saw some," said another.

"Those big ones are wolf tracks," said Bearie.

"They're following them into the forest," Joshua said.

"Looking for rabbits," Bearie said.

"No, looking for you," Joshua said.

"And that's fresh wolf poop," John said.

Annie and Rachael followed the others, who had reached the other side of the creek.

"No, Rug. No," yelled his brother Bearie.

John rushed back to stop Ruggles, but the ice broke, and his boot got soaked.

Ruggles ran toward Rachael, who, like Annie, was now following the wolf towards the forest. Abner and Joshua followed behind.

Joshua and Bearie kept throwing snowballs at each other. Everyone around them, except John, with his wet foot, ended up rolling and fumbling in the snow.

"Polly, we have to go," John said. "We can't stay here. There's wolves."

Polly stared at the trees, which looked really close. The treeline on both sides was only about fifty feet from each other. "Yeah, they could be in there right now," she said. "And there'd be lots of them."

"I heard them say that there's mountain lions, wildcats, and even bears out here," said John.

"They went in there. Abner, you afeared?" hollered Bearie.

"Why don't you go?" Joshua told him.

"Yeah, we should go back," said John.

"If they come for us, we'll feed them Rug," Joshua said.

"No, how about Polly?" Bearie said.

Once Abner got close to his sisters, he said, "Annie. Rachael, come on. We gotta go."

He tried to grab Annie's hand, but she kept following the wolf tracks in.

"Annie, don't. We have to go. Momma's not in there."

He lobbed a snowball in front of her. "Thinking it is, is not going to make it so."

Rachael returned one of hers, but it fell short. Abner beckoned her to come closer. "Annie, Poppa is waiting."

"Not for Momma," Annie replied.

Rachael got close to him and landed another one on his stomach. He took a few steps back toward the clearing and plopped back into the snow, feigning injury. Both Annie and her sister threw snowballs at him and started laughing.

"Boys, you're all useless," Polly hollered. "You're supposed to be helping," she said as she scooted the younger children to safer places away from the cracked ice patches.

Bearie went into the forest, following the wolf tracks first, and others followed. Joshua told them he heard something. John, who was the last one in, told them that he thought he had heard something, too, and then all of them started running. John fell and banged his knee. After he was out, he picked up Ruggles, who was headed in a different direction.

Rachael laughed at everyone who was racing to get to the other side of the creek.

Abner noticed that the sky hadn't cleared up at all. It was still cloudy. He also thought he heard something moving through the forest. Feeling his father's stern glare at the back of his neck, he told them, "They's coming for us."

⟿⟾

Thomas had asked London to check on the skis of his sled. "Some grease might help with traction," he said.

Philemon came by to check on the sleigh, which was behind his.

"I know there's work for the new men once we're at our property, but what about now? Thomas asked. What can they do for us on the way?"

"Whatever Bill Morewood tells them," Philemon said. "Get us some fresh game, perhaps. Can any of them cook?"

"Matthew was persuasive, but in the light of day, I'm having serious thoughts about dealing with another crew. I've broached this with Bill, so I'm giving you a heads-up. Might be a flare-up in the next day or two. Might also be a good time to get rid of some of Bill's deadwood. In the meantime,

Philemon, do what you do best—keep the men inspired. Brave new world, farming paradise, new town, water power, milling—you know, with the usual touch-ups. I'll leave you to it."

Before Philemon was able to say anything, Thomas quickly left. He flagged Samuel with the intention of continuing ongoing discussions about ways to make business connections in Montreal. Due to an intrusion of two new arrivals, their conversation was short-lived. The men came into camp with a buck strapped over the back of each of their horses.

James Savage and Aaron Johnson introduced themselves. James wore a coonskin hat and had an old burn mark on his neck. Aaron looked part Injun, and had a bent nose, which was likely a remnant from some past brawl. Both came from Springfield, which was in the western part of Massachusetts.

Thomas learned that the others weren't far behind. At Philemon's prompting, James offered to cook the meat. Aaron and a couple of Bill's crew did the preparations.

At supper, Philemon interrupted his brother and handed him a venison supper plate. London, from the other side, offered Missus Abigail the same.

"So, what woodcutters are you going to leave behind?" Philemon asked.

"That's being petty. Don't you think? Philemon, don't you have something to do? I'm sure if you ask London here, he'll have some suggestions."

London left before Thomas had finished his sentence.

"Philemon, the rest are coming," said Thomas. "We'll see what that brings."

—◦◉◦—

Abner cautiously carried bowls of soup for the settlers but froze when a couple of new faces appeared from the dark. They looked dirty, wasted, and sickly. He passed the bowls out to the children and quickly returned to get some more. He pointed them out to his father. "Winter fever, maybe," he said.

"Never you mind. I'll have Bill Moorwood deal with them. Ugh, on second thought, keep the girls away from them."

As Abner kept on with his chores, he watched the men being taken away by Bill Moorwood, the crew chief.

About ten minutes later, he froze again and accidentally spilled a bowl, almost scalding Philemon's wife's sister—Lavina.

"What are you doing?" her husband yelled.

"Yeah. Watch out," Joshua whined.

Abner bowed his head and slipped away to get another. He pulled on Joshua's sleeve and waved for him to follow.

"What?" Joshua squirmed.

Abner nodded toward a man with a toque and a long greatcoat. He approached Thomas Wright. Another six men walked with him. He shook Thomas Wright's hand, and his expression lit up as Abner had seen before. The stranger kept an arm wrapped around Thomas's shoulder as they walked along.

"It's him," Abner said.

"I thought you said he was an Injun."

"Different hat, but it's him. I'm sure it is. I don't like him one bit. He's scary. You know—he was at Abigail's funeral. Remember? And did you see those other men that came in? Dark circles around the eyes; Don't look well. Hungover, maybe? Wrights aren't going to take to that, are they?" said Abner.

"The tea, remember?" said Joshua. "Missus Abigail, the dead girl's momma is coming for us. You don't want that. Come on. Let's finish this."

When London approached the oxen, he found one of the new men there. "The buck you cooked up was fine-tasting, Mr. Savage. You don't need to worry about feeding the livestock. I make sure they're treated just right.

"Mighty obliged," London said. "Two of your men don't look well. I was surprised that the crew chief wasn't worried."

"David Wells and Wyatt Little, you mean? I don't know what's wrong with them for sure. When we left them, they looked just fine, but I've seen others get sickly looking like that. I've seen men with that condition appear with Matthew and with no good reason. Was told that they'd follow along later, but that's the last I've heard of them. I don't have a reason to believe that folks can catch it, but I'm telling you, I don't like that Matthew. I wouldn't trust him for nothing."

After James left, Tom Jr. rode in. When he dismounted, he offered London the reins, but London didn't take it. "The line for the horses is there. Do it yourself," he replied.

"That's your job," Thomas said.

"Who's taking care of my girls?"

"Bearie."

"Did you see your cousin with them?"

"Maybe Polly. Father wants you to verify that the new men know what's expected of them on the trip."

"You mean no drinking?"

"I gotta go," the boy said and rushed off after he tied up his horse.

"Damned, damned, and damned," London said. "Again, no one's taking care of the girls." He gave the horse some hay and patted it. London knew in his gut that drinking wasn't what was making those men sick. He was suspicious that it might not be winter fever either."

In the morning, while Thomas discussed the route with Samuel Choate, Philemon again attempted to talk with Matthew. Thomas got up, abruptly cut him off, and patted Matthew's shoulder. "Philemon, this is Matthew."

"That's what they call me," the man said, and he tipped his hat. It belonged to Thomas.

"How do you know each other?" Philemon asked.

"Met him on the road to town. I don't know how the subject came up, but he told me that he had connections with a team of workmen in the western part of the state. I was in a hurry, but he was convincing."

"I heard that it was James Savage who knew the men," Philemon said.

"Yes, we're familiar with James," Matthew said.

"Are you going to help clear the land, tree cutting, or—"

"You'll find that we have many talents. Don't worry about things. We're here to serve. You're a very capable gentleman, sir. I'm sure, if you were so inclined for politics, you would find the experience captivating."

"Do you really believe so?" Philemon asked.

"I sincerely do, sir," Matthew said. He clapped Thomas on the shoulder and escorted him to the far side of the sleigh.

Philemon grinned. "Samuel, I understand that you have more questions about where we're going." While he talked to Samuel, he kept an eye on what the other two were hiding.

Philemon Wright acquired a dish of fruits and breads. He rubbed his fingers around his bowl of tea and then flicked them as if to get rid of the cold. "Best to 'nip it in the bud.' Oh, Sam, let's get this over with."

A tall, long-bearded woodsman, with a coonskin cap, blocked Philemon's path from the settler's fire circle.

"Mr. Wright, it's me—James Savage."

"Yes, of course, James. Is this something London can't deal with?"

"No, siree. 'Twas me that told Mr. Thomas where to find the new men. Was Matthew that was supposed to get them.

"There's men missing. I'm wondering if you've heard anything about the Davidson brothers, and McCaskill and Simmons."

"It's good that you're concerned, isn't it Phil?" said Matthew.

Philemon was caught off guard. The man had surprised him. He seemed to appear from nowhere.

"Don't worry yourself, James," the man who was dressed in black leather continued. "They're big boys." He was still wearing Thomas's hat.

"And Kevin McCaskill and Frank Simmons from Sturbridge—what happened to them? I saw them with you in Lunenburg. Like David and Wyatt, they weren't looking well. What happened?"

"They weren't up to it. Must have been something they ate, I guess. They're not here with us. That's all that matters."

Philemon kept looking for Samuel Choate, but he wasn't with any of the settlers.

Matthew walked over to James and tried to put a hand on his shoulder, but the man backed off. "What's wrong with you? Keep the touchy stuff to yourself. I told you that before."

"Men, relax. No need for things to get out of hand, is there? A peaceful camp is what we want. If that's not possible, folks can leave, is all I can say about that," said Philemon.

"As long as we're getting paid, we'll be glad to work for you," James said.

Philemon turned to Matthew, "And it will remain a dry one, you hear? There's much to be made and done for hardworking men. There's more than clearing land. We've got big plans. We're going to build ourselves a town. It'll be a place of industry that no one will want to miss. I'm sure both of you, after spending your coin, will want to bring us more hardworking and god-fearing folk. Now, if you don't mind, I've got to find someone before this tea gets cold."

After stepping away, Philemon looked back and noticed that both men had disappeared. His brother-in-law, Samuel Choate was sitting at the woodsman's fire.

"Sam, I see you have your tea," Philemon said and offered his plate.

"Treats, too; yes, don't mind if I do. Do you have an answer to my questions?"

Philemon took a sip of tea and replied, "As soon as we get there, yes, of course, I'll show you a choice of land applotments."

"But surely you can show me the plot plan."

"I took to heart your comments about circling the camp. I know you've been discussing that with my brother. Placing the lean-tos against the wagons was a good idea."

"The maps, Philemon. I'm an engineer. You know—"

"Yes, of course, Sam. They're buried under the tarp like everything else. We'll unload when we get there. In the meantime, we'd like more of your support for planning the mill. The site has waterfalls and rapids. More power there than you can imagine. There's lots to plan for—a house of worship, a town, a school, stores, and who knows what else."

"But Philemon, I'd like to plan the layout of my farm."

"Focus on the mill, maybe a steamship line. I'm sure we'll be able to export our bounty abroad. With vision and discipline, our capabilities are only limited by our imagination." He noticed that Samuel's wife, Margaret, who was about fifteen feet away, was listening carefully.

"And how about a prayer service at dinner, around the fire?" Philemon asked. "It's about time, don't you think?"

"I'm not against it," Samuel said.

"Wonderful. And how's Margaret?"

"Four under six."

"And in our new found land, you can have twice as many. Buck up, Sam. As I said, anything is possible."

Samuel put down his soup.

"I hear my men calling," Philemon said. "Try the chutney, if you will—Abigail's special."

After Philemon left, Samuel's wife joined him.

"I heard Philemon recommend a prayer service. I've been saying that since we started. There needs to be more."

"Yes, dear. Of course."

"And what did he say?" she asked.

"The usual. Not much."

⁓◉⁓

The settlers slept in, but Joshua, like the Oxfords and the workmen, didn't.

As Abner and Joshua were hauling water back to camp, Abner struggled to keep up. "Wait up," Abner said. "I heard something last night."

"What else is new?"

"Why are you always a fool?" Abner complained. "No wonder you're alone."

Joshua dropped the bucket and clenched his fists.

"What's that supposed to mean? Why's someone like you complaining about me? You stupid turd. Come here and I'll knock your head off."

Abner kept walking.

"Your father didn't think much of you mouthing off yesterday, did he?" Joshua said.

"The creek? It was you and Polly."

"Shut up."

The quiet on the next water runs was blistering.

"Do you remember your dad?" Abner asked, trying to break the tension.

"No, I was just seven."

"I's going to forget my ma'am?"

"What?" Joshua said, stopping and looking back.

"I was the same when she died. How could I not remember?"

"I don't need this. Don't be such a fool," Joshua said as he tramped back into camp.

As Joshua poured water into a large pot, Abner said, "How come you don't want to remember?"

"I don't need nobody. Go away."

On the way back to the stream, again they didn't talk to each other. As Abner filled up his bucket, Joshua asked, "What did you hear?"

"What?"

"You said you heard something last night."

"I heard wolves howling. Then some yips."

"Yeah, I guess I did too. Sounded like they was in pain."

"Don't know about that."

"After having a shit, I heard someone leaving camp and going toward the sound of the wolves," Abner said. "I followed the tracks this morning, and guess what I found?"

"What? Your pants?"

"I found two dead wolves. Want to see?"

Joshua cautiously looked around. "Yeah, but we better be quick. No way anyone would less go back there."

The boys left the buckets at the stream and followed the human tracks in the snow that led into the woods. They kept following until they reached a clearing, where they came across a pair of wolf tracks. The path turned into a trail of blood. It led to a pair of dead wolves.

Claw marks were ripped across the side and snout of one of the fallen animals. "The cut on its neck must have been what killed it," Joshua said.

The other one, about a dozen feet away, didn't seem to have a mark on it. A man's footprints encircled both of them.

"I might have heard them yesterday," Abner said.

"This happened last night," Joshua said.

Abner wondered if he got close to the one that wasn't marked, if it would wake and attack him. "Maybe they're sick," he said. "They're all white. No colour at all. Ever see something like that?"

"Abner, those aren't bite marks."

"Cougar?"

"Look, the only tracks here belong to a person, and there was only one here when this was done. The cut on the neck is kind of small for a hunting knife. It's not what I'd expect." Joshua grabbed a stick, lifted a paw of the one that didn't seem to have a mark on it, and let it flop back.

"And yeah, this one's dead alright."

"Maybe someone put a spell on them."

"And all the blood?"

"I guess not," Abner said.

"Maybe someone bashed that one with the end of an axe," Joshua said.

"You'd think there'd be some blood showing. Turn it over."

"You turn it over."

"So you think that it might not be dead?" asked Abner.

"I'm thinking that whoever did this might not want us here."

"If one of the woodsmen looked at it, I'm sure they'd have something to say."

"Yeah, like piss off."

Abner was quiet while walking back.

"Did that scare you?" Joshua taunted.

"Annie thinks my momma has something to do with wolves."

"Just don't forget her," Joshua said.

"What?"

"Just don't let them go, if they're important—your memories, I mean. If you don't let them go, you won't forget."

"I'm never going to forget my momma."

Joshua kicked the snow.

"If you want it then, hold on. For us that don't want the memories, just leave us alone, is all."

"Thanks," Abner said, kicking the snow like Joshua.

When they returned to camp, Abner said, "Shouldn't we tell someone?"

"Why didn't they bring back at least one of them for their fur? I think we should just be careful, is all. Maybe after chores. What do you think?"

"Injuns, maybe?"

"No. Tracks come from here."

With different tasks dished out, the boys didn't see each other until later in the afternoon.

London dropped some more firewood next to the settler's fire. "Yes, ma'am," London said when Abigail approached him.

"There's a prayer service this evening. Philemon needs reminding. Tell him, please. He needs to select the readings."

"Yes, ma'am. Will look for him as soon as I find my girls."

"I'm sure they're in fine hands with Abner. This is important, London.

A few minutes won't make any difference. Oh, and get Joshua to bring more buckets of water before dinner."

Lavina came over and said, "Something from Psalms, Abigail.

When London noticed that other women were getting up, he said, "Sorry ma'am, I've got to go."

"And tell Bearie to bring Lucy and Ruggles back. I mean it," Abigail called.

At the workmen's fire, he found Abner piling wood next to the fire.

"That's not your job. It's the woodcutters," London said. "And where's the girls?"

"With James," he said as he pointed to the bulky lumberjack. He was facing the woods and blocking the view of his daughters.

"And who was taking care of them all day?"

"Polly, maybe," Abner said. "They were here when I arrived, so I don't know exactly."

He walked over to Rachael and saw that she was throwing a rock at a tree. Her scarf was on the ground.

"Rachael, what are you doing?" he asked.

"Just teaching her how to hit a target," James Savage said. "Don't hurt to teach her how to defend herself. Never know when you have to stand off a cougar or a wolf in these parts."

"Probably better to climb a tree," London replied. He wrapped the scarf around Rachael's neck. "Girl, you won't want to lose this, so please keep it on. James, on second thought, children up trees and throwing rocks, in these parts, that's a bad idea. By the way, Missa Aaron Johnson needs you to carve and preserve the second buck. Says, he's roasting."

"Don't know about that," James gruffed.

Both girls kept throwing rocks at the tree. Annie almost hit the axe that was stuck in it.

London knelt, attempting to embrace them, but both stepped away.

"She told us to go away," Rachael said.

"It was Lucy," Annie said. She told Rachael that she didn't want to play with no coloureds.

London hugged Rachael. "Yes, they can be mean. Life can be mean. That's why I want Abner to be with you." He looked back at his son and called, "Abner, don't let them out of your sight. I'll see you at the other fire, you hear me?"

"Why?" complained Abner.

London nearly bumped into one of the new men. The look of him was terrible. He had sickly black eyes, a ghostly face, and cracked lips. "Damned," London muttered. And stepping away, the man behind looked the same.

Seeing the foreman, he hurried to reach him. "Bill, why are those men still here, and why shouldn't we be worried that the rest of us won't get what they got?"

"They seem to be getting better. No fever. No shakes, and they swallow what's given to them. Anyways, the decision to let them go is up to Thomas. He told me that they can stay only so long as they can keep up, which means if they can walk to the next camp, they can stay. If you got a problem with that, you best take it up with him."

He found Missa Thomas being lectured to by his wife behind the ring of sleighs.

"Matthew," Thomas repeated to her.

"What's wrong with you?" Mary asked.

London stopped ten feet away.

"London, this doesn't concern you," Mary said.

"Abner is supposed to mind my girl when I'm not around. So why are people telling him not to?"

"I was told Polly—"

"Nope. She says she was doing something else."

"Then tell him and Joshua to mind the children and your girls again," Mary said. "Polly is doing something else."

"Missa Philemon is supposed to choose the readings for tonight," London said. "Just thought I'd say."

London hurried away before he got himself caught up in something. He routed a couple of requests about dinner to Aaron Johnson and tried to avoid any more family questions. He checked his arms to see if there were any patches of white.

When Abner caught up to Joshua, he noticed that there was a cut across his hand. "How did that happen?" he asked.

"Was chasing a couple of those runts in the woods. Got sliced from a broken branch."

"Them in the woods is the last thing we need," Abner said.

"That Christopher is a wily one."

"Anyway, I talked to one of the contractors. It was James Savage," Abner said. "He told me that Trevor Byrnes bragged that he was the best hunter in camp. Maybe we should ask him about the wolves? James told me that his jacket has a tear on the shoulder."

"Doesn't mean he knows much about anything, but sure, why not?" Joshua said.

When they found him, Abner told him, "I heard that you told folks that you know about hunting."

"Been around. Why do you ask?" said Trevor.

"We's seen something mighty strange," said Joshua.

"We found a couple of dead wolves in the woods near here," said Abner.

"Something clawed one of them bad," Joshua said.

"Predators go for the back feet and neck usually. Wolves, you say. Maybe a mountain lion, but they'd take a noticeable bite out of it."

"But somebody from the camp went there," Abner said.

"Somebody as curious as you, I bet."

"But there weren't any other prints in the snow. Just those and ours," Joshua said.

"There wasn't any cuts showing on the other one. Just real small marks. And they was almost completely white."

"Sounds like it might have been sick. Maybe that's why the other one was so easy to kill," said Trevor. "Did you turn it over?"

"Well, not really," Joshua said.

"Maybe it was hit with an axe and smashed on the side you weren't looking at."

"But there wasn't claw marks on the other one," Joshua said.

"Sharp hunting knife maybe," Trevor said. "Don't know. I'd have to see it. I'll have a look at it before I leave."

Abner told him where the path was.

"Now if you don't mind, leave me be. I've got my own things I gotta do."

"What do you think?" Abner asked after they'd walked away from Trevor.

"He's got some points," Joshua said.

"Didn't think much of it, but I'm sure he'll have something useful to say once he sees what we saw."

Cravings

London returned to the workman's area. James Savage wasn't around. Abner and Rachael were watching men throw knives at each other. Annie tried talking to a sickly-looking man, but he just plopped off a log by the fire.

"Poppa, he's tired," Annie said.

"I can see that, but we have to go. Annie, aren't you hungry?" When Abner looked at him, London beckoned for him to follow along with Rachael.

At supper, London, with his back to the fire, did his best to be with his girls. "How come Polly's not around?"

"Wants to be with Bearie and his sister," Annie said.

"The older children," London said. "I heard that Missus Margaret's going to teach reading and writing. Being able to read is a good thing. Maybe even Missus Abigail."

"Not Rachael and the younger ones," she said.

"If not, I's going to teach you like my poppa did for me. Reading is a good thing. It's hard, but you know, you can write secret messages to your sister. Like me and your momma used to do. And don't tell no one, but I can do it better than Missa Philemon, maybe even Missa Thomas."

"Why'd she go?" Rachael asked.

"Momma, you mean. I know what they told me, but I don't rightly know. They say she drowned, but nobody could tell me why she went off without saying. Never made sense to me, but one thing for sure—she's in heaven now, and no one can tell us different."

"If we pray, can she hear us?" asked Rachael. "Missa Abigail says so."

"I sure hope so. I mean, yes, of course. I pray to her every day, so she's always with me. Of course, Momma listens, real good."

London noticed that Matthew had refused anything except a bowl of water. Leaning against a tree, he kept away from the other men and the campfire. For the most part, he kept quiet, using sign language with the workmen when he had to.

Isn't he cold? London thought. *He's looking for something. Wonder what?*

London also noticed that the couple of men who looked tired and undernourished earlier in the day now, this evening, had a ravenous appetite for meat and water—lots and lots of water.

—◦◉◦—

"London, Phil's horse needs to be looked at," said James Savage. He was carrying animal feed to the livestock.

"It's his attention that needs to be looked at," London said. "Was totally unprepared for the service last night. Picked the readings out of his ass. Doubt anyone could tell the difference."

"Was referring to young Phil. It's the back leg."

"It's probably the cold. I'll see what I can do. And how is it between you and Matthew?"

"More I see him, the more I don't like him. This evening, he tried to bait me into a fight. Not sure what that was even about, but I'm telling you, Thomas Wright has got to get rid of him. He's like an infection. Nothing good will come of him being here."

"I hear what you're saying, James. I'm concerned. I just hope nothing stops us from getting out of this place tomorrow. No way I wanna stay here another night."

The next morning, the caravan packed up and continued on its journey. At the end of the day, they camped in a small field. The sleighs were left on the trail.

While bringing food to Thomas and his wife, London heard screams coming from the opposite side of the campfire. It was Polly.

"She did not," Abner shouted back.

Ruggles was laughing. Lucy was crying, and Rachael threw another stone at her.

As London rushed over, he heard Missus Mary say, "Thomas, didn't I tell you this wasn't working?"

"What's happening here?" London asked.

"Nothing," Polly said.

Lucy threw a stone back at Rachael.

"Polly was told to mind her sisters, but she didn't, so she's blaming me," said Abner. "'Cause Lucy wandered off."

"London, a better example has to be set. This is not acceptable," ordered Missus Mary. "Girls, go over there, where I can keep an eye on you. This is not a request. Move. Shoo."

She gave London a glare and moved away.

"But," said Abner.

"I know," replied his father. "No arguing with them when they're embarrassed. You and Joshua are minding the little ones tomorrow night."

"But," said Abner.

"I know. And Rachael, why are you throwing stones at little Lucy?"

"She didn't want to play with me," said Rachael.

"I can see why. You throw things at each other. What about Lizzie?"

"Bearie," she said.

"There's lots of others. And there's a lot worse. They could tell us to leave. And there's stories about the Iroquois that don't need repeating. I hear they'd skin us like rabbits." He tickled Rachael and then Annie. "And what about Ruggles?"

London watched her run after Annie and Ruggles, who were playing. He noticed that Thomas Wright was still sitting quietly by himself. It wasn't like him.

The strange thing about what had just happened, when Polly was getting blamed, was that Lucy, who was his favourite little girl, was the one screaming. He didn't even move.

I wonder what's wrong with him, thought London.

He noticed that the new man, Matthew, was sitting with the settlers by the fire. It was also unusual that he wasn't with the other woodcutters. When it got dark, London didn't see him for the rest of the night.

In the morning, the workmen made breakfast and provisions for the day. London and the Wrights were eager to have an early start.

Everyone was up and around before daylight, except James Savage, who awoke with a paralyzed leg. He was supported by two others at the settlers' fire circle. The large crowd that encircled him was curious about his disability.

"Give him a horse," Samuel Choate said.

James tried to stand but wasn't able to. He couldn't move his leg at all.

"No good to us," said Philemon.

"I'll be all right," the big man said. "I just need some time, is all."

"Have some Christian charity," Abigail Wright said.

"Then ride with the coloureds," Philemon said. "They's got room."

"But we's—" said Abner.

"You sure it's not broke, or something?" Samuel asked.

"Nothing like that. Just give me a chance. Just for a day or two is all," James said.

"Stay off of it for a couple of days. London, you can make him a crutch. After that, we'll see what my brother has to say about it."

"It's his men. That's their job," Abner said.

"That's not necessary," his father said.

"But there's no room," Joshua added. "There's barely enough room in the back as is."

"We'll move some gear to the sleigh behind, so never you mind," London said.

London followed the sleighs ahead as the caravan moved on. The start of the morning had an overcast gloom about it. A disabled workman rode with them, and Joshua and his girls continued to vent that they needed to get out because there wasn't enough room for them in the back.

James sat between London and his son.

"Can you feel anything?" Abner asked.

"It's all numb," James said. "Like all life drained from it. I got no strength, either. Feel real tired."

"When did you first see this Matthew fellow?" London asked.

"Jack Davidson and his brother rounded up the men. Matthew was with them. When I saw Jack, he looked nervous. Always thirsty. Reminded me of someone who got hydrophobia. You know they're always thirsty. He couldn't keep anything down. We went on ahead. I expected that he, like McCaskill and Simmons, would catch up to us in time."

"Who?"

"I last saw the other two at Lunenburg. They and Matthew were supposed to bring more men. Matthew returned alone and just told us that they made other arrangements."

"That's a mighty strange story," Joshua said from behind them.

"I don't disagree at all. I'm just telling you what I know. Honest truth is all." That was followed by James throwing up.

"At least you missed your boots," London said.

"Sorry about that."

"It didn't miss mine," Abner said.

"There's snow on top of the canvas. Clean it with that," London said.

Within the hour, James dozed off, after which Joshua and Abner helped him slip into the back.

"Looks like he needs rest. By the looks of him, I don't think he can afford to lose what he ate."

"Do you think he's still sleeping back there?" Joshua asked.

"Ask him," London said.

"Do you think he's got hydrophobia?" Joshua asked.

"Nah. He wasn't thirsty. He said you have to be thirsty."

"Those who get hydrophobia go mad," Joshua said.

"You think he's going to go mad? What about Annie and Rachael?"

"You two, you stop that," said London. "I think he just needs lots of rest. That's all. Maybe he got a bad case of frostbite."

"Should we have taken his boot off?" Abner asked.

"You want him to hit you in the head? Go ahead," Joshua said.

"Yeah, I guess you're right," Abner said.

"Abner, have the girls make sure his legs are covered with blankets," London said. "Just in case frostbite is what he got."

"I heard that if it's frozen bad, they can lose their foot," Joshua said. "Chop it right off. Right at the bone."

"We's not going to chop anyone up," London said. "Focus on what's ahead. More chance of Injuns or robbers running at us from the trees; maybe Matthews got friends."

"Why us?" asked Abner.

"Look at all the stuff that we're carrying."

"But what about them?" he said, as he looked back at the men in the distance who walked behind the caravan.

"So there could be a lot of them. Besides, what does it matter if there's just one or a whole bunch? It only takes one of them to cut your throats. The two of you, keep a lookout. That's your job."

"Shouldn't I have a knife?" Abner asked.

"Next time both of you get the kindling, find yourself a good staff. Nice oak would be good."

"But—?"

"In the meantime, just keep your eyes open."

"Where are we going to stay?" asked Abner.

"Don't rightly know. Why don't you ask that feller when he wakes up?"

"Not if he's got hydrophobia," Joshua said.

The wider, more-travelled trail permitted the horseman to ride alongside the sleighs. The caravan eventually entered a small town.

"You think they's going to stop?" Abner asked.

"Nope. We got all we need packed up in these sleighs. Wrights would have to pay if we stopped, and they's not going to do that. Besides, we's in a hurry. Got to get up north before the ice starts to melt."

Thomas, his brother John Allen, Samuel, and Matthew passed them on horseback. They were heading back to town.

"Well, isn't that a surprise?" London said. "Must be going to that inn. It's supposed to be a dry trip. That's not like the Missa Thomas that I know."

When the caravan stopped, they entered a spacious clearing. The seven sleighs formed a loose half-circle.

"How's James?" asked London. "Is he dead or what? Joshua, you git back there and check on him. And if he tries to bite you, don't let him." London laughed.

Less than a minute later, James climbed out of the back and jumped off the sleigh, landing on both feet. He madly starts devouring snow.

"Lord," said London. "Boys, stay back." He climbed down his side and cautiously walked in front of the ox. "You all right there, James?"

"Parched. Absolutely gotta get me something to drink."

"I'll get you something," London said. "Too much will go bad on ya."

Ignoring what London said, James started pounding through the snow. Each step went up to his knee.

"Well, will you look at that? He couldn't walk, but it looks like he can run," said London.

James was almost at the creek when London yelled, "James, that water might be rancid. Better if you let us melt the snow on a fire."

James didn't stop. He jumped on the creek. When the ice broke, he didn't try to get out; he just kept scooping the water and drinking it.

London looked back, and he saw the boys lowering the girls to the ground.

"Lord," he told them. "Maybe he does have hydrophobia. Stay back, all of you. Abner, find us a loaf of bread. Anything more and I think he'll throw it all up."

At dinner time, London was filling bowls of stew for the girls when he heard a yell.

"Poppa, what's he doing?" asked Annie.

"Is he going to die?" asked Rachael.

James used his fingers to devour his bowl of porridge. He beckoned Abner for another.

His boots were off, and his bare feet were close to the fire.

"Girl. Girls, you'll scare the horses," London said. "No frostbite, I see."

"Nah, I feel just fine," James said. "Don't know what it was. Like life was sucked right out of me. Got meself some sleep and grub. I'm feeling so much better. Thanks. Got some chills, but being by the fire is what I need."

"Good to hear, James," said London. "I don't know what to think of what you got. I just hope that's the end of it."

—⁂—

Abner and Joshua helped their father lug fresh water. The two girls followed behind.

"There goes Missa Philemon," Abner said.

"He's riding with his brothers-in-law John Allen and Samuel Choate back to town," his father said. "They's even taking another pair of contractors. "They're off to do some serious drinking, and the women folk definitely won't be pleased. Abner, best you keep your head down. They might want to take this out on us."

John walked over to Joshua and passed on some orders.

"They want us to do what?" Abner said.

"Take care of Ruggles, Elizabeth, Lucy, and your sisters," London said.

"What about Polly and John?"

"They're with the younger ones."

"Pooper duper," said Joshua.

"That's you too," Abner added.

From the contractor's circle, London kept a surreptitious watch on the four wives as they huddled together, planning vengeance.

Left Behind

As the caravan moved out, London believed that he had just witnessed something earth-shaking. He had seen the women take drastic measures.

"Something for the history books," London said.

Missus Mary had Philemon Jr. sit up front. He gave her an earful for not being allowed to be on horseback with the rest. She sat next to Lavina. John Allen must have loved listening to the lady's business. *Oh, and poor Samuel with Margaret and Abigail,* he thought. *They all must be having a time. Looks like Missus Mary's doing. She must be mighty distraught. This was earth-shaking. It's a time like no other. Those poor men—so cold under the covers.* London smiled. *And the journey is long and cold. Doubt they'll even last the night.*

Despite it all, that Matthew character is still sitting up front next to Thomas. The one responsible doesn't seem to be concerned one bit.

The wind had a bite to it. London held the reins with one hand raised, his other holding his scarf over his cheeks.

"Was strange about James Savage, wasn't it?" Joshua said.

"Any of you boys seen him this morning? London asked. "He usually helps me get the sleighs ready. Was just Wyatt Little and me this morning."

"Haven't seen him," Abner replied. "Maybe they let him sleep in."

"Judging by what I saw last night, he would have to be pretty sick not to get something to eat. I was concerned about him having to do all that walking and all."

"Anybody say anything?" asked Joshua.

"Bill Moorwood told me to never mind. He loves to tell people their business but doesn't know much, that one. I didn't see the Wright boys this morning either. They must have slept in as well. Late night, I'd expect.

"Abner, no use standing up. They got a late start. You won't see nothing. You both might want to consider huddling up in the back under blankets. Feels like it's going to get worse before it gets better."

The two remained where they were and didn't say much for a long while.

"Are we in Canada yet?" Abner asked.

"New Hampshire. Not even Vermont yet."

"Poppa, a long time ago, you told me a story about Grandpa and some Injuns. There was a prisoner. What was his name?"

"Matantu. I remember 'cause I kept having questions about the Injuns. Poppa kept repeating the story, and when he got older, he didn't want me to forget any of it, 'cause he thought it was real important. 'It was something real, and it was no story,' he kept telling me."

"Matantu. Ain't that like Matthew? Ain't that funny?"

"Like maybe a sneeze in the middle. Whoever Matantu was, he's long dead and buried. You think this is his grandson or something?"

"I don't know what. I'm just saying it's mighty curious he's got those snake stripes on his neck, and that hat and even the name is mighty similar. I'm just saying."

"There's a lot of Injuns from a lot of different places, and they're all not going to want to cut your head off."

"Poppa, I'm telling you, I got a mighty bad feeling about him. They's something wrong with him."

"Missa Thomas believes he's a good man. I wouldn't worry. We've got dozens of hardworking men with axes and all sorts of weapons."

"But he brought men with him, Poppa. Don't you get it?"

"James Savage is one. Seems good enough to me. It's up to Missa Thomas to decide what he's gonna do. You gotta prove something has been done. Ya can't just try to tell the man to leave just because you don't like the look of him. I mean, for that matter, if the Wrights was honest about what's going on, most would just run off. Just be careful."

"You think they're not going to be paid?" asked Joshua.

"There's enough of that talk. I have no reason to think that will be a problem. Don't let the Wrights hear you say that 'cause you'll be on your own, walking back."

"Didn't mean anything by it," Joshua said.

"If you boys are finished now, I'd like to give my attention to this girl. Don't need to have her wander off."

"What was you all talking about, Abner?" asked Joshua. "Whose Matantu?"

Abner repeated the story about how his grandfather and a girl he met were rescued. He left out the part about getting a stone.

When the story was done, Joshua said, "You know, Matthew didn't give Mr. Wright no mind. He was quiet in the beginning and kept to himself, but when he started talking, he was plenty different."

"What do you mean?"

"He'd just go up to Mr. Wright direct-like. Now he kind of sounds and acts like Mr. Thomas himself. The rest of the contractors wouldn't be like that. Matthew patting him on the back like that, when you think about it, was kind of strange. Maybe he's not an Injun at all."

"You mean he's pretending?" asked Abner.

"Not rightly sure."

"Me, I'm glad we got help," said London. "We got dozens of men to help us out. You know, where we're going, there's nothing. Just trees like that there."

Joshua climbed into the back and disappeared.

At the next camp, before dinner, when Abner was passing out bowls of tea, he didn't see James anywhere. He confronted some workmen.

"Where's Mr. Savage?" Abner asked a man with torn boots.

"Didn't like it here. He's gone."

"He told you that?"

"I heard Matthew telling someone."

"When?"

"This morning, he said. That's what he heard when he saw him leave."

"Anyone else talk to him before he left?"

Gary Straw interrupted. "I saw him last night, but he didn't say nothing," he said.

"Anyone else?"

"I also heard Matthew say he left real early this morning," said Bill Moorwood, the crew chief.

"Did he take a horse?"

"No, he just left, is what I heard," Bill said. "Maybe Mister Wright can tell you more. Did he take something from ya?"

"No, just wondering that's all."

At the other campfire, Abner asked Mister Thomas if he knew why James left.

"Peculiar man. I heard he was on the mend. I was told this morning that he went home."

"So he didn't speak to you?"

"Was the crew chief that told us," Thomas said.

"Bill Moorwood?"

Thomas shook his head. "These things happen. We could have used him, but thanks to Matthew, we have more than enough men to get what needs to get done. We'll push on. Since you're up, I could use another bowl of tea. Bring us another if you would."

Missa Thomas continued to look a bit weak-footed, Abner noticed as he stepped away. *Wonder if he's catching what Mr. Savage got,* he thought. *Maybe we should all leave like Mr. Savage. If we don't, maybe we'll get what Missa Wright's got.*

—◦◉◦—

When London was feeding the livestock, he watched the crowd of women sneak out to the deserted wagon trail.

"That's not important," he heard Mary say.

"Don't swat at flies," Margaret said.

"Oh, shut up," said her oldest sister.

"Abigail, you can be so condescending," Mary said. "That's not very nice."

"Don't be a turd," Lavina said.

"Dozens and dozens of men in this camp—Ladies, we have to stand together, or it all will come apart," said Mary.

"All will be lost—a sure fall from God's grace," Abigail said.

"Keep cutting them off. Yes, cut them off," said Margaret.

"What are you talking about? I just want to keep the community dry," said Lavina.

"Babies, babies, babies. I don't know about you, but I could use a break," said Abigail. "Make sure they're always busy. Fill them dreams and all the work they got to do. Those new pastures, fencing, new crops, or whatever. Get them so exhausted, they'll just fall into bed.

"And, Mary, that man of yours, keep him on the farm," Margaret said. "Looking for investments in town or scouring the country will come to no good. Keep a close eye. That's God's will."

"Never you mind about my business," Mary said.

"That new man—Matthew, needs to be put in his place," said Lavina. "He doesn't do much but seems to be causing lots of trouble, I hear."

"Got to get them on their knees," said Margaret.

"They have to confess their sins," said Abigail.

"Tarnation. Absolutely. They got to return to the righteous path," said Lavina.

"Yes, ladies, the righteous path. Back to our say-so," said Mary.

Mary had the group walk back to camp so she could flag London's attention.

"Damn," London muttered.

She directed him to organize an evening prayer service.

In the morning, after the girls crawled into the back, Abner and Joshua climbed aboard.

"I didn't see you leading the girls to the shitter," Joshua said.

"That's your job," Abner said.

"They have you wipe their butts?"

"I told Missus Abigail."

"Told her what?"

"That I saw wolves last night," said Abner.

"She must have liked that."

"Two men with axes went in ahead of them," Joshua said.

"I'd do that if they gave me an axe. As long as it was a real sharp one," Abner said.

"And if there were six of them?"

"No problem. Wap, wap, wap." Abner swung his arms madly.

Matthew appeared. He and Trevor Byrnes came from the camp and were walking towards them.

Abner cringed at the sight of them.

"Glad to see that you're going to defend us, young sir," Matthew said. He patted Joshua's leg and stared at Abner.

Shocked by their sudden appearance, he folded his arms and shifted toward his father.

"Joshua here thinks you got rid of James," said Trevor Byrnes, who walked alongside Matthew. "Personally, I don't think so. I think he was just a lazy layabout."

"You stupid shit," Joshua said as Trevor was leaving. "You don't know what you're—"

"Good to hear that someone is keeping an eye on things," said Matthew, not looking at anything. "It's unfortunate that we're a man short."

Matthew had started to walk ahead. He looked back at Abner and replied, grinning, "More work for everyone, don't you think?" As soon as he climbed aboard Thomas Wright's sleigh, the sleighs headed out.

London whipped the reins, and their ox followed in line with the rest of the caravan.

"That monster. He got rid of James Savage. I know it," Joshua said.

London took a drink from his flask.

"And Byrnes, that good-for-nothing. No way he looked at them wolves. Hope he gets hydrophobia like James."

"Joshua, you're a fool," Abner said. "How could you have trusted such a—"

"I'm driving," London said. You're going to spook Missy here."

"So, if he got scared off—just a minute." He crawled into the back. A couple of minutes later, he stood up with a blanket in his hand. "Look at this. I forgot about this. It belonged to James. He left both of them. He wouldn't have left without them. No way. Don't you understand?"

"Maybe he just didn't want it?" London said. "Or maybe he took another one."

"Then there was the Davidsons and those others."

"Nobody knows nothing about them," Joshua said.

"And Missa Thomas doesn't look right. And what do you think he's going to do if he thinks we know?" Abner said.

"More work in the latrines?"

"We gotta tell someone," Abner said. "Missa Philemon, maybe?"

"Why don't you walk?"

"Think I will, mud face," said Joshua, and then he jumped off.

London didn't say a thing. He just took another drink.

—❧◉—

At the next camp, while unstrapping an ox, London noticed Matthew walking around the campsite. While the others were clearing up, as usual, he didn't seem to be doing much to help.

Bill Moorwood approached Thomas, who was standing near the settler's bonfire. Bill had James's coonskin cap and offered it to Thomas. Matthew came over and stopped him. He whispered something, and Thomas, in turn, passed it on to Matthew.

So much for hand signals, London thought. After getting the straps off, London led the ox out. He noticed that Matthew put the coonskin cap on as he walked away.

While London was hitching the ox to a line fastened between trees, Thomas approached him. "How's the cold affecting them?" he asked.

"As long as they're not too far from the fire, and they got good feed, I expect they'll keep up.

"You know, Missa Thomas, we haven't had a chance to talk."

"Go right ahead, London. What's on your mind?"

"Since your father died, we've helped support the farm. I'd like to know what to expect from this place we're going to."

"We could definitely use some help with setting up," Thomas replied. "Beyond that, I expect that you can pretty well do whatever you like. There's probably coloured folk in Montreal. And there's work along the river that runs to York. There should be lots of fine places up there to raise those girls of yours."

"But the children could help out."

"We've been thinking of relying on Polly more. She needs to develop those mothering skills. Won't be long before they're ready for families of their own. The way time flies, it'll happen for her before you know it."

"Don't mean to disagree, but they're—"

"Once we get crops in, there won't be any shortage of new folks wanting to come up. Should be a lot of work for Abner if he's interested. When those new folks come in, I'm sure we won't have a problem with getting us another nanny, if we need one. And by then, Mary will probably have another three. The way things go, maybe more."

He patted London's shoulder. "Anyway, those are just possibilities. I am sure when we get to the promised land, everything will work out. Don't fret none, just keep on. It will sort out in time."

Saying nothing, and offering nothing, is not what I expected from him, thought London. He yearned to walk away somewhere but was unsure of where to turn.

He turned to the ox. "Tied and fed, you're like me." He led her away and wondered if he could find a quiet place to think and drink.

Abner approached Polly, who was scolding Ruggles and Maryanne for running away from her. He asked if she wanted some more.

"Of what?"

"Tea?"

"How about cornbread and beans?" she asked.

"Is your father sick?" Abner said.

"I don't know. Maybe just tired. Aren't you getting me something?"

"Yes, of course. What about Matthew?"

Polly gave him a blank look.

"Who's he? Did you notice? He never eats." Abner said.

"So, he already ate."

"But everyone eats after prayers."

"Do I have to get my food for myself?" Polly asks.

"Oh yeah. Just give me a minute."

After giving her a bowl of beans and cornbread, he proceeded to pour tea for other folk around the bonfire.

Polly dropped her bowl in order to chase after two escaping children.

He overheard Lavina say, "John Allen, what about your Christian charity? For the Lord's sake—he's my nephew."

The chin of Lavina's husband was round, on a clean-shaven face, which was supported by a small, wiry, square beard. When there was conflict, as now, he spoke with a baritone voice from his beefy frame. His thick, strong, stubby hands were more suited for pockets, which he didn't have, and working the land. "Do him a world of good," he told her. "Being with the coloureds will put Joshua right. That layabout attitude—from what I see, he'll be just like his father."

"Don't," Lavina replied.

Matthew marched into the circle, where everyone noticed him.

He stood without a hat, and his bare hands clasped his lapels like an English fella.

"Thomas has welcomed everyone to the dinner circle," Matthew said. "Fine teams of woodsmen have accompanied us. He has requested that his wife, Mary, lead us in prayer and thanksgiving. Thank the Lord for the bounty before us." After saying closing "Amens," he left the camp.

No hat, mitts, or even a scarf tonight, thought Abner. Joshua was right; he was just pretending to be an Injun. This was real creepy.

Abner watched Matthew return to the Wrights. As soon as the man squatted next to Thomas and his wife, Philemon showed up.

"So, Thomas, when did you start letting someone else speak for you?" Philemon asked.

"Excellent," said Matthew. "Thomas told us about your elaborate plans. Mills, waterworks, and farms for everyone. This is the place to set the spark. Show everyone what's possible." He raised his palms up toward Philemon. "If I'm not too bold, Philemon, how about taking the reins?"

Philemon rose to the occasion. For another twenty minutes, he emphasized with his hands his plans and expectations for their new world agrarian utopia. It would be a massive undertaking, with no judicial or economic constraints to prevent what needed to get done. When Matthew touched his shoulder, he became even more animated about his visions for an agrarian utopia.

Afterword, Abner followed Matthew to the contractor's camp, where he saw the man puff up someone else's ego in a public forum. This time it was with David Wells.

In the morning, when Abner and Joshua were cleaning up, Abner said, "Come on, we don't have time."

"You can see, I can't leave right now," Joshua said as he washed the breakfast bowls.

"This can't wait. Trust me."

"And why don't you help me?"

"There's no time."

"What about your sisters? Mrs. Wright and my aunt—"

"Now. We have to go now," Abner said as he turned and started to walk away. He stopped and beckoned him to hurry.

"What could be this important?" Joshua huffed.

"This," Abner said as he pointed to tracks in the snow.

"So what? What is it?"

"David Wells. Last night, Matthew took him in there."

Abner was pointing to a set of tracks that went into the woods.

"Matthew heard him try to tell folks that Trevor wouldn't have left without his axe. I found these tracks last night, and this morning, he's gone missing."

"Why don't you have someone else follow them?"

"No one will listen because Matthew has convinced them not to worry. I think we should check this out before they force us to leave."

"What do we do if we find something?"

Abner kept walking. "Maybe he's hurt."

"Two sets of tracks going in, and only one set goes out," Joshua said.

"And why'd they come here? Just trees. Just more and more trees. They could have gone for a walk along the trail. No one to bother them and definitely no deep snow to trudge through."

The path led into a thick wall of cedars.

"They say wildcats don't like the snow," Joshua said.

"You afraid?"

Joshua went into the woods. It was dark and haunting. The stand led to a patch of dead trees, with a floor of decaying branches.

"Maybe they'll forget us like they did James Savage," Abner said.

"You're the one that wants to be here. Now you want to leave?"

The decayed wood cracked beneath their feet as they walked.

"They'll hear us," Joshua said.

"Who?"

"I don't know."

Abner stopped. "It's him. I can see his clothes," he said.

"What?"

Abner pointed. Fifty feet off, there was something on the ground. As they got close, they could tell it was the shape of a man. But when they were ten feet away, it wasn't clear what they were looking at.

"Man's clothes all right, but the hairs were grey," said Joshua "Skin's as dry as a corpse. And those eyes. Dark like a skull. He's definitely dead. Must be somebody else. This guy's old. Must have been here forever."

"Nope. He doesn't have much snow on him. Two tracks come in. Look. One's his."

"But where's the blood? He must have just keeled over.

"Who are you?" Abner asked the corpse. "Can't be Trevor Byrnes."

"You think he's going to tell you?"

"Look. Look at that. There's a tear in his boot."

"And?" Joshua asked.

"Missa Wells had a tear like that. And that's his thick sweater."

"But look at his hands. They're all dried out. Kind of like paper. Betcha if you touch it, it'd fall off. Why don't you?"

"Stop it." Abner said.

"I'd say he's real sick, and we'd better get out of here. What you looking at?"

"Wildcat tracks."

"Where?"

"There is none. Just looking, that's all."

"Come on, we better run. We've been gone too long."

They trudged back until they were out of breath. "Do you think they brought somebody sick here to die, or were they made sick?" Abner asked.

"You said that's David Wells's clothes. Was he normal-looking when you saw him last night?"

"Looked strong enough to me," said Abner.

"You know what that means?"

"We better tell Mister Wright."

"It means if someone did that to him, they'd do it to us," Joshua said.

"Yeah, but—"

Joshua ran ahead and didn't stop until he was out of the forest. When Abner caught up, he saw his father's sleigh waiting. All the rest of the caravan had gone.

—❦—

London gave a snap of the whip. The oxen pulled on. The boys who sat beside him, emptied snow from their boots.

"And what did you boys think you were doing? And Annie almost got kicked by a horse. This is a dangerous place.

"There was no end of complaints about you two. And you have no idea of the trouble you got us into. Missa Philemon wasn't going to let me stay. 'Gonna take off and steal the sleigh,' he said. Saying we were useless and was gonna send us back to the plantation where we belong.'

"I don't think Missa Thomas knew what to do. He still looks weak. I would have gone looking for you, but no way I was leaving my girls. Definitely no way I was taking them looking for the likes of you."

"Sorry, Poppa."

"So are they going to let you stay?" asked Joshua.

"Bill Moorwood told them he expects to see us at camp. If not, they'll haul the sleigh back in the morning."

"You mean without us?" asked Abner.

"Best we make up for the time we lost."

"Do you know where they're setting up camp?" asked Joshua.

"Somewhere up there, that's all," London said as he pointed to the single road ahead.

"But what if there's two or three roads?" asked Abner.

"Well, you better pray we'll be able to see which way they went."

"What was you looking for that was so important?" his father asked.

"Was looking for Missa David Wells," said Abner.

Joshua elbowed him in the ribs.

"And what did you find?"

Abner looked at his sisters, who were standing behind him.

"Nothing, I guess."

"Well, that was a mighty waste of time. You should apologize to your sisters. At one point, they was in a state of tears. And the way Philemon Wright was hollering, things didn't look good at all. I hope we can sort this up tonight, or I don't know what we're going to do."

Abner looked at Joshua and drew a line across his neck. He slouched down.

They did come to a crossroads. The sleigh tracks and horses made well-worn impressions on the right-hand path.

"Thank the stars, Abner," said his father. "If it snowed, or even worse, or if it rained, we'd be in a bad place."

"But, Poppa, I think that's where we're going."

"What?"

"A bad place."

Much Too Close

As they travelled, London noticed the cut of the trail rise and fall along a hard-to-see background of tall, rolling, snow-streaked hills through breaks in the canopies. Crystallized forest sleeves bent and stretched over the trail in attempts to touch amputated branches on the other side. A shallow, partially covered brook marked the foot of the eastern perimeter of the forest. London parked at the end of a line of sleighs. He and the boys were hesitant on what to say when the beast in front of him stopped.

Neither the Wright brothers nor Bill Moorwood seemed to notice or mind that they'd arrived late. Although London felt lucky, their lack of concern was disconcerting.

Thomas was sulky, spiritless, and lacked motivation. His missus ignored him and let him sit and mope.

Philemon was entertaining Samuel Choate and the contractors with his ideas for building ferries, stone buildings, and a mine and ripping out trees. *Always has big ideas, but how's he going to pay for any of them?* London wondered.

A couple of new men, who London wasn't familiar with,

were handling his chores. The change bothered him more than anything.

—◦◦◉◦—

Abner felt that the tree cover was squeezing in on them. He hadn't seen any sign of Matthew, but he cringed at the possibility that he might have gone back and discovered their footprints.

He hesitated to slurp another taste of his soup. Polly plopped down beside him. She was sitting way too close.

"You know something, don't you?" she asked.

"About what?"

"Him," she says, pointing to the oxen.

"Who?"

"That man you asked me about."

"What? You mean he's here?"

She pointed to the other campfire.

"Lord," he gasped. "Uh, that's not a good thing. You know he's a friend of your father's."

"My mother knows better. She knows that he's a problem, but she's got four little ones to worry about."

"Yes, he's a really bad man, but you know there's a lot more of us than him. The problem is that no one is going to disagree with your father."

"He doesn't talk to any of us anymore, and I think my brothers John and Tom are fools."

"I've seen them. They like it when nobody is telling them nothing."

"Who says that he's dangerous?"

"I just knows."

As she got up, Abner said, "Bearie's useless, and you'll find Phil's just like your brothers."

—◦◦◉◦—

London approached Thomas, who stood near the secured line of oxen.

"But it belongs to Missa Choate, and he told me that your boys were supposed to pen it in," London complained.

"The whereabouts of those boys is not my concern, London," Thomas Wright said.

"There's a calf, and I just—"

"What? Of all the lunatic … That can't happen. Oh yeah, and John Allen is complaining that his sleigh is pulling off-centre."

"It's 'cause he doesn't or won't pack it right."

"Do what you can," Thomas said as he patted his coat and looked elsewhere.

"And Missus Abigail is complaining about those men being too close to her Maryanne."

"Speak to Philemon."

"And they's following your Polly."

"Speak to Bill Moorwood."

He's not thinking, London thought. *Polly may only be twelve, but she's surrounded by dozens of single, powerful young, able men, and some not all too bright.* "That's who she's been talking to," London said. "Missus Abigail doesn't like him."

"Lord—drives a man to intemperance," said Thomas. "I know you're busy, but we have the utmost confidence in you, London." Thomas waved to someone and walked away.

"Shit," London mumbled.

"He noticed Thomas's daughter was moving toward him. When he veered toward the livestock, she kept following.

Behind him, Polly said, "I heard that there's a calf coming."

"That's right," he said as he continued walking. "Not coming right away, but she's farther along than we expected. Shouldn't have happened, but when males are determined, they can find a way."

"But killing her because she can't keep up seems so cruel."

"Life is savage, isn't it? Young Abigail and my Jane, for instance."

"That's different. Giving birth isn't like being sick."

"You believe my Jane caught what Abigail had?"

"My brother John told me that she looked the same when they found her."

"Just him and your father found her?"

"We was told not to speak about it. Expect that they were afraid of catching it."

"I'm sure we'll be safe now. We're a long way from it. Who else was there, when they found her?"

"It was in Medford, which wasn't far away. They met a minister and some people from the church. Was my father and the boys that got her."

"Polly, I don't expect you'll listen to your father or me, but it would not be smart for you girls to be around those men by yourselves. You know what I mean?"

"Maryanne was with me."

"Hmmm. Well, stay close to camp, is all—within hollering distance. And best not talk too much about that disease. Like your parents say—don't want to make folks upset, do you?"

London approached a cow that was tethered to a tree.

"Now, if you don't mind, you should leave real quick. I got to reach into this lady's backside, and it's not very lady-like for you to be here, if you know what I mean."

When the girl was out of range, he tried to calm the cow, but it didn't help. He nervously reached in with his right hand. "Damn it, girl," he moaned. "Jane, why, oh why?"

"London, you look like you're in pain," said a grinning Phil as he approached.

"Attracts flies, doesn't it?" replied London.

"How's the girl look?" asked Phil Jr. "How many months?"

"Three at the outside. She really shouldn't be here. Phil, what was my Jane looking for in Medford?"

He shuffled back and looked away. "Nothing, I thought—"

"The bridle, I heard you say it was wearing out and—"

"I could do with another. My father said—"

"Don't worry about that."

"Maybe it wouldn't hurt, I guess. A nanny—my cousins said that she was looking for another Negro to look after the young ones. I was told that you were moving to Boston. The minister there was in contact with people that we believed could help out. That's all that I know. I'm sure you know the rest."

"Weren't they afraid they'd catch what Abigail had?"

"Don't know much about that, but when they came back, my mother told me to stay away from them. I thought maybe it had something to do with chores, but maybe it had to do with something like that. Sorry, that's all I know. Does any of our stock have something that I should be concerned about?"

"Goats should be closer to the fire. Watch them joints."

London went to slap his shoulder, and Phil Jr. screamed, "Hey," and hurried back.

"Sorry," London said while smiling. "I should wash up, shouldn't I?"

Polly chased after Abner and grabbed his arm.

"What do you want?" he asked. "Gotta haul water."

"Why not boil the snow?"

"Sometimes they's fine with that. They don't know their own minds."

Polly caressed an old scar on her hand. "I think he's poisoning my father."

"Matthew?"

"I know it."

"So feed it back to him."

"Never seen him eat anything."

"Me neither. I think he does, but he takes it with him into the bush."

"I want you to take my father's bowl before he eats."

"So what's he going to eat?"

"Yours. Change it for yours."

"No way I'm eating no poison. Get someone else to do it. How come you're not going to do it?"

"Well, if he asks for seconds, guess I could do something."

"I noticed that when he's in a group, he doesn't do much talking," Abner said.

"Yeah, it's Matthew or my uncle."

"Yeah, nobody better than Missa Philemon for talking."

"I'll see what they want me to do, and then we'll see what's possible," Abner said.

"You know they might have you boys hauling water just to keep you busy, ever think of that?"

Not knowing what to say, he just looked around for Joshua.

Abigail was circling Ruggles and Lucy to keep them from wandering off and getting too close to the fire.

"Mrs. Abigail, if I may," said London.

"What's on your mind?" she asked.

"Missa Thomas was concerned that your daughter Maryanne shouldn't be visiting the single men without the accompaniment of one of the older brothers."

"The boys are always busy. I'll be glad when this is all done with. It's so unmanageable, you know."

"Yes, Missus Abigail. I was really taken by the last prayer service we had. He blessed himself. Was definitely a good thing. Folks really need it."

"Thank you, London. It's a privilege to do the Lord's work."

"That got me thinking. Did you hear if my Jane found another Negro after she left?"

Abigail hesitated. "Thought she drowned," she said, as she looked down.

"Are they hard to find?" London blessed himself.

"I did hear she expected to speak to someone about it, but obviously that never happened."

"Obviously," London repeated, and he blessed himself again.

-◦◎◦-

London found John patting and feeding his horse.

"Hello, John. Feeding her too much might not be a good thing."

He was surprised and dropped the grain.

"Have you seen my girls around?" London asked.

"No. Doesn't your son take care of them?"

"I guess I'll keep looking. By the way, maybe you could help me out. Your father gave a real good sermon the other day. We appreciated it very much. There was some good words of consolation. I prays to my Jane every night. I tells her about the girls growing up so fast and how strong Abner has become. Would make more prayerful-like to learn more about her last days. She'd appreciate us knowing. John, when you boys found her, where did you find her?

"The Mystic River."

"Yeah, I've heard that. "But where was she found?"

"Boston."

"Medford, you mean?" asked London.

"Well, sort of."

"How far from the church?"

"Oh. Was a couple of miles. I heard that she was going to Boston."

"But she wasn't in Boston?"

"Well, no, but the river goes there."

"I see. What did she look like?" London asked.

"You should talk to my father."

"He's mighty busy; you know that. Besides, you was there and would know. Did she look like Abigail?"

"Don't know because they didn't let me see her."

"Well?" London asked.

"She was old-looking. There was no colour on her skin."

"Look dried out?"

John looked around for others.

"Don't worry, I won't tell no one," London said. "We'll just keep it between you and me. I would just like Jane to be at peace when I talk to her, you know. It's the Lord's plan that she gets to have her peace and all. Did she look dried out?"

John nodded.

"How come she went alone?"

"She wasn't supposed to, but one of the ladies said she was nervous about something. Did she know Negroes in Medford?"

"Not many Negroes in these parts, and no reason to fear any of the ladies at church," said London. "Not familiar with those parts, was probably what it was. Thanks for your time. I'm sure I'll find what I'm searching for. Boys get scarce when there's work, don't they?"

"I thought you were looking for your girls," John asked.

London kept walking away and didn't reply.

When Abner approached Mister Thomas, he was standing within a group of workmen. Bill Moorwood, the crew chief, and Matthew were closest to him. Matthew had a bowl of stew in hand. He stared at Abner and deliberately offered Thomas his bowl.

Abner saw Polly in the distance, with her fingers beckoning him to come over. He stumbled, spilling his bowl on Thomas's jacket and knocking what was in his hand to the ground.

"Sorry, sorry. It was an accident. So sorry," Abner said.

Thomas's curses were drowned out by the workmen's laughter and taunts. Matthew put his hand on Thomas's shoulder and persuaded him to give Abner his jacket. When Abner returned with another couple of bowls, he saw that Thomas had almost finished another one. He was huddling close to the fire with the two men on each side of him. Matthew again was patting him on the back.

"Too slow and unnecessary. Matthew beat you to it," Thomas said.

"My poppa is cleaning your jacket and is going to watch over it until it dries."

When Abner saw Polly, he humbly shooed her away.

—❦—

London was looking for feed in the last sleigh that carried farm equipment. Philemon walked towards him from camp.

"London, Abigail tells me that you were asking questions earlier," he said.

"Your brother said that someone complained that single men were seen with his daughter," London said. "I let Abigail know of his concern and that your Maryanne was with her."

"Oh, she didn't mention that."

"We got talking about prayers, which led to me asking about Jane's last days. Why was my Jane looking for a Negro woman in Boston?"

"Oh. Was that why she was there? Some folks at the church wanted to get a Negro nanny for themselves. She told Mary she had some contacts. Maybe that's why she went."

"Did she catch what Abigail had?"

"Oh."

London blessed himself.

"Rightly, I don't know."

London glared at him, waiting.

"Maybe. I mean, I don't know what it was that she had. But yes, she did look the same. Skin dried out. Her skin and hair lost colour."

"By the way, I noticed that your Maryanne went with Polly again to the men's camp. Best have a word with her before it gets dark."

When he was out of hearing range, he muttered, "Jane volunteered—I don't believe a word of it."

—❦—

London approached Missa Thomas by the fire. Most folk, other than a handful of workmen, had settled in for the night.

"I've seen two new men in camp tonight—Gabe Taylor and Bradley Rogers," said London.

"I was told that David Wells had business in town. Hopes to rejoin us when he's able. Was told that he recommended these men," said Thomas.

"Matthew told you this?" London asked.

"Well, yes."

"There's a lot of young men in camp now. Guess you know what you're doing, Missa Thomas," London said. "Another thing, though, if you don't mind. I've been thinking a lot about Jane lately. Been asking around, trying to figure some things out. I was wondering if you know, Missa Thomas. What took my Jane from me?"

"I thought we covered this, London. We picked her up by the river. She drowned."

"Where did you say?"

"Boston, I believe."

"Where exactly?"

"Near the docks. It's rough down there. Church folk found her, and we came as soon as we could, but you know all that."

"Clearer now. Much clearer. I hear ya."

Abner wondered if he'd ever sleep again. The flashing orange and brown colours from the fire weren't the problem. It was the wild, roaring yellow that kept him awake.

What if Matthew lights up the cedars above our heads?

Do I drag Rachael out? Do I pull both of them by their feet? Annie would probably kick me in the head, and we'd all die. Damn.

His father rolled toward him.

Or will he try to turn Poppa into one of those dead things? He'd have to take him away, or does he?

Abner stared at the fire's ever-changing colours as his father snored beside him. Abner was determined not to sleep. He felt that Matthew's eyes were still on him. He was convinced that the man was committed to killing every last one of them. And nothing was going to persuade his father to leave this place. Maybe he should have told Poppa about the dead man, but no way, no how, was he ever going to give away the last thing that he had of his momma—her necklace.

Little Fishies

The train of sleighs followed the east side of the Connecticut River toward the Canadas. The river flowed the other way. It ran back to the United States. More than a couple of woodcutters had been mulling the same consideration.

The majestic Green Mountains, which lined the Vermont border, ascended on the far side of the valley. For the next few days, the caravan was going to stay at Bellows Falls.

Once the travellers stopped and gathered around their campfires, they had a clear view of the river, and they could hear the sounds of the babbling rapids and cascading waterfalls. Like the opposite shore of the river valley, the rising hills beyond were steep and had a thick forested coat.

On Sunday, after breakfast, Abner negotiated down a craggy, brush-covered slope to the rapids' shore.

Thomas Wright and his brother's brothers-in-law, John Allen and Samuel Choate, followed behind. Two people were already fishing in a calm spot above the rapids. The waterfall pounded steadily in the background.

Matthew was in the water, but his black greatcoat was left on shore.

His shirt and pants matched the thick, tar-black of the snake marks around his neck. The icy water didn't seem to bother him. The river reached his mid-thighs. Four salmon wiggled desperately onshore.

Bearie stood on the beach holding a line from the water's edge. Relative to the others in his family, he had a blocky face and a brawny frame. His hair was thin and wispy, and he carried an attitude of practical determination. He was made for a good day's work. Spending hours that seemed idle, just waiting for the fish to bite, was a challenge. On the Lord's day, it was a sacrifice he was willing to carry, especially when folks kept reminding him.

"What a wonderful place to celebrate a day of rest," said John Allen. He almost lost his footing as he gingerly slid down the embankment. Under the thick snow was slippery rock. "A magnificent, winding river filled with God's splendour. By the looks of it, we may even get some sunshine. And Matthew told me that he'll get us some salmon for dinner tonight."

"Hey there, boy," Thomas called to Abner. "Could you help Matthew with preparations, please?"

"Yes, sir, Missa Thomas," Abner replied.

Thomas turned to Bearie and said, "Bearie, bring in some fine eating for dinner, too, do you hear?"

The boy tipped his long-brimmed hat back to his uncle.

The four men tramped on, upriver.

"Here, catch," Matthew said to Abner as he lobbed a salmon in front of him. Abner stepped back.

"How you doing that?" Abner asked.

"Come here, boy," Matthew said.

Abner approached the water's edge, and for a few long minutes, Matthew said nothing while he bent over and stared at the water. His face almost touched the surface, and his arms were submerged above his elbows.

Abner took off a mitt and touched the stream with a bare hand. It was as cold as ice.

"I need you to bring me something," Matthew said.

Abner quickly put his mitt back on.

"Like what?"

Matthew threw another fish at him. It bounced off his chest. Abner tried to catch it on the rebound, but it slipped through his hands and plopped into the snow. As it wiggled toward the water, he grabbed it. *How could anyone bear the numbing cold?* Abner wondered. He moved next to the other ones.

"There's a green stone I need, and I want you to bring it to me."

"A green stone?"

"You know the one."

"What green stone?"

"I'm sure young Annie would be more than helpful if I asked."

"You leave my sister alone, or I'll—" Abner looked at Bearie and the others upstream. They weren't looking. He didn't think they could hear what was being said, and Matthew didn't seem to care if they could.

"Or you'll what? Complain to your father? To Thomas or his brother? Do you think that's wise? James said you had some concerns. Young Joshua says you think I had something to do with his leaving."

"He didn't like you at all."

"No, I suppose he didn't."

"I don't think Mister Wells did either."

"Figured that's where you were. Not many places to go in those woods, is there? You'll have fewer concerns if you hand it over."

"What makes you think I know anything about it?"

"We all have our secrets, don't we? Would be a shame to lose little Rachael, wouldn't it?" Before Abner could say anything, Matthew lobbed another salmon at him. If Abner hadn't stepped out of the way, it would have hit him again.

"Don't just stand there, kill it."

It flopped on the ground and wiggled like the others.

"You don't know nothing. You don't kill them; you string them on a line and keep them in the water."

"Exactly." Matthew threw a smaller fish at his feet. "Just seeing if you were awake. Don't stand around; get Bearie to show you."

Abner picked up a couple and brought them to Bearie, who still hadn't caught anything.

"Obviously, I'm using the wrong kind of bait," he said. Bearie showed Abner how to secure them to a line in the water.

As Abner picked up another pair of the beached fish, Matthew yelled, "A special one." The man raised another big salmon from the water. As it twisted, he held it with both hands, with the fish's head facing up. As his eyes glared into Abner, the fish stilled. "Too, too bad," Matthew said, as he let the dead fish float away.

"Abner, the gills. Fingers in the gills," Bearie said.

"Put your fingers in it," Matthew repeated with a smile. "Listen to what he says. You're running around like a chicken with its head cut off. Hard to do what you need to do like that."

Abner strung the remaining fish and hefted it out of the water.

"Where you going?" Bearie asked.

"They need it," he said, as he hurried to get away.

"Nowhere to run, young man," Matthew hollered.

Abner slipped and fell on the ice-covered rocks.

"That's no place to hurry, Abner," repeated Bearie, with a laugh.

London hated it when food wasn't drawn from the stores. Getting grub from the day's fish catch was nice, but way too many new hands cooking got involved. Margaret, at the behest of her husband, Samuel Choate, attempted to take over the meal preparation, but Aaron Johnson, who was one of the hunters, had already gotten Bill Morewood's permission to do the frying. After an irksome tirade, she offered to do the rest. The regular cook, of course, was left with nothing to do but complain and criticize. London was tagged to do the filleting as a ruse to maintain order. None of them paid him attention because they didn't believe they had to. London brought some herbs to the skirmish. It bought him a few seconds of respite, but not much more.

Abner and Joshua hauled staples and supplies from the last sleigh for the cooks.

"The way Missa Philemon goes on, young Bearie is some fisherman," London said.

"Two trout is what he got," said Abner. "It was Matthew that got the rest."

"The Injun?"

"He's no Injun, Pop. Don't know what he is, but he's no Injun. He's a monster, is what he is."

"You really don't like him?"

"It's about Annie and Rachael."

"Don't worry yourself about that. Leave that to me."

Missus Margaret motioned to London that she needed the fish. London knew she meant Aaron.

"Yes, Missus," he said while biting his lip. He was resigned to try to stay out of everyone's way.

"But, Poppa."

In a soft tone, London said, "Abner, you don't want to scare the women folk, do you?"

When Margaret wasn't so close, Abner leaned in close to London. "No, sir, but the men are dead, and I saw him kill that fish with my own eyes. And what he's doing with Missa Wright and the others—There's a heap load of trouble."

"Dead? Fish?" his father repeated. "What?"

"There's so much bad that he's capable of," Abner continued.

Aaron and the cook, who weren't supposed to be doing anything, were trying to get London's attention.

London lifted the tray of fillets. "Son, I hear what you're saying."

"But, Pop."

"No, I really do. Now take those buckets to the slop pit and tell folks that Missa Thomas wants them to get ready for prayers."

"But—"

"Go on. Folks are waiting to eat. You don't want them to come at us, do you?"

—❧—

Joshua joined Abner, who was standing next to trays of food.

"Looks like you don't know what you're doing?" Joshua said.

"That's because I don't. All I see is trouble."

"There's another one."

"What?"

"Wyatt Little," Joshua said. "Look at him. See those circles around his eyes?"

The man was lazily waddling about on his own around the settlers' bonfire. He almost bumped into Ruggles.

"Wasn't he minding the horses?" Abner asked.

"He didn't look right."

"He threatened my family."

"Wyatt?"

"You know who. He's watching. He killed a fish. I saw it."

Joshua returned a frowning look.

"Tell you later," Abner said. "Is your aunt taking you with them tomorrow?"

"Don't think so."

"They don't like you, right?"

Polly surprised them and appeared next to Abner. "Stop it," she said.

"Me?" Joshua asked.

"Abner, you were right. There's something wrong with people, and I really don't like Matthew," she said.

"Shouldn't be here. He's watching," said Joshua.

She gave Joshua a pretentious stare, but on reflection, decided that he was right. "I better go," she said.

—❧—

Influenced by their wives, the husbands arranged for the contractors to show up for the nightly prayer service. It was like an outdoor church service but without a minister. A wall of towering men surrounded a small circle of five couples and a swarm of young children, who were corralled around the blazing bonfire. The sky was starless. On one side there was a dark, haunting background of rising trees, and the other was open to the waterway and a display of star-like lights coming from distant village windows. The view became less open when the tall, young, virile, and powerful contractors moved their formation closer in to keep warm.

Matthew came out of the dark forest and approached Thomas and his family, who were sitting across from London. He placed his hand on Thomas's shoulder, said a few words, and was invited to sit down. The pair of Thomas's oldest daughters joined their mother and the other children on the other side of their father.

Samuel Choate stood and gave prayers of thanks.

After the prayer, Matthew stood up and held his hat against his chest. "I am honoured to share scripture with you. God's grace is true. His words, like the flames in front of us, show us what matters. We are grateful for the abundant bounty the Lord makes available to us this evening." He gazed around the circle of listeners and gave a steely grin.

Matthew waved an open Bible. "Romans, twelve, one, says, 'I beseech you therefore, brethren, by the mercies of God, that ye present your bodies a living sacrifice, holy, acceptable unto God, which is your reasonable service.'"

The man in black closed the bible and, from memory, said, "Philippians twelve eight–'And being found in appearance as a man, he humbled himself by becoming obedient to death—even death on a cross!'

"Amen, Amen," Matthew said loudly, and the others repeated.

"John one one–'The Word Became Flesh,'" he said as he stared at Abner. "'O fear the Lord, ye his saints, for there is no want to them that fear him,' Amen, Amen," he said loudly, and the others repeated.

Matthew glared at London and said, "But fear not. From Isaiah forty, twenty-nine to thirty-one, we know, 'He gives strength to the weary and increases the power of the weak. Even youths grow tired and weary, and young men stumble and fall, but those who hope in the LORD will renew their strength. They will soar on wings like eagles; they will run and not grow weary; they will walk and not be faint.'"

London checked for Abner or Joshua but didn't see either of them.

As the man in black quietly stared into the fire, Samuel Choate nervously added a pair of "Amens," which the others dutifully mimicked.

After supper, there were only a few people left around the settlers' fire. Most like Abigail's sisters were sitting with their backs to it because they were staring and listening to the water.

"I wish those boys would get along," Lavina said to her sister Margaret. They both had toddlers waddling in front of them.

"Philemon has to have his say, is all," added Margaret Choate.

London handed a bowl of tea to Lavina and asked, "Why is Missa Philemon so hard on Thomas? I know he doesn't like to be told, but there's something more there between them."

"They were both in the Revolutionary War," Lavina said. "The way Philemon sees it, his brother left him to fend for himself at the Battle of Bunker Hill. It was real bad. He was only fifteen. It was their father's fault. He told Thomas that he'd be disinherited if he didn't come home. He needed at least one son to carry on.

"Really affected Philemon, you know. Deep down, he believes that his father and brother left him alone. They left him to die. And there's something about you being brought into the household. Heard hints of it, but don't know really what it was about."

"Their father always had to have his way, didn't he?" Margaret said. "Elizabeth was like him—smart, direct, and ordered. Thomas won't admit it, but he misses her. She had a way of sorting the boys out."

"You know, he didn't have to move you into the house," said Lavina.

"With Philemon moving out, they could have managed the crops differently. Particularly when you had a family. It would have been easier on Thomas if you had kept a place of your own. His father was looking ahead. He gave them a push. It was not just for his children, but the ones after."

"I wouldn't have figured Thomas for wanting his son to leave Woburn."

"It's one thing when you're alive, but it's different when you know you're going to be gone."

"You never know what the Good Lord has in mind for any of us," said London.

"Best to keep this to yourself. Need to know your place. Knowing too much could come back and bite you, if you know what I mean."

"Yes, ma'am. Yes, indeed, I do."

—⁂—

After checking on the livestock, London returned to the girls. They were asleep, but Abner was sitting up.

"What are we going to do?"

"About what?" London asked as he sat and wrapped blankets around him.

"The girls."

"Shush. You're going to wake them. Now lie down."

"Matthew. We need to keep him away."

"I told you, don't worry about it. I'll take care of it."

"And what can you do?"

"Count sheep."

"What?"

"To make sure nothing's getting the livestock. I'm just messing with you. Now go to sleep. I'm here, and no one's going to bother anyone tonight."

"But—"

"Hush. That's enough." He lit his pipe and took a puff.

Abner rolled away and eventually managed to fall asleep, at least until a loud sound woke him up. A towering figure stamped in front of him. Abner quickly sat up and backed away. The man had an axe at his belt. He was staring at him. It was Bill Moorwood, the crew chief. He ordered him to settle down and go back to sleep.

Abner noticed that his father had fallen asleep. He was sitting, but had fallen away from the girls. Abner asked if anyone else was around, and Bill told him that Matthew had been by. Abner pulled his blankets tighter and sat there, eyeing the dark. Afraid that Matthew was going to come for him, he didn't know what to do. Captivated with fear, Abner refused to sleep. After what seemed a short snap of time, someone shook him.

"Wake up, Abner," his father said. "We gotta make breakfast, and it won't make itself. Don't wake the girls." Abner was shivering.

The next campsite was set up on the shore of the Black River. The settlers stopped just south of Springfield. The trail looked flat, but the land was overrun with towering stands of trees shadowing the outer edges of the trail and the river. It was about fifty feet between each shoreline, but the water was shallow.

To commemorate the first stop in Vermont, the Wrights convinced contractors to do some trout fishing. With the fires and lean-tos against the sleighs being right next to the river, there were a lot of complaints about frozen and soaked feet.

In the morning, John and Bearie joined Abner, who stood next to a vacant sleigh.

"You found a dead man?" asked John.

"Who told you that?"

"Who do you think?"

"Joshua?" asked Abner.

"Horse shit," said John. "He's not good for nothing."

"So, it was him," said Abner.

"What was it like?" asked Bearie.

"Not here," Abner said and pointed them to the bush on the opposite side of the road where the caravan was camped. Once inside, it didn't feel like anyone was following them.

"You tell me about Abigail first. What did she look like?"

"We don't need to tell you nothing," said John.

"Me neither, then."

"There's something about my father," said John. He stared at Bearie. "I thought she just got sick, is all. Like winter fever. We found her in our barn. Couldn't tell it was her. When ma'am came, she recognized what she was wearing, and she had those beads of hers. But she was like an old woman. Only six, and her hair was grey with some white even."

"Yeah, that's how my brother Phil explained it," Bearie said.

Abner was looking around to see if anyone else could hear them.

"You expecting someone?" asked John.

"The man that's dead and all dried up," Abner replied. "He kinda looked like that. He was like a skeleton."

"So who is it?" asked John.

"It was Missa Wells. He had skin like paper."

"Woah," said John. I was told that he just left."

"No, he's dead. We saw him. It was really him."

"Yeah, Abigail had that too," Bearie said.

"I've seen that once before myself," said John. "Well, I don't know if I should say. I'd get in trouble."

"What are you talking about?" asked Abner.

"That's what happened to Abner's ma'am. It was the exact same thing. Figured it was her because she was coloured, but it sure didn't look like her."

"What?" said Abner.

"Are we all going to get it? Is it like a plague? What we going to do?" Bearie complained.

"My ma'am?"

"Sorry, Abner. We didn't know what it was. Couldn't go spreading it around. That's why we had to burn the barn."

"We didn't burn ours, but we burnt everything that was in it," said Bearie.

"Obviously, it wasn't enough," said John.

"But the last case was more than two years ago," Bearie said.

"Not a disease. It's Matthew," Abner said.

"But he's not sick," said John.

"Don't know," said Abner. "But Matthew led Missa Wells from camp. The next morning, we followed their tracks, and we found him dead. And I saw him kill a fish."

"Fish; what?"

"Uh, never mind."

"I wonder if my dad's got it," John said. "He doesn't look right. He's not acting right." John turned to Bearie. "Abner's right about one thing: I don't like Matthew. Dad seems to agree with everything he says. He and my ma'am were always arguing about it."

"But what can we do? Turn around?" asked Bearie.

"Matthew kills people," said Abner.

"John, we better be careful who we talk to," said Bearie.

"What about telling our brothers? What about Phil and Tom?"

"Maybe, but they might not listen, and I don't know what they'd say. I wasn't supposed to tell anyone about Abner's ma'am. Don't want it getting out to anyone else, especially now. And we don't want to give him cause to come after us."

"He threatened my sisters," said Abner.

"If you learn something else, don't talk to us when anyone else can see," said Bearie.

"If this gets real bad, maybe we should run off and join the army. Bearie, what do you think?" asked John.

He shrugged and turned to leave. John followed him out.

"Somebody killed my ma'am," Abner muttered quietly in the dark. He was surrounded by an army of towering bare trunks. The place looked lifeless and cold. Broken, rotted branches poked through a thin layer of snow.

Whatever monsters watched him from the dark couldn't be as bad as what waited for him at the bonfire. He wiped the snot from his nose. "And there's just me, Joshua, and maybe Polly," Abner muttered. "I gotta find Polly."

—◦◦—

"It's about time you showed up," Polly complained. "And where were you? There's just Maryanne and me, and look at them." Eight children were running around the fire. Another seven, who were closer, were toddlers.

"We should talk," Abner said.

"Where were you?" Rachael repeated.

"I'm here now."

"Come on. Come on," yelled Ruggles as he grabbed Abner's hand.

"Fine," said Abner. "Polly, I got to ask," but before he could finish, Ruggles lost his grip and flopped to the ground.

He grabbed Ruggles' wrist and swung him around and around in circles. There was not much space between the stands of trees and the blazing bonfire, but Abner did his best to keep the children entertained. Lucy was next, then Annie, who was really heavy. Rachael was followed by Maryanne and Elizabeth. Toddlers were yelling, "Me too. Me too."

Seeing his daughter almost tossed into the fire, Philemon rushed over in a rage. "What in tarnation do you think you're doing here, boy? No more of this. There'll be no more."

The children grew silent.

"And Polly, what were you doing? How did you let this get out of hand? We expect more."

Abner was disappointed that Polly didn't stick up for him, but when her uncle left, she told him, "Wouldn't have helped saying anything."

"Again," yelled Elizabeth.

"Tag, you're it, Lizzie. Go get Rug," Abner said.

Bill Moorwood got up from his seat by the fire. "You got to take them out," he said. "Someone's going to get hurt."

"But we just brought them back."

"I know, Polly," Bill replied. "But the three of you are going to have to round them up. I'll get three of my men to watch over you."

"Polly, you think three men with axes, gonna stop a pack of wolves in the dark?" asked Abner.

"Then go get Joshua. They'll eat both of you, and we'll be fine."

"Actually, I'd prefer something sharp," Abner muttered.

Abner ran over to Joshua and told him that he had to help mind the children.

"She called me?" asked Joshua.

"She was telling me what she likes about you."

"Yeah?"

After pulling his axe from a tree, Bill Moorwood slipped it into a holster. He swore and gave a second torch to another woodsman. They followed the children to a pitch-dark wagon trail and reluctantly listened for the sound of wolves.

Abner was looking for another blanket under the canvas in the back of the sleigh, while the children played nearby with Polly and Joshua. Matthew came from behind and surprised him.

"You have something of mine," Matthew said, patting his open palm.

"Go away," yelled Abner.

Matthew drew closer.

"Leave us alone."

Matthew pointed to his hand. "Give me what I want." He gazed at the children around Polly. "Lots of other little fishies, aren't there?"

A woodcutter stepped in. "Boy doesn't want to be bothered. Do what he says."

"It's Joe Carver, isn't it? Matthew said, eyeing the man. "Came with James Savage's crew, right? You do know you're here because of me?"

"That doesn't give you the right."

"Who says I'm bothering this boy? He's got something of mine, and I want it back. That's all."

Joe gave the boy a back-end wave, and Abner left with a blanket in hand.

"Nothing so important to ruin anyone's day. I've heard that you like your sleep," Matthew said. "Minding the horses in the dead of night. Terrible thing. Some say that I have influence." He repeated a backhand wave, and Joe Carver, upon leaving, tipped his hat.

Once London confirmed that his children were sound asleep in the back of their sleigh, he went looking for the man in black. He found him sitting on a log talking to Philemon's brother-in-law, John Allen.

"Give him time, John," London heard him say. "Philemon is light on details, but his intentions are good. They always have been. We all know that." He looked up and saw London. "What can we do for you, London?"

"We've got something to discuss." Looking at Mister Allen, he said, "Private-like."

"It's getting late," Matthew said. "We've a long drive in the morning." John Allen gave him a polite nod and left.

"My boy keeps telling me that you's been bothering him. He thinks you're going to hurt my girls. You even—"

"Wouldn't dream of it, London. I'm sure it's a misunderstanding. You know when boys get to be a certain age, they crave adventure. Wasn't you like that at his age?"

"Maybe, but what's that got to—"

"I've heard a lot of great things about you and your boy from Thomas and Philemon. That you're going to have a cabin of your own and more land than either of them had at Woburn. I mean the very idea of it. You, a Black man—free, with a farm. Your own cattle, even. Being able to do what you please. When you please. That would be quite something, wouldn't it,

London?"

"Yeah, but—"

"Philemon does have an interesting temperament," said Matthew. "Sometimes he can get out of sorts, can't he? Don't you worry yourself about that. Leave it in my hands, and it will all work itself out."

London stared at him and didn't know what to say.

"You're going to catch a chill. Better get yourself some blankets, don't you think?" Matthew turned away and threw something into the fire. It looked like a piece of bone.

"It would be best if we all get what we want."

When London returned to the fire circle with a toque and thick blankets, he noticed that Matthew was talking to Wyatt Little. The big man was getting thinner by the day. And there was something wrong with his hand. Much of it had turned black. Matthew was holding it.

The ride out, although sunny, was cold. Thick blankets secured with scarves covered their layers of wool clothes, but the windchill was still biting. Abner stepped from the back of the sleigh and squeezed between his father and Joshua.

"Get any sleep last night?" asked his father.

"Every night there's wolves howling," Joshua said. "It's like there's more and more. And getting louder and closer."

"Missa Thomas hired men for that. They stay up all night," London said.

"Last couple of nights, I've only seen one," said Joshua.

"I'll talk to Missa Thomas about it."

"I don't think a couple of axes are enough," Abner said. "Like, what if there's a whole lot of them? What then?"

"Count your blessings?" London said.

"What?"

"Cause it can always get worse, that's what," London said.

"What you thinking?"

"I need me an axe," Joshua said.

"Better sleep in the woods then," London said.

"What?"

"No one's going to be near the likes of you. You'll be the first one they get. That'll be best for all of us, won't it?"

Joshua punched Abner in the arm.

"You going to go for another walk?" asked Abner, as the caravan of sleighs steadily moved ahead.

"Your turn," Joshua said as he punched him in the shoulder again.

Abner side-pushed him.

"Hey," yelled his father. "You want them to have you both?"

"I was threatened yesterday," Abner said.

London saw that his expression had changed. "Was it, Matthew?"

Reluctantly, he nodded.

"Can't stand being around him. Feels like he's the kind that would cut your throat for no reason," Joshua said.

"Why's he bothering you?"

"He's plain bad."

"I warned him to stay away. Then he tried to be nice to me last night," London said. "Not sure why."

"You said you were going to ride with your aunt," said Abner.

Joshua just shrugged.

"It's not you, boy. It's just those aunts picking on their brother, is all. I know it's not fair, and it's not right."

"Do you have a family?" asked Joshua.

"None to speak of," London said.

"How did you get Coffey's necklace? Why didn't it go to someone else?"

"Zach and Patte passed after the war. The others? No idea. They was sold long ago. Patte gave it to me because I was free. She knew the others didn't have the same chance."

"It's gone, and so is your momma. No screaming is going to change that." His shoulders dropped as he leaned forward.

"*Little fishies*," Abner muttered. He was tired. He didn't get much sleep last night. There were the wolves, and there were the nightmares. Worse still, he had to pee.

The next camp was hill bound on both sides of the trail. There was enough clearing to make a half circle around the settler's bonfire. Before supper, Abner and Joshua, with Polly and Maryanne, collected all the children that could walk.

"We're supposed to tire them out before dinner," Polly said.

"You'd think they would get tired of racing," Abner complained.

"If they're running down the track that the sleighs and livestock made, they're all going to get covered in animal shit," said Joshua.

"If you'd been helping us out, you'd know that little legs can't go far in the snow."

"And that's a bad thing?"

"Joshua, are you doing this or not?" asked Polly.

"A swarm of them covered in shit. Sure, why not?"

"No sooner do we clean them up, it's coming out the other end."

"There's worse things," Abner said.

"What do you think Matthew's doing?" asked Polly.

"Haven't seen him all day," said Abner. "No good, whatever it is. I think something has got him distracted. I think he's just waiting to kill us. He's got me so afraid I haven't been able to sleep for three nights. And I don't think Joshua takes this seriously. I told him not to tell anyone about James Savage, and what does he do? He tells Matthew. We're lucky we're not dead by now."

"I told you already. I hate him. So what is it?" Joshua said.

"My cousin Abigail and Abner's mom—he killed them," she said.

"Woah," Joshua said. "God Almighty. None of us are safe now. Maybe we never was."

When they returned the children to the fire, they saw Matthew talking with the four housewives. He was bouncing a one-year-old on his knee.

"Look at them, peaceful as cows at milking. Won't be like that when he kills one of them," Joshua whispered. "Or do you think they'll even catch on?"

"Abigail was almost as old as Rachael," Abner added. "But they're not going to listen."

"Not to them," Polly said. She walked over to the woodsman's crew chief, who was adding logs to the fire.

"Mister Moorwood," she said loudly. "You keep him away from us. You keep him away from me."

"What?"

"I was doing my business in the woods, and he was watching. That's just wrong. He's sick. It's him." she pointed at Matthew. "And I've seen the way he looks at Mrs. Allen when she's sleeping. You keep him away. You keep him far, far away. Do you hear?"

"What's that, Polly?" her mother asked.

Mrs. Allen quickly snatched her daughter from Matthew.

"What is it that you saw, Polly?"

"Couldn't sleep last night, and there he was."

"Just a flight of someone's growing imagination is all," Matthew said. "Surely, she was mistaken." He stood up and reached for Thomas Wright's wife, Mary. She quickly moved back and shuffled her toddlers away from him.

"Ladies, no trouble from my men. I promise," Bill said. "I'm sure he didn't mean anything by it. Men folk usually keep to their own at the other fire."

Matthew approached him, but Bill stepped away. "No need to go into this, Matthew," he said, pointing to the other fire. His other hand held an axe that he used for splitting kindling.

"Ladies," Matthew said as he scanned the women who had scooted their children away from him. For the first time in a long time, he was at a loss for words.

Polly rushed over to her mother and wrapped her arms around her. "Mother, you've got to believe me. Keep him away."

"Yes, yes, of course I do." She squeezed an arm around her. Next, she gave her the two-year-old and told her to mind the seven-year-old while she scooted back her other two young ones.

Mrs. Choate was going to say something in the man's defence, but she, like the others, locked hands with her children. "Sir, Mr. Moorwood asked you to leave here. Please go."

"Bill," said Abigail, and waved them away. "From now on, we're sleeping in the sleighs."

Matthew avoided the other campfire and walked off into the dark line of trees.

Thomas Wright weakly stumbled into the altercation with a pained, confused look. He took his hat off.

"Thomas, it's Polly," Mary said, while glaring at him. "I know you overheard. It's our Polly, for Lord's sake."

"Yes, yes." He shook his head. "There's something terribly wrong here," he moaned while staring at the ground. He looked at his daughter and then his wife as he moved next to her. "Yes, it's true, there is something terribly wrong," he repeated. "We can't have this." He nodded at Abigail.

Polly shivered. She was terrified, wondering what was going to happen to them next.

Loose Ends

Something touched Abner's shoulder. He heard someone say in a soft voice, "Time to get up, sleepyhead." Abner groaned.

When someone grabbed his arm, he awoke with a start. "Hey," he yelled.

When he saw that it was Matthew, he sat up quickly.

"Let go of me," he said.

"You slept in. Everyone's been up for a while. We need to talk," the man in black said.

Others were huddled around the morning campfires.

"What do you want?" Abner asked.

"You know what I want—your mother's green stone. It's mine."

"What?"

"I told you, your mother had it."

"I don't know what you're talking about."

"Coffey, your grandpa, had it and passed it on."

"Coffey? But would you—"

"I saw it."

"You're Matantu?"

He grinned and tipped a pretend hat.

"But you don't look old at all," Abner said.

"Can you give it to me?"

"Jack gave it to us. It wasn't yours."

"The Wìsakedjàk? No, that's not true. Listen it would be better if we were cordial about this," Matthew said as he approached and attempted to touch his shoulder.

"Get away from me," Abner said as he slipped backward and looked around for the contractors. "And Jack Wizak will come for you," he whimpered.

"You'll find him much worse than me. He'll leave nothing left standing, everything that you know will disappear, and he'll do anything to find her. He knows that I'm the only one who can locate her. He didn't know that then, but he does now."

"Wekatesk?"

"So you do know where it is? Why are you stalling?"

Abner pointed to the contractors. "They'll stop you."

"You won't do that because any one of them will take it from you. You'll give it to me because it's mine. By the way, your Annie would be very upset with you."

"Where is she?"

"I'm sure you'll find her if you give it to me."

"Poppa says that somebody stole it."

Matthew placed a hand on the side of his face and stared at him. "But you know where it is, don't you?"

"You're not getting it until I know Annie is all right."

"Enough of this," Matthew ordered, and he reached for Abner's shoulder.

Abner moved back. "I can find it, but only if you don't hurt my sisters."

Matthew stepped forward and reached as if he was going to tickle his chin. "It's your life we are bartering with. Last chance."

Abner got up and stepped back. "And what are you going to do with it?"

"It's a key."

Matthew took a step closer.

"John took it," Abner said.

"Let's hope that you're not wasting my time."

"What are you going to do with it?"

Matthew shooed him away with a flick of his hand.

"But where are my sisters?"

"How would I know? You're supposed to be looking after them. Go find them yourself." He looked back and saw Philemon's wife thundering toward them. "By the looks of it, someone wants to have a word with you. I'll leave you to it."

When she got close, Abner turned toward her. "Yes, Missa Abigail. Right away. Just had to get something."

"Now is not the time. You gotta do what you're supposed to. Go on. Hurry it up. Shoo."

Abner ran along the sleighs in the direction Philemon's wife had pointed.

"Looking for the children?" John Allen asked. "I's told they're up there."

Abner followed footsteps through the trees to the sounds of yelling. There were about a dozen of them. Except for Joshua, they were all ten years of age or less. Joshua sat on a deadfall, sharpening a stick. Annie and Rachael were nearby. Annie was throwing snowballs at Ruggles.

"Did that man in black talk to you?" Abner asked Annie.

"Who?"

"Matthew?"

She shrugged.

"That's a no, I guess," said Abner.

"Rachael, what about you?"

She didn't listen to him. She was busy packing down a snowball between her mittens.

Abner walked over to Joshua, still sharpening his stick.

"Where's Polly?"

"Don't know. Just left, that's all."

"Missus Abigail doesn't want you here. What're you doing?"

"What does it look like? If something comes for me, I'm going to need something." He lunged his wooden spear several times into the snow.

"He's going to take it."

"What?"

"He wants something of my mother's, and I think he's going to do bad things with it. He threatened me, and he's going to hurt my sisters."

"Maybe he's feeding people to something," Joshua said.

"Poison. Yeah, I think it's poison, just like Polly said."

"That might be it. Maybe we can get him to leave," Joshua said. "Don't know about you, but I don't want to look like those dead folk. And there's more that are looking sickly."

"We gotta get them out of here," Abner said. "Missus Abigail is mad that they're here. We gotta take them back."

When Abner led the children back into camp, Polly came storming towards him.

"You bloody prig. Who do you think you are?" She pushed the back of his arm.

Stunned, Abner spun away. "What the hell?"

"Who are you to tell me what to do?"

"What are you talking about?"

Abner saw Missus Thomas talking to her son, Ruggles.

"I didn't say anything to nobody. Somebody else must have complained that you didn't mind them."

"Where's Joshua?"

Abner turned around, realizing Joshua hadn't come back with them. "I need to talk to my Poppa."

"Try the shitter," she said. She left him to rejoin her cousin Bearie.

Abner doubted that she knew much about anything, but he did find his father, who was leaning on a log, hovered, over a snow covered latrine pit.

"Abner, there's a lot of log here to share," his father said.

"Don't gotta go, but I do have to say something."

London finished up with bits of spruce branches. "Well, go on," London said as he adjusted his pants.

"Poppa, you got to listen. We gotta go."

"Is this about the sickness?"

Abner folded his arms as he rocked back and forth.

"He gave it to Momma."

"Why do you say that?"

"Momma was the same as Abigail. He had to take it from her."

"What?"

"Her necklace. John says that he saw her, and she looked the same as Abigail, and he knows that I know who he is."

"Who's that?"

"He's Matantu."

"Who?"

"The story. You know Coffey's Matantu. He told me who he is."

"Can't be. He'd be really, really old." London put his hand in his food pocket.

"That's what he told me."

"You keep the girls safe. I'll take care of the rest. Careful who you talk to. Folks aren't what they appear, and I've seen that fella charm them to do things they normally wouldn't do."

A problem with one of the sleighs prevented the camp from moving out. Mary, with her husband, drove ahead. She wanted to get her husband away from the camp. Their oldest sons rode on ahead on horseback. Mary had arranged for four workmen to watch over Polly, Maryanne, and the children while they were gone. Thomas dismounted to look at an old bridge that the caravan would have to cross. While he was pounding it with a wood staff ,the boys kept riding.

"The bickering hasn't started yet," John said.

"You can go back if you miss it," Tom said.

"Nah. To the corner—a race; You in?" Without waiting for an answer, he darted off.

His brother, with not even enough time for swearing, raced after him. Tom cussed a blue streak once he reached the bend in the road.

John laughed. "If you paid more attention, you wouldn't have to complain so much. Anyways, I thought we'd see something of Rutland by now. Maybe we're not as close as Father said."

Ahead of them, Matthew emerged from the woods.

"Whoa," said Tom as he squeezed the reins.

"Tarnation," his brother muttered.

"I saw your parents back there. Looked like they were enjoying the sights. Find anything interesting, boys?"

The boys didn't reply. John knew that Matthew wasn't someone he wanted to be alone with. At the moment, he was captivated by the change in the man's appearance. Matthew's clothes had changed colour and texture. The black leather pants, vest, jacket, and greatcoat were replaced with a similar set that was dark grey with a barely visible trace of fur.

Matthew walked up to John's horse and stared at him. "How are you, John?"

"What are you doing here?" he replied.

Matthew put a hand on the neck of the horse, its front legs bent, and John fell. Matthew supported his elbow and pivoted him into a standing position, and then he put his hand on his shoulder.

"Relax, John. You're in good hands," Matthew said.

"What's wrong with my horse?"

"I'd expect it would appreciate you more if you fed it something." He put a hand on his shoulder. "Feel better?"

"I'm fine. Just what are you doing?" John asked. He tried to push him away, but quickly began to lose strength and his attention.

"I'm told that you have a stone of mine."

"I do? What colour is it?"

"Green. It's part of a necklace. You got it from the coloured boy."

"Me. No. Never seen it. If Abner had it, he probably still does."

"You're feeling good?" Matthew repeated.

"Wasn't, but yes, I'm feeling good. Yes, actually really good. Anything else I can do for you?"

Matthew let him go, glared menacingly, and again asked, "Are you absolutely certain that you've never seen it?"

"No, sir. Never."

"The boy stole it from me." Matthew patted the boy on the back.

"When you boys find out where it is, you'll tell me won't you?" He put his hand on John's neck again and stared at his eyes and then at his brothers.

"No problem," John said. "We'll let you know, right away."

Matthew glared at Tom, who, in turn, replied with, "No problem. If we learn something—"

"You mean when you learn something?"yo

"Absolutely."

"Thanks for your patience, gentlemen. I'll take my leave. I have to get me some more little fishies."

Richard James lumbered back to a circle of half-awake workmen, with his coveted bowl of stew and a small loaf.

"Richard, fook off," said a man with his back to the fire.

"Howard, that's not nice," said Richard.

"Shut up, or I'll tear out your balls and feed them to your momma."

"Nice to know you're thinking of me," Richard said as he sat down beside him. He took a quick bite of his bread. "So, what you looking at?"

"The coloured. He's staring at me."

"He's coming for you. Better eat up, or he's gonna take it."

"Richard, just shut up. It was so quiet before you came along."

London carried a pot and some cups. "Howard, you didn't take your tea."

"Mister Simpson, to you. Don't you know nothing?" Howard replied. "Don't want none."

"You can give me some though. Richard James raised an almost-empty bowl.

"That Matthew sure is different, isn't he?" London said as he filled the bowl.

"Why's that?" asked Howard.

"Never seen him eat. Just nothing at all. Never."

"Thomas Wright must be giving him something."

"If Missa Wright wanted us to prepare something, I'd know, wouldn't I?" said London.

"Maybe Injuns get their own," said Richard.

"No way he's an Injun. He acts like one of Thomas's boys. Him with short hair now, and a vest and good boots," said Howard.

"He doesn't have the long hair, or that ugly hat anymore. I rarely see that long coat either. And that wild stink he had is gone. Something he ate, maybe? When you think about it, that's strange, ain't it?" said Richard.

"Not natural," Howard said. "Definitely not. London, I changed my mind. Give me some more tea."

"I betcha that you've also noticed that he disappears into the woods at night. Who knows where he's going, or what he's doing," London said.

"London, you's bring us another bowl of that stew, and we'd like to hear more. Won't we, Howard?"

Howard laughed. "Sure. London, we'd be mighty appreciative."

London nodded and left.

"So, what's Matthew doing?" Richard asked.

"Getting rabbits? Maybe London doesn't know what he's talking about."

"When it comes to food, I don't have no reason to disbelieve him. If that feller is trapping, he must have a camp set up. I've never seen him carry anything more than what he was wearing, and we've moved a few times. You'd think we'd see him carry some game or pots or something.

"If he was an Injun, he could be joining another camp that's following us. Iroquois, maybe."

"Since he's not an Injun, he must be joining other folk."

"Robbers, you think?" asked Howard. "Pretty easy pickings from this bunch, with all the children and women folk. Looks like Matthew has a lot to answer for."

"Maybe we should follow him at night. Should show us what we need to know. If something doesn't go right, we'll blame the coloured boy."

London brought Howard and Richard more stew and bread.

"I don't know about you folk, but I'd really like to find out what the man is doing," London said.

"Maybe he's doing stuff for the Wrights."

"No. I know he's not."

"So you think he's up to no good," said Howard.

London nodded.

"I'd like to follow his tracks to-night before it gets too dark. I need a couple of powerful men who know the bush better than me, and who knows how to take care of themselves real good. You boys should be good at that, I'd expect—I'm thinking that if my hunch is right, putting in good words to the Wrights could be worth something. You know, they're giving out land."

"I've heard that, but they haven't offered it to us."

"So, given the right circumstance …"

"Let's do it, then. Better not mention it to anyone. It might just spook the bastard. Fortunately, we don't have to stay up tonight, but I guess you already knew that."

London grinned. Since he had seen Matthew leave already, he convinced the others to get up and go. Each of them wanted to get back before dark.

The men, a couple of hours before sunset, followed Matthew's footsteps along a winding path into a thick forest. Both woodsmen carried axes and sharp knives. Richard's knife was sheathed to the calf, and Howard's to his belt. London followed.

Wild runs across fields, and furry drag marks in the snow implied that Matthew had been hunting for game.

"He was in a mad run. Look at the distance between each of his steps. Can that fella run or what?" said Howard. "Twenty feet after crossing its tracks, the deer succumbed."

"This could be trouble," said Richard.

"What do you mean?"

"He hasn't butchered it, and he's been dragging the whole thing. He's stronger than he looks."

They came to a snow pit. A mound of snow encircled it. An uprooted root ball of a fallen tree, about ten feet in diameter, served as a backstop to the hole. In the hole, there were pairs of deer and raccoons. They looked old, white, and emaciated.

"They're diseased. Like they got the plague. Don't go near them," said Richard.

"The bodies have cut marks on their sides. Those aren't knife wounds," said Howard.

"Look at this mark in the snow. He must have been lying between the pair. I don't see any signs of cook pots. Not even a fire. I'd say he's out of his mind. I don't like the looks of this."

London had stepped off the path behind a patch of young, bushy cedars.

"Where is he?" Howard asked.

Richard, who was staring at the footsteps that went around and to the right of the raised root ball, stepped backward. Matthew came out from the other side.

"What a sick bastard," Howard said.

"Kind of late for a walk, don't you think?" Matthew said. He was only about five feet from where Howard stood.

"Aren't you boys supposed to be working? You do remember that I brought you here. You folks taking a holiday paints me in a poor light. Are the conditions at the camp up to your expectations?"

"Better grub, maybe," said Howard.

"I suppose we should all get back," Richard said. "It will be getting dark soon. We don't want to lose our way."

"You've brought up a very good point, Richard. It's time to go."

Howard stared at the dead carcasses. "Yeah. Yes, it's time to go," he said as he backed away.

Matthew stepped forward.

"Stay back," Howard said. As he took two steps back, he pulled his knife from the sheath attached to his leg. Matthew lunged at him, causing both of them to fall into the small pit.

Howard managed to slice Matthew's collarbone. Matthew smashed his face. Seeing what looked like blood, Richard also jumped down. As soon as he landed, he repeatedly stabbed Matthew in the abdomen.

Matthew fell to the ground beside Howard, who was moaning. After sheathing his knife, he froze in shock. "Good God," he groaned.

Howard fell back. Tendrils from Matthew's left hand were attached to Howard's stomach. Thin black vine-like growths started to stretch from Matthew's other hand.

"What the fook?" muttered Richard. He quickly tried to crawl back out of the hole. Richard felt a thin vine attach to the side of his calf. Terrified, he tried to stand on one leg and smash it with his other foot, but he stumbled back. "No, no, no," he murmured as he tried to pull out the axe on his belt. He got it out and raised it. The thin vines had thickened and stretched throughout his leg. Realizing that he could no longer move, he noticed that Howard's face had turned pale white. The axe dropped, and he fell. As he was pulled across the hole toward Matthew, he saw that the man was alert and smiling.

As the vine-like tendrils burrowed into Richard's chest, he and Howard were pulled to each side of the man in black over top of the other carcasses.

⁓⊙⁓

At the woodcutter's camp, Abner faced Tom Jr. and a contractor named Bill Harris. Joshua was chasing after Annie and Rachael.

"Can't you see what's happening?" Abner shouted. "Tom, your father is dying. Matthew's poisoning him."

Bill, whatever you do, don't let Matthew touch you," Tom said.

Tom stared at Bill Harris. "And what are you going to do about it?"

"Me? What would you expect me to do?" Bill asked while looking at Tom Jr.

"Don't like him. Abner's right, I think he has something to do with making Father sick, but I don't believe that all the men that left are dead. It's been weeks and folks would have noticed."

"A lot of them, folk didn't have enough time to get to know them," said Tom.

"But I'm telling you that both me and Joshua have seen it," Abner said. "Tom, you gotta get your father far away from him. He's told me that he's going to kill my sisters. Damn, he's going to kill us all. Don't you get it?"

"Why aren't you saying this to Philemon?" asked Bill. "He's in charge."

"Damn. Look at him," said Tom. "He's getting sick like my father. There's nothing he wouldn't do for Matthew."

"Boys, I know you don't like it here, but when we get to where we're going things will get better. You just got to give it a chance."

Joshua came back with Annie on his shoulders. "Give up on it, Abner," he said. If we can't persuade him, we're not going to be able to change anybody else's minds."

"But you could take Missa Philemon, away from that man," Abner said. "We're almost at the lake. There must be a town you could stay at. I betcha he'll get better."

"Burlington. But even if I believed you, and was sure about most of it, no way would my mom go along with it." Tom stared at the woodcutters. "That's not going to happen. Too many would think we're running away. I appreciate your concern, but it's not going to happen." Tom said, "Sorry," as he walked away.

Joshua put down Annie, and she ran back to see her sister.

"Then just tell her that you're going to Burlington to find a doctor," Abner yelled.

"Come on," Joshua said. "I told you they wouldn't listen."

"I'm thinking of getting one of their horses," Abner said.

"And go where?"

"Back home, I guess," Abner said. He then ran after Rachael, who was heading toward the settler's fire. She was running after little Ruggles.

—⁓◉⁓—

London, from a nook within a small cedar bush, watched the men that he had travelled with become as emaciated as the earlier prey. As the black tendrils reached deep into the bodies of Richard and Howard, London saw the axe wound on Matthew's shoulder close. The oozing from his abdomen had stopped, but was slow to close. Even the tear in his jacket was mended.

London tried to wipe his footsteps away from the path the others had made. He was shivering with fear and the damp cold. The persistent running and huge leaps taken to catch the wolf meant that Matthew was fast, agile, and determined. Like Richard had said, Matthew was a lot stronger than he looked.

The predator left the hole as the sun started to set. Matthew stopped near London. He looked around and breathed as if smelling for intruders. Although London couldn't make out a remaining cut mark on the jacket's shoulder, there were still tear marks on his vest by his abdomen.

Eventually, Matthew turned and walked back the way he'd come. London didn't move for a long time after he heard Matthew step away. He didn't move when his leg fell asleep or when he needed to pee. He didn't walk back to camp until it was very dark and late into the night. There wasn't a moment when he wasn't expecting Matthew, whatever he was, to come for him.

—⁓◉⁓—

As the light of the full moon leaked out from some thick clouds, and a lone wolf howled, Abner froze.

"What are you doing?" Rachael asked.

He looked around for any sign of Matthew and then focused on the horses.

"Just getting some stuff," Abner said as he grabbed some things from their sleigh and tossed them into a shoulder sling. He put a blanket over his shoulder.

Following the howl of the wolf, he caught sight of Matthew. He quickly grabbed his sister's hand. "Come on, we gotta go now," he'd ordered. "We don't have time."

"Annie," Rachael asked. "Where's Annie?"

"With Joshua. Later. Right now, we gotta go."

He rushed over to the woodcutter's fire circle. "Missa Harris, mind if we stay with you folk," he asked. "The feller I told you about is back, and he means us serious harm."

"No problem," Bill replied.

Abner scooted his sister away from the fire.

The figure in black emerged from the night and marched toward them. He was clenching his fists.

Bill noticed that Abner wasn't moving, so he walked towards Matthew to intercept him.

"The coloured thinks you're going to do something."

"Bill, is it?" Matthew attempted to touch his shoulder.

"No, don't think so," Bill said and backed away. "I'm kind of touchy about that sort of thing. Don't know what this is about. Don't need to know. Just don't want no trouble here."

"I guess there's all kinds," Matthew said. He raised a hand and stepped over to another woodcutter who was sitting near the fire. "It's Kerry Williams, isn't it?"

"Yes, sir, it is. Is there something we can help you with?"

"Has Philemon told you about his idea about putting up a mill? You look like the kind of able body that could do the job. Could be a good bit of stonework. That pays well, if you know what I mean." Matthew put his hand on Kerry's shoulder as soon as he got a smile. He turned him around and steered him toward Abner and his sister.

Abner, seeing that Kerry was being used as a shield against Bill, quickly moved away from the fire with his sister. He had decided to make a run to the horses.

"Stone, I'm good with stone," muttered Kerry.

Bill, again, stood in Matthew's way.

"I'm sure there's no reason for concern, Bill," Kerry said. "It's a beautiful evening."

"Kerry, I've never heard you use the word 'beautiful' for anything," Bill said. "Are you feeling all right?"

"Never better. Feel like I could fight a bear."

"Where are you going, Matthew?" asked Bill as they passed him by.

Looking back, Abner saw that Kerry's face had changed. The man quickly appeared to become weakened and confused.

Matthew ran after them, and Bill followed. At the main trail, Matthew attempted to grab Bill's arm. The man, in turn, punched him in the face with his other hand.

Near the horses, Rachael asked her brother, "Where we goin?"

Abner looked back and saw the fight behind them. "They're fighting bad. We gotta leave," he said, and he pulled her arm to make her run faster.

Rachael tried to turn around, and Abner saw Matthew try to grab Bill Harris's shoulder, and then sharp dark tendrils ejected from his fingers and elongated throughout the man's body."

"Rachael," Abner screamed. "You have to come with me. Now."

"No, I don't want to."

"Rachael, do you remember when I told you that bad men were trying to take me?"

"Yeah."

"This is way worse. Now be quiet." Abner wrapped his sister in a blanket, picked her up, and ran with her the rest of the way.

He untied the horse and walked over a fallen tree. With great effort, the tree fall enabled him to step up and mount both of them onto the horse. Abner had ridden before, but his father was always there for him. At that moment, he felt helpless.

Abner heard Matthew running. Looking back, the figure approaching looked more like a hungry cougar than a man. Abner whipped the horse and kicked. His sister screamed and rocked wildly in his grip as the horse raced on. But with the monster racing after them, Abner felt like they were floating in slow motion, waiting to be bitten.

PART 4: Crossings

Trailing

When London returned to camp, he was rattled by what he had seen Matthew do. That creature was a mortal threat to everyone. He didn't know how to explain, even to himself, the unbelievable, unnatural monstrosity that he'd witnessed. The creature's footsteps had veered away from the original set of tracks about midway on the return trip, and London was still expecting him to jump out at him at any minute.

It was late, dark, and quiet. He was shivering by the time he got back to camp. Everyone seemed to be asleep except for a pair of woodsmen who were minding the bonfires. London grabbed some blankets. After finding a spot that had a pile of spruce boughs already laid out, next to the contractor's bonfire, he crumpled into a tight curl and succumbed to sleep that took him.

About an hour before dawn, Philemon nudged London and told him to wake up. Once he sat up, he told him, "No wonder, I didn't find you. You were over here."

"What's that?" London asked.

"He told me that there was something important that you had to get."

"Who? Matthew?"

"Yes, he was here, but he didn't say much, but he was adamant that I give you this," Philemon said. He passed him a folded piece of paper that was sealed with a wax stamp. "Apparently, it's a private matter."

London broke the seal. When Philemon leaned over to see, London leaned away so he wouldn't be able to read it.

Matthew's message was bland but clear.

> I would appreciate it if you would return what is rightfully mine. I am sure you will be able to track it down.
>
> On a sour note, little Annie tells me that she is very distraught, and she would very much like to see you. She doesn't like the cold.
>
> I convinced Philemon to hold off on leaving for another day. It's best if you hurry.
>
> Mtt.

"When did he leave?"

"I don't know, but there's something else. Apparently, your Abner rode off with one of our horses."

"What? What happened?"

"It was just before it got dark. One of my men is going to track them down."

"Them?"

"He took Rachael with him."

"Annie? Have you seen Annie?"

"With Joshua, maybe?"

"Maybe?"

London put his boots back on and marched to his sleigh. When he pushed the canvas back, he saw only Joshua.

He shook him and told him, "Joshua, get up. Where is she?"

"Ouch," he moaned. Hot rocks kept you warm, but you had to avoid rolling on them.

"What?"

"Where is she? Where's Annie?"

"Matthew. Matthew took her," Joshua said as he sat up. "He walked away with her, and Mister Wright ordered me to do some chores. I looked for her, but no one saw her."

"Damnation," London muttered. "Lord. Lord Almighty."

"And Abner left with Rachael. They went south. They were all in a fury about that, being a coloured stealing a horse and all."

"It was probably Matthew's doing," London said.

"I was thinking about leaving myself, but no way was I going to steal a horse."

"You wouldn't have survived the walk back, Joshua. You would have needed to convince an adult to get you outta here. Matthew has my Annie —you say.

"I'm going to have to get her."

"Did you see Matthew leave?"

"No, but I heard that he had arguments with Kerry Williams and Bill Harris. It was near where the horses were tied up. That's where Matthew chased after Abner."

Joshua, if I don't come back, tell Abner and Rachael I know what they did was right. And all I want for them is to be safe. And when the Wrights look for me, tell them that Matthew took me with him. Got that?"

London returned to the contractor's fire and asked a woodcutter, "Where's Bill Harris?"

"Nobody has seen him since yesterday. We all found it strange. He was supposed to mind the fire for a spell."

"Mr. Wright told me to get a good knife. I got a good axe myself, but I need a good hunting knife. Got one I can borrow?"

The woodcutter returned with one. Here's a stone. "You'll need to sharpen it yourself," he said. "Why do you need it?"

"Something I gotta do for Mr. Philemon. He's particular about things. Don't rightfully know, but thanks."

London woke Kerry up. He told him that he saw Matthew arguing with him. After an exchange of blows, Matthew took him into the woods.

London let him go back to sleep and checked out the tracks around the horses. After following a set that went into the bush, he found Bill Harris's corpse. He noticed that there were multiple return trails, which suggested that he wasn't killed outright. The creature kept coming back for more.

"Disgusting," he said as he imagined the creature's black vines slithering through the corpse. "Sweet Lord Almighty, that's gonna be me."

He took off his mitt and felt nicks on the axe blade. "Could have chosen something better, couldn't I?"

After taking a leak, London bit the sleeve of his winter mitt and pulled it on tight. He cut some brush to test the blades' bite and then re-secured the broad axe to his belt.

He left the camp on a trail that led to rockier terrain.

The creature's stride was unnatural. It leapt around intimidating crags and woodland shadows, like something that was a cross between a deer and a big cat. The added weight of his daughter didn't seem to matter in the slightest.

And why the hell am I the only one? He thought. *Describing him as a monster didn't work. With my boy taking a horse and them not believing me. No wonder. Gahd, why didn't I show them Bill Harris?*

"I'm not thinking right," he said. "No, sir."

"Shit. Damn! God Almighty!" he screamed as his hat got swiped by another branch. "It's got Annie and gettin' farther away. Dear Jesus, I'm gonna lose her," he moaned as he bent to pick it up.

"Jane Ammon, it's only me, how's I going to do it?" He nervously checked around as he tightened his scarf.

Last thing we need is to get spooked, he thought. *Gotta get our own and keep them safe. Guess that means we gotta kill it. God Almighty, he sucked Bill Harris dry, didn't he? And me here, losing my shit. Ain't we going to have a time?*

Well, the tracks aren't weaseling around much. With my girl in his arms, he's not wasting time covering his tracks. Looks like he knows where he's going. His tracks follow the mountain.

When we had you, baby girl, it was so special, you couldn't imagine. And that kind of special is thanks to your momma. What a gal.

I accompanied Missa Thomas to *Boston, which is where I met your mother. Actually, I think it was her that found me. She got help from friends. I think she was looking for somewhere safe. When you were born, I think it was the first time she wasn't afraid. Missa Thomas didn't know she was a runaway. At least I don't think so. Well, at least he didn't ask. Guess he might have thought something when there was no one on her side at the wedding. Anyway, he let me work and make money so I could convince her I was a good catch.*

And Annie, you were the best catch there ever was. Don't know what I'd do if . . .

And Abner's gone. Don't know where he's going. Dear Lord, they's going to starve, and there's a lot of bad folk. There's money for taking them.

If you was here, this would be too much. Of all the things in life, this would be too much. Maybe, dear Lord, that's why it was your time. That was bad, but this. It's just sheer cruelty. That's what it is.

Thinking on the situation, he realized that he was choosing his baby over the others in the camp.

I gotta save her. She's got no one. Rachael has Abner. Even if it goes bad, she's got her brother. So I definitely gotta save my girl. Jane wouldn't forgive me.

The tracks led through an open field. The snow was soft and deep. It was a slow trudge until he entered the treeline again. The tracks now looked more like a big cat, and by what he could tell from its stride, it looked like it was moving faster. The trail kept in a steady line until it crossed tracks with a pack of wolves. The tracks turned and followed. Hours later, he found them dead. Emaciated wolves lay in a hole in front of a large tree. Looked like there were half a dozen of them. The corpses were shredded before being drained of life. He saw where he put her in the snow. One of them would have been next to her. He used her to bait them.

"At least it looks like she's still alive." The impression she made in the snow was like an angel. There was no blood or anything to suggest that something was broken.

Maybe Matthew is baiting me like he did the wolves, he thought. *Should have paid more attention to Abner. Maybe I could have persuaded the rest to kill him.* "Yeah, me a black man." *Sounds unlikely when I actually say it.*

In Poppa's story, he was all roped up. All I got is a big wood chopper. A feel for his axe verified he still had it.

He was freezing just like he was when he returned to camp. Knowing how fast it moved highlighted the obvious fact that he didn't have the slightest idea how to fight it.

Damned, I should have made arrangements with somebody. Lord Almighty, how's the boy going to manage on his own?

—◦◉◦—

Abner squeezed Rachael and the reins tight. She cried hysterically. He was determined not to fall off and wasn't going to let that creature touch them. No way. No how.

"Down. I want down," she yelled.

"Stop moving," Abner replied. "You're gonna make me fall."

"Stop. Stop," she yelled.

"Can't," he said.

She elbowed him in the stomach.

"Ouch," he cried.

When the horse slowed, Rachael asked, "What are you doing?"

"We had to leave." Abner checked back, and he didn't see anyone following.

"We're in trouble?"

"No."

"Where's Poppa? And Annie?"

"There's a bad thing back there. I'm trying to keep you safe."

"I'm cold. Something to eat?"

"No, I don't have anything."

"Does Poppa?"

"In time, maybe. Stop it. I'm thinkin'."

"You sure we're going the right way?"

Abner, staring at the darkness in the stand of trees they were passing, realized that there could be lots of things that might want to come at them. The caravan had the woodsmen, and they had axes, and some even had muskets. All they had was this horse, and it was going to get hungry, too.

Aren't we going the wrong way?"

"Doin' like Grandpa Coffey and the Injuns, is all," Abner said. He told her the long story but didn't tell her about the green stone and Matthew.

"Grandpa's massa was a bad man?" asked Rachael.

"Yeah, by my reckoning, I guess there's all kinds, but that thing back there was a special kind of bad."

"I miss Momma too. Miss Poppa and Annie too."

"You ever think about Momma?" he asked.

"Best cooking," Rachael said, "and I remember her tucking me in and lots of good stories."

"I used to think she could do magic," Abner said. "White folks did what they was told and looked like she could fix things, all sorts of things, and then ..."

"What?"

"Maybe real magic doesn't work on monsters."

"What kind?"

"I don't know."

"Well, I thought I heard her," Rachael said.

"When?"

"Back there."

"Maybe I did too.

"What?"

"You scared me and the horse so bad we left him way back there. Damn, I think maybe you even scared him."

Rachael laughed.

"Don't think I could have gotten out of there, if it wasn't for you," Abner said. "Momma does have magic. We's still here, aren't we? And we's here because we did it together. He leaned over and spit at the ground. Holding her tight as she leaned, he let the world below have it.

London's knife was tucked in a sheath at his back. What little food he managed to grab was stuffed in his pockets.

The tree cover was a mix of evergreens and leafless trees. The woodcutters had told him that the lay of the land generally went north, but with all the meandering that Matthew was doing, he didn't know if that was true.

Stepping through deep snow in the open was exhausting. It was like the snow's softness and brightness pressed him back. Matthew's stride was a lot longer than his.

That axe wound healing up. The black blood drying up, he thought. *What's there to be done against such a thing? And the black hand—if it was cut off, would it grow back? And if it was cut off and the blackness was inside, would it still take over the insides?*

Don't know what he is. Maybe it ain't natural, but the important thing is I've seen him bleed, and devils don't bleed. And when he's cut, he don't like it, one bit.

London stopped. The land rose in front of him. It was rocky, and the trees were thicker. *Still, it kind of makes you wanta fall down and die right here,* he thought. He took his hat off to feel the freezing wind on his ears. He licked his lips and swiped his axe into the snow.

"Dear God in heaven," he said as he put his hat back on. "Sweet, sweet Annie."

London had tramped a couple of miles to get here. He wondered if the creature was in those trees, waiting for him. He looked back in a faint hope that he might hear someone or something following. It was terrible to think that her survival depended only on him. The wind was already obliterating some of their footsteps.

It killed my Jane. He licked his lips again and checked his knife blade at his back. *Damnation.* He remembered the eyes staring at him from the black water. London felt vulnerable because he knew that he was watching. Resigned to his fate and determined to get the trek over with, he tightly clenched his axe and tramped onward, up and across a rising, rocky, treed hillscape.

—◦⊚◦—

Riding through the night, Abner almost fell off his horse several times. His sister, however, still managed to sleep in his arms. Without blankets or covers, they were freezing. When the sun came up, Rachael told him, she had to pee. They rolled off, and Abner managed to tie the horse at the treeline before rolling against the tree and falling asleep. After she had taken a pee in the bitter cold, she curled up on his lap, and they both fell asleep.

Abner felt something shaking him. A voice groaned, "Boy, wake up. Wake up, or you're going to die."

Abner heard a horse snort. As he slowly opened his eyes, he saw that a strange man was shaking him. He was freezing. And he didn't want to wake up.

"You have to wake up," the man repeated. He wore a thick-furred hat, coat, mitts, and boots.

Abner felt his sister shivering in his arms.

"We, we're, cold, sir," Abner said as he started shaking like his sister.

"I want you to stay awake and watch me while I make us a fire. Can you do that for me?" He took off his coat and draped it around the children as he moved them into a simple lean-to shelter. The man brought their horse closer to the fire, and they all rested on cedar branches. The man sat in the middle, hugging the children, and they all shared his coat. He heated the snow in a wooden bowl and dropped bits from a pouch he carried.

"Is this better?"

"Yes, sir. Thank you kindly."

"That's a little soup I'm making, in case you're wondering."

"I'm Abner, and this is my sister Rachael. What's your name, sir?"

"Some call me Wìsakedjàk."

"Jack Wizak. You're Jack Wizak?"

"Uh, I haven't heard that in a long time."

"No way. You're dead."

"Well, I don't feel dead."

"My Poppa told us about you," Abner said.

"Says you're an Injun," said Rachael.

"That's what white folk say, unfortunately."

"But you was alive when my grandpa was a young feller. You don't look like you're as old as my Poppa, so it can't be."

"Don't know what to tell you, but it's me."

"Rachael, Jack is the one I was telling you about in Grampa's story. You know the one about Grandpa Coffey Oxford getting to marry his Nelle, and he got Buckmaster's to say it was all right."

"Well, that was a long time ago. I expect that it worked out in the end because here you are."

"Yes, and we's free folk."

"And your father was the only one who got to be free."

"So you know our Poppa."

"That's why I'm up this way. I'm looking for someone called Matantu. He wears black. He has a reputation for causing trouble."

"Poppa …" said Rachael.

Abner stared at his sister, shook his head, and told her, "I'll tell him. Yes, we saw him. People call him Matthew. Folks died and turned all white. It's like he brought a plague or something."

"Where did you see him last?"

"Near Bellow's Falls."

"You might catch him there." His sister was going to say something, so Abner kicked her under the coat.

"Wyatt Little was killed at camp. I saw him dead. Don't think he got buried. People were afraid they'd catch it. The sleighs are going to the Canadas."

"Did you find your girl, Wekatesk?"

"Wekatesk? Who told you that?"

"My Poppa's Coffey."

"Well, at least I know she's still alive. There are folk who make it their business to make it next to impossible to talk to her."

Jack shared his bowl of soup. Abner shared bread and dried fruit. For a while, they ate in silence.

"I'm going to have to leave soon, and you can't come with me," Wìsakedjàk said. "If I hadn't come along, you and your horse would have died. You're going to have to find shelter and more supplies. You might consider returning from where you came from."

"Sir, we're going back to Woburn."

"That's a long way to go for children like you. Keeping the fire alive will feel good for today, but there's a lot more cold coming this way. Wish I could do more, but I have to leave."

"Why can't we go with you?" asked Rachael.

"Sorry, but that's not possible. Someone's coming to take you back. Considering the lack of alternatives, you'd better go with him." Jack quickly stomped back into the forest.

After Jack left, Rachael turned to Abner. "Why'd you kick me?" she asked.

"I was told that Jack might be worse than Matthew."

"Who says?"

"Matthew."

"He's scary. Do you believe him?"

"If somebody that scary is afraid of someone else, I'd rather keep away. That's what I'm thinkin'."

In late morning, Aaron Johnson, from the caravan, rode up to the children's fire.

"The Wrights sent me here. You took their horse, and they want it back. They told me to bring it back and leave you."

"Is Matthew still there?" Abner asked.

"He left last night. I heard that your father went after him."

"We left because he was chasing us. We had to leave. He was going to kill us. Just like Wyatt Little and Bill Harris."

"What you talking about?"

"You don't know nothing."

"Don't matter; I'm taking the horse with me. You don't mean nothing to me."

As he attempted to untie the horse, Abner said, "We changed our minds. We're going back."

Aaron got up and put the fire out. He helped Abner and his sister mount up. As they rode alongside Aaron, Abner added, "We're going back to take care of Annie."

"That won't be possible because Matthew took her."

"I hope you brought it," Matthew said. The voice came from beyond the trees that were above him.

London kept climbing.

"Where's Annie?" London asked. "I want to see her."

"You'll find her when I get what is mine. Did you bring the stone?"

"What makes you think I'd bring it with me?"

"She doesn't have much time."

"Show me where she is, and I'll tell you where I put it."

The voice seemed to come from above and to the right.

"Come up, and we'll discuss this," Matthew said.

London stepped up the hill but angled to the left.

"My son told me that you believe Jack Wizak is something worse than you. Why's that?"

"Where I come from, they keep us like animals. Like livestock. They want us because we can give life. They treat us like cows."

"He's worse because …?"

"We value our freedom," Matthew said as he stopped for a moment and let London continue his climb.

"He takes my people back to be tortured. I think you can appreciate my concern."

"Considering what you have done to us, it sounds real good to me."

"You take the deer, boar, or bear with great pride, don't you? No qualms about that at all."

"They's not people. You take them. Not my Annie. Hell, no one's going to bother you about taking wildlife."

"You haven't talked to the Iroquois or the Anishinaabe, have you? They might disagree."

"So, the stone's going to help you free your friends."

"We'll see."

"You must be really old."

"Best not waste your time on irrelevant distractions," Matthew said.

The top of the slope flattened. The clearing was a large, open space. When London reached it, Matthew, like a big cat, leaped behind him. His clothes had changed to a light grey with noticeable fur. It was not much darker than shadows cast across rolling hills of snow.

"Where is she?" London asked.

"Wrapped in the snow. That will do for my purposes."

"But you said …"

"I didn't promise anything. My people at the border will finish the rest of your acquaintances, and then we'll continue with our business."

"Releasing your people," muttered London.

Tendrils stretched from Matthew's right hand to caress London's face. Matthew grinned. The tendrils started to shrink but then shot out. They ripped the axe from his hand and flipped it away. "You won't be needing that," Matthew said, as the tendrils retreated into his fingers.

London stepped back. Matthew stepped forward. London's hands and legs began to shake nervously.

The tendrils on both of Matthew's hands snaked out slightly from the ends of his fingers. Matthew raised the palm of his right hand. "As I said, you have something that I want." The tendrils extended and curled menacingly like small snakes.

London licked his lips. It reminded him of when he was buried underground. There was that air pipe. *The taste of air—it saved me,* he remembered. He took a calm breath. "There's folks always asking for more than they can chew. Why would you be any different?"

Matthew gave another grin. "Funny you should ask that." The tendrils shot out, but London spun away. Matthew kept lashing out with the tendrils, making London turn around several times until he almost lost his balance. London attempted to reach for a kitchen knife but discovered it was gone. The creature had taken it from him without his knowing.

Matthew stepped forward, grabbed London's left elbow, and wouldn't let go when his prey tried to pull away. London kicked Matthew's arm and managed to get free, but fell on his back. Matthew tried to step on London, but he rolled and manoeuvred onto all fours. He was unsure what to do and realized that time was running out. London remembered collecting firewood with Abner on the farm. That was when the boy told him how determined his father was in getting Nelle. London grabbed what he could from the ground.

The creature bent his knees and put his hand on London's shoulder.

"Let me up," London said. "It's the stone you want, isn't it?"

Near London's face, Matthew's fingernail-like tendrils started to extend from the ends of his fingers. "Absolutely," Matthew said.

London put his hand forward and dropped a stone. Matthew moved his hand away so he could catch it. Realizing it wasn't the emerald, Matthew dropped it. Waves of skin grew from the black marks on his neck and collarbone and stretched out. Like a reptile, he was positioning to attack. He made a fist and bashed London on the side of the head.

With a sturdy, sharp piece of wood that he had picked up, London, despite a weakened back, tried to lunge his left hand toward Matthew's abdomen.

Matthew smashed London's arm, causing him to fall and lose his weapon. He rolled back to a crawling stance. When Matthew tried to grab his head, London smashed his hand and bit hard on a finger. He had only seen the tendrils grow from the ends and not anywhere else, so he didn't stop until he bit the finger right off.

When London rolled, he had grabbed another knife from a sheath in his boot. It had belonged to Richard James. Like Richard, he drove it deep into the creature's midsection. Unlike Matthew's shoulder, it still had wound marks. They were left over from Richard James' multiple knife cuts.

Matthew hit London hard in the side. London licked his lips again and managed to reach inside the cut and grab something inside. He knew he had to stop the cut from closing. With a foot on Matthew's thigh, he heaved on what was inside with all his might. Matthew smashed London hard a couple of times. London lost his grip, but not before having yanked out some of the creature's intestines. They were slowly being pulled back in. London lunged forward again and managed to pull out more. He stepped on Matthew's abdomen and heaved again. Matthew struck his arm and his chest with closed fists. He was thrown ten feet away. The reptile-like folds on his neck retracted.

London got up and removed his jacket. He slung it on his arm to make a shield. He pulled his axe from the snow.

The creature leaned forward to protect its bleeding-out wound. The tendrils tried to wrap around the jacket to pull it off. London managed to slice its ankle and then hit a wrist. Not being ready to stand, it was vulnerable when London tried to hit its back. He managed to cut a shoulder.

Matthew attempted to retreat to a more defensible position next to a bush and a tree. Chops on its shoulder affected the use of an arm. London kept swinging high until he managed to cut off the creature's head and hands. It was slow, messy work, but London kept at it while continuously reciting the names of his wife and daughter until he was done.

Most of the clothes the creature was wearing morphed into something that looked like leathery skin. London plumped down on the ground, exhausted. Matthew moved again, and London lifted his axe and kept chopping.

He stared at the black marks on the creature's shoulder and neck. London wasn't sure why it wasn't used in the first fight he witnessed, but he realized he was within seconds of being paralyzed, and it scared the hell out of him. Again, he chopped madly. London wanted to burn the body, but at the moment, there were more pressing concerns.

"He's a liar," he said. "My God, my God. I hope he's a liar."

"Annie!" he yelled. He didn't hear anything.

London followed Matthew's footsteps around the hill, calling her name as he went, but found nothing. He returned to where he first heard Matthew and kept screaming for her.

From within the forest, he heard a barely audible moaning. London tracked the sound. It was coming from high up in a tall pine tree. He climbed the tree and found a package secured to branches. It was about seventy feet above the ground. Once he carried it down, he removed an outer deerskin wrapping. Under it, Matthew had used strings of human skin to secure her. At least that is what London thought it was. "My baby. My baby. Annie girl," moaned London as he rocked her back and forth. There was some life in her, but she was frozen.

In his race to warm her up, he cut his leg open. He managed to bring her back to where he left Matthew's corpse. London wrapped her up in his coat and made a simple lean-to covered with cedar branches next to a raging bonfire. He held her tightly in his arms, and they faced the blaze. "You're safe now, Annie. He's gone. It will never bother you again, ever."

"Are you sure?" she asked.

"Yes, I'm sure. He will never bother you ever again. He's gone."

He got up and threw Matthew's severed body parts into the fire.

While watching its feet burn, he fed Annie bits of bread and dried apples from his pockets.

She gave the trees an "Ah-whoo," howl. London chuckled and hugged his young wolf caller tight for a moment. To hide his tears, he tossed another couple of branches onto the pyre.

As she fell asleep in his arms, the centre of the inferno reminded him of when he was made free. He wasn't much older than Abner when Philemon got him.

He didn't have a chance to talk to anyone but his Poppa. He was crying. *I asked Poppa, why? He just told me to never mind. It was 'just tears of joy,' he* said. I had no idea what he was talking about. Seemed to be just some foolish old man thing. Missa Philemon told me that I had to go with him. I asked why, and that I didn't want to leave my Poppa.

'Cause, I'm going to make you free. I'm going to buy you.'

'How's I going to be free if someone buys me?' I said. 'That's not the same thing.'

"It is what it is," Philemon Wright said. "I won't force you to come with me."

"Like it or not, boy, you're leaving,' said his Poppa. 'This man tells me that you're going to be free. You don't have a choice. Now stop whining and get. I never, in your whole life, want you to come back here. Never, you hear? Never. I love you, but our time together is over." He put something in my hand and then said, "Bye."

And that was the last I ever saw my Poppa. I learned later that the state of Massachusetts declared that coloureds were free and couldn't be owned. That wasn't particularly true, but most owners sold to plantations in the South. "They needed to get a good price for what they had," my poppa told me. "But the master is crying out," Coffey said. 'They're taking advantage of us,' he shouted. "How's that for a load of horse shit?"

It was Missa Philemon who learned that when all of us was sent away, Poppa passed. In that goddamn place, my poppa was left alone and struggling hard.

In this moment with Annie in his arms, staring at the crumbling outline of a blazing corpse, brought back a well of tears that washed over long-forgotten, festering wounds. In the blaze, he saw himself as a young boy, in bare feet, leaving his family forever. All that he had left of them was the stone in his clenched fist.

Persuasion

London and Annie, in the morning, followed the caravan's tracks north. Although they walked slowly and were hungry, he considered the moments with her precious. It was hard listening to Annie ask why he'd arrived so late.

"I heard ya, but when you got me I thought that we was going to fall," she said.

"Never," he said, as he picked her up and tried to carry her, but with her winter clothes, she was heavy and he almost dropped her. "I think I'll be better at it when the snow is gone. Let's pray for all this snow to be gone."

"How we going to carry everything if it all melts?"

"I guess, you're right. We got to be careful what we pray for. You think God froze the river to let Moses get to the promised land?"

She shrugged, and then London repeated his story about how his father met his wife, Nelle. He got depressed because she couldn't tell Momma like Abner did. When she told him she was going to tell it to Rachael, it made him feel proud.

"There's my girl," he said. He also felt a bit of a spark when she noticed that the girl in the story had the same name as her.

"You love saving people," she said.

"No. Just you, Annie," he replied. "Just you."

That night it snowed, and the temperature plummeted. The wind was bone-chilling. London had lost his flint. He tried to hurry, afraid that he was going to lose his tracks back to the caravan, but Annie's little feet could only go so fast in the deep snow. Although convinced that the cold might take them, at least he'd gotten his little girl free of that monster. Twice, he lost the trail. When he didn't think he could go any farther, he stopped, hugged, and lifted her above the snow. "Just a little farther," he repeated. The next day was a long one. By the time they reached the caravan, it had been dark for a long time.

Bill Moorwood and Kerry Williams helped them get changed and covered close to the bonfire. Abner noticed something that looked like black muck on his father's hands, pants, and shirt. His shirt was ripped with a four-inch tear under his arm, and cedar bark was wrapped like a rope around a leg wound.

After staring at the black blood and the tear, London laughed and said, "Looks like I need a new shirt." He was shivering.

London beckoned his children close. He gave them a wrapped embrace and said, "I have …" with a crackling voice. "I have never, never been so happy." His breath stalled from another wave of tears, but he forced, "So happy, so very happy to see … you."

"But what about Matth—"

"Never you mind, Abner," London said. "He's gone."

"How can he? You sure?"

"More sure than anyone can be. I'm telling you he's never coming back. We saw him die."

London and Annie were set up close to the fire and covered with layers of blankets.

After looking at his leg wood, "Not good," Bill said. "But it doesn't look like we'll have to cut anything off."

"Abner, if he comes anywhere near me with anything sharp, you wake me up, you hear?" London muttered as he shivered.

"Where did you go?" Bradley Rogers asked.

"I needed to relieve myself," London said. It took a while, but it came out all right."

London and his Annie fell sound asleep in seconds.

⟶◦⟵

When London woke, Kerry Williams offered him some hot soup. The sun was up, and no one looked like they were packing up for another move.

"You weren't looking good last night," he said.

"Not looking forward to today's drive, but it's got to be done, doesn't it?" London downed his soup in nearly one swallow. "Could I bother you for another?" he said.

After London got a refill, he told him, "Your man took my little girl. She almost died."

"I wasn't with him. It's the Wrights that pay me."

Three other men crowded around.

"Anyway, Matthew's not coming back," London said. "He won't be bothering any of us or our children."

"The likes of you admitting that you killed a man," said Bradley Rogers. "And a good, God-fearing man at that. This is outrageous."

"Bradley, hear him out," said Kerry Williams.

"How could you be so blind? He was a monster," London said. "Him a god-fearing man? He's not even a man. And there wasn't a plague. It was him. Look at what's happened to Missa Thomas. And what about Wyatt Little?"

"I say we should put this man on trial," said Joe Carver.

"The Wrights would be the ones," said Gabe Taylor. "Now let's not be too hasty. Didn't like Matthew. He was way too slippery. Never trusted him."

"Philemon is getting as bad off as his brother. No. It's just us," said Kerry.

"We could bring him to the next town," said Joe.

"You should listen to me. They're waiting at the border and intend to kill you," said London.

"What, you going on about?" Bradley asked.

"Then let me speak.

"Matthew told me that there will be men like him, waiting by the border to kill all these folks. It was Matthew who killed Bill Harris. Missa Williams, my son Abner told me that you saw him the night before last and that you would have seen him attacking my children."

"Must admit that feller was acting peculiar," said Kerry Williams.

"I was told that Missa Harris's body was left in the bushes near the trail at the last camp. You'll find him dried up like the rest. Don't expect any of you to know how bad they looked when he kills them, though. You folk better toughen up because we're heading into big trouble."

"I'd like to see that," said Gabe.

"What do those folks want with us at the border?"

"I told you. They're like Matthew."

"That's ridiculous," said Joe Carver. "It's the coloured that will feel the pull of the noose and all."

"You want to go ask them why they want to kill you? Just go ahead. Do your best, but just not with the rest waiting on."

Kerry realized that the men around him, like himself, were brought here by Matthew. "Best lower your voice, Joe. I have no idea what London is saying about the border, but folks have been in a real bad state about possibly getting sick from the plague. The rest of the folk are blaming those of us who came with Matthew for making people sick. I'd say it's in our interests to check this out for ourselves before getting anyone else riled up."

"But the coloured already admitted to murder," Joe said.

"If it was Matthew that brought the plague, do you think folks will stop with him? They and the Wrights might end up blaming you or the rest of us. Then what?" said Kerry. "London, are you sure you know where those bodies are?"

"I didn't see the body of Mr. Harris, but you could probably find him, right? As far as Howard Simpson and Richard James, I followed a path of footprints, but with the lot of us, it shouldn't be difficult to find them. Better hurry, though. Wolves might get them. I could also take you to Matthew's body, or what's left of it, if you want. I'll arrange to get us some horses. I'll need a good excuse, though."

"Better include Jim and Aaron on this," Bradley said.

"Kerry, if he's lying, you better be prepared to do something. I'm not going to be made a fool of by a coloured," Joe said.

"Joe, if you're coming, you better calm it down a notch," said Kerry.

"London, we'll need seven horses. We'll leave in a couple of hours, so keep warm in the meantime. Gabe, find out where the next couple of camps are. We'll be gone for a couple of days."

"We'll just tell folk that we're going to be doing some hunting," Bradley said. "That's not far from the truth, and I don't know about you, but I might be in the mood for killing something."

When London told Abner and Joshua that he had to leave again, both demanded to go along because they knew where other corpses were located.

"Boys, stay out of it. You got to mind the girls."

"No. He killed my momma," Abner said.

"He also killed young Abigail," Joshua said.

"You do know that if the settlers hear any of this, they're all going home. It could turn into more of a mess than it already is," London said. "I'll be back in a couple of days."

"You'll never guess who I met," Abner said.

London shrugged his shoulders.

"Jack Wizak."

"Not possible."

"You've seen Matantu with your own eyes. They must be similar people."

"What did he want?"

"I sent him to Bellows Falls."

"Matantu was really afraid of him."

"Would he help us or not?"

"Matantu doesn't think so, but he helped my Poppa a lot. I really can't say."

—◦◎◦—

The seven riders rode back to the last campsite. From Kerry William's recollections, they were able to locate
Bill Harris's corpse.

"Sure is withered, isn't he? That's him, alright. That's his hat."

"Take off that shirt, and you'll find those marks I was telling you about," said London.

"You do it. That's why you're here," Bradley said.

"No, I'm not."

Kerry unbuttoned the shirt, which revealed a string of holes on his back below the shoulder and purplish bruising throughout his torso. The body was extremely emaciated and pale.

"Looks like he got the plague or something, but that doesn't explain all those marks on his chest," said Gabe.

"Doesn't that mean that we gotta stay away from him?" Bradley said.

"It means that you're chopping wood for the funeral pyre. Anybody, want his boots? Bradley, how about you?" asked Joe Carver.

The body was dropped into a hole in the snow and covered with dried firewood. It was not a Viking-style funeral fire by any standard. Most of the men considered that the man was infected with something.

While watching the flames, London asked, "Kerry, do you believe me now?"

"I didn't want to, but I experienced something like what you said."

"What do you mean?"

"Whoever or whatever he is, can do things just by touching. I watched your son run away from him, and Bill Harris smashed him in the nose. His touching me made me useless. It was like being comfortably drunk. The man was fighting, and I wasn't in a state to do anything but stand there."

The men didn't stay long and were quick to leave. At the next site, London led them to the corpses of Howard and Richard.

"What was left of them was like the animals they lay next to. Like Bill Harris, the faces and hair of these men got no colour at all."

"That's Howard, all right," said Joe Carver. That's his belt, and that's his hat."

"It happened real quick," London said. "I saw Matthew do it to both of them in minutes."

The men quickly burnt the bodies and set up camp at another site.

When they returned to the campsite, which London had returned to a couple of days earlier, the caravan had moved on without them. London brought them to the site where he had burnt the body. A piece of Matthew's arm that wasn't completely burnt remained. By puncturing it with a stick, he was able to show them that gooey black blood came out.

"He's not like us," London said.

"Not like me," Bradley said.

London raised the stick with the black goo to his face and sneered. It caused him to stumble backward into the snow.

"Bradley, you can stay here if you want, but I'm going back to the horses," said Kerry. "I'd like to get a good night's rest before hunting tomorrow. The caravan's relying on me."

As the others were leaving, Bradley yelled, "But what about the arm?"

"Burn it if you like, but don't be long. We'll be back at camp."

On the way back to camp, Kerry said, "London, frankly, I would have preferred if you were lying."

"Meaning?"

"It's going to be hard to convince anyone else about this. And if there's more like him at the border, there will be a lot more than melting ice to worry about."

London stared at the footprints in the snow ahead. *We better not run into any trouble,* he thought. *There's no way any of you have any idea what we're up against.*

—◦◎◦—

Abner met London as he rode back into the new campsite.

"Where's the rest of them?" Abner asked.

"Kerry and me came back to make sure the camp wasn't going to leave the men behind. They're still hunting."

"They took the necklace," Abner said.

"What? What are you talking about?"

"I found Momma's necklace, and Matthew tried to steal it. That's why me and Rachael had to leave. I believe that Jack Wizak can use it to track down that missing woman. That's Wekatesk in Grandpa's story. Matthew was going to use it to release others of his kind."

"Who has it?"

"John told Missus Wright."

"John knew, but I didn't?"

"Matthew threatened the girls, so I told him that he had it.

"When Aaron brought us back to camp, Missus Wright sent Bill Moorwood to get it from us. I made a pocket for it in my pants. Missa Moorwood told me that I had to give it to him or he'd send me away without my sister. He told me that I couldn't wait for you or talk to anyone. Said he was told to give it to Missa Wright."

"So, Missa Thomas has it. Well, they can't have it because it's ours," London said. "Let me take care of this."

"But—"

"Don't worry about it. Just leave it to me."

—◦◎◦—

"Kerry, who's preparing the meal tonight? The ladies or someone else?" asked

London.

"My men, as you know, brought in some game. Joe Carver and Aaron Johnson are preparing the feast."

And is one or all of the ladies going to have a hand with the cooking? London thought, then smiled.

"By the way, Master Philemon has been asking for you," Kerry said.

London walked over to where the Wrights were sitting and offered a bowl of tea and a couple of biscuits to Philemon's wife, Abigail.

Philemon, who was sitting next to her, said, "And where have you been? The place has been going to hell. Sorry, Abigail. Just not feeling like myself."

"Tea, sir?" As London passed it to him, he saw that, like his brother, he was sickly looking. His eye sockets were dark, and his skin pale.

"For dinner tonight, everyone will appreciate the venison the hunters brought back. If you can keep it down, it should help you get back some of your strength."

"Maybe as a soup for me, thanks."

When London returned to the cooking crew, Abigail followed.

"Missus Abigail, can I get you something?"

"Philemon's not well. I'm worried about him," she said.

"I haven't seen Missa Thomas. How is he?"

"He left camp some days ago," she said. "Mary and her children convinced him to go ahead to Burlington. Apparently, there's a doctor there. That John wouldn't take no for an answer. I've never seen him so excited about anything. He must have infected Tiberius with his spirited determination. The two of them. Good Lord—what a pair."

"So why haven't you all gone with Thomas?"

"Because he's stubborn."

"Maybe he's concerned about Injuns. How about an escort of woodcutters? Things are in hand here. Why don't you go ahead? The caravan will only be a couple of days behind." London saw Philemon waving. "Looks like he wants his soup, ma'am. Missus Abigail, I suggest you think on it, and I'll have a word with Bill Moorwood. Maybe he can provide Philemon with a little more coaxing and persuasion, if you know what I mean?"

Once she left, London felt perplexed. *Don't know what Philemon's expecting from me. They haven't even started cooking the damn meat.* He wasn't sure what else to give him. *Don't know what's going on with him,* London thought. *Now that the leech was gone, he should be getting better, not worse.*

—◦◦—

"Kerry, Missus Abigail convinced Missa Philemon to get medical help," said London. "They're going to leave early for Burlington so they can find the right medicine. They've asked for an escort."

"Talk to Bill," Kerry said.

"Too late. I told him that your men are going along."

"You should have asked first," Kerry said, with some anger in his voice.

"Matthew has some of his own waiting for us at the border. I know because he told me. We need to get us a scouting party."

"How many will be waiting for us?" Kerry asked.

"Don't know anything about them. Just know they're up there waiting. It's your men that have to come. They're the only ones that know what they're capable of."

"Oh Lord, that's a hell of a thing—demon creatures waiting for us."

"Burlington is on Lake Champlain, and the border is just a cut above. It's not far."

"Not sure if any of them will want to go. Hell, I don't know if I want to go. We don't even have muskets, for God's sake."

"We're not planning on fighting these things. They won't be expecting us. We just need to find out how many and where they are. If we find them, maybe we can get someone else to do the work."

"They might be more receptive on a full stomach. I'll see what I can come up with at dinner. If I can't convince them, it will have to be Bill Moorwood's boys."

"And forget Bradley Rogers," London said. "He's too much of a hothead. He'll get us all killed."

Stalking Northern Critters

There wasn't a track of any kind across the trail for as far as could be seen. For a moment, it seemed like the ox and London were the only creatures in this wilderness. Philemon's coughs broke the illusion. He stared at the man nibbling on things he had taken from his pocket. Since he didn't look away, Philemon took another dried apple from his pocket and offered it to him.

"The air must agree with you. Looks like your appetite is returning."

Philemon leaned forward again, staring at his feet.

"Why aren't the riders in front?"

"I told them, but Kerry says they're guarding from the rear," London said.

"They should be clearing the trail."

"Safer this way," they said.

"Lazy no-goods." At that, he seemed to nod off. London couldn't quite tell, so he poked him.

"What you doin?"

"You was gonna fall off. You were staring at your boots."

"What you talking about? Stop it. Mind your business. I'll make you walk."

London smiled and wished he had something to drink.

Their sleigh left a couple of hours before the rest, and they were going to keep moving until they reached Burlington. It wasn't until that morning that Kerry told him he needed seven horses and that Bearie was coming along with them.

"So who's staying?" London asked.

"Phil and Tom. Bearie is behind us."

"Why's Bradley here?"

"Joe Carver came because Bradley was going. The other three followed Joe. It's just the way it worked out."

"Tarnation."

From that point on, he didn't want to look at them.

"It was your boots my brother was supposed to have," Philemon mumbled.

The words shook London from his thoughts.

"Terrible to see someone die," Philemon mumbled.

"What?" London said. "Yeah, I suppose it is. War is a terrible thing."

"Your brother tried to join the army, you know."

"Zach?"

"He escaped from Buckmaster. He was in the enlistment line with us and was real persistent. He would have made a good fighter. He snuck out of the plantation to help fight, and you know why they didn't take him?"

"Cause he was coloured?"

"Cause they were ignorant, and he didn't have boots. It took another year for the army to learn that they needed boys like him. We needed more bodies. We didn't want to fight, but he did. Oh did he ever. I remember him saying, he wouldn't take no for an answer."

"I heard that you were at Bunker Hill," London said. "I heard that it was bad."

"Don't want to talk about it."

"I never knew what happened to him. Poppa just told me he was gone."

"The army made him leave. Didn't feed him or anything." Philemon coughed. "We thought about him when we were fighting. I thought he deserved better; that's all. I heard that he returned to Buckmaster, but he was sent away."

"Why?"

"Was a misunderstanding."

"What happened to him?"

"He's dead. I was told that it was cholera."

When Maryanne climbed out from the back, the conversation ended.

⁓◎

London left Philemon's family and Bearie in Burlington as arranged. London rode off on Bearie's horse, heading north along the lake toward the border.

"London, if they're like you say, how we gonna kill them?" asked Aaron Johnson.

"You don't believe me."

"Honestly, I'd like not to. Gabe thinks they're Injuns."

"I see your point. No, they ain't Injuns. Injuns might be able to do better than us."

"Why do you say that?"

"They know how to hunt."

"I know how to hunt," said Aron.

"With an axe and a knife?"

"Traps. I make traps."

"And have you got any? You don't know what we're dealing with."

"I'll use you as bait."

"I'll keep that in mind," London said.

When the sun began to set, Kerry asked, "You look distracted."

"There's something you need to know," London said.

"You don't know where we're going," Bradley said.

"If you try to cut them, they can heal up, and if you let them touch you, they'll kill you."

"That's a bit hard to swallow," Kerry said.

"If I was you, I don't think I'd be convinced either. You don't need to believe me, but I am telling you that there are very good reasons why you don't want them to see you. Just be on your guard, is all that I'm saying."

"Can they see in the dark?" asked Gabe.

"What if there are dozens of them?" asked Jim.

"I think I just need a long piece of good hardwood. I'll stick it down their throats," said Bradley.

"How did you kill Matthew?" asked Kerry.

"Howard cut him good in the gut. It hadn't healed well, so I jabbed him in the same place. Then I chopped him up with an axe and threw him into a fire."

"Boys, I sure as hell hope this boy is lying. I don't want to deal with any of this, if it's true."

"Me. I still believe they's just Injuns," said Gabe.

"Possessed Injuns, maybe," said Aaron. "Demon Injuns."

"That's just foolishness," London said.

"How are we going to stop them?" asked Kerry.

"I got something they want. It's a rock."

"You're kidding me," said Bradley.

"They think they can use it for something."

"Great, I can give them all sorts of rocks, and then I'll stuff my piece of wood down their throats."

When the men arrived at St. Albans, the sun had been down for more than an hour. The Vermont town lay along the Lake Champlain shoreline. The men didn't camp outside. It took some bargaining, but they managed to persuade a public house to let them in.

—◦◉◦—

In the morning, they interviewed folks in and around town. They came across stories about dead people being found on the other side of the border. The corpses were dried out and ghostly-looking. People told them that they heard the stories from folks living on the peninsula, which bit into Lake Champlain from the north. It cut much of the lake in two. Most of the witnesses lived in Alburgh.

After riding upcountry for a few miles, the men carefully led their horses across an ice-covered strait. The slippery ice stretched for almost a mile. At Alburgh, they scoured the area in three groups. Jim went with Bradley and Joe to interview farmers immediately north and west of town. London accompanied Kerry to interrogate the town folk. Gabe and Aaron went south.

When the men returned in the afternoon, they exchanged their stories at a local tavern in Alburgh. They were all cold and desperate to get close to the blazing fireplace.

"We met an old fella that was concerned about his neighbour," said Jim. "The farmer went across the border to discuss selling a bull. He's been gone for five days, and he told us that no one has been milking his neighbour's two cows."

"Although we found suspicious tracks, we didn't find anyone," said Gabe. The length of the stride looked strange.

"Yeah, we also ran into a man who complained that a friend had been missing for four days," said Aaron. "But as we were leaving, his wife told us that he's probably looking for work."

"A woman told us that she saw a couple of dead folks," said London.

"Yeah, she was nuts," said Kerry. "Absolutely around the bend. For the last year and a half, she believed she saw them walking."

"Yeah," London said. "I didn't think she was all there, if you know what I mean."

"So how about we camp out at that farm?" said Bradley. "Won't cost us anything. If he's dead, he's not going to complain, is he?"

"Since this is the last of our money, I hope we can find us some food," Gabe said.

"Well, at least he's got two cows," said Jim.

When the men went to the farm, they found it deserted. The cows were missing. They did, however, find a sufficiently stocked root cellar and lots of firewood and kindling for the fireplace.

In the morning, the men rode off in the same groups. Aaron and Gabe rode three miles north into Canada. Jim, Bradley, and Joe visited farms immediately on the east side of the peninsula. London and Kerry rode back into town and then scouted along the western coast.

—◦◦◎◦—

"I didn't sign on for this shit," said Gabe as he pushed back his large fur hat. "Why we following this feller's tracks? Wouldn't there be a bunch of them?"

"Keep it down," Aaron said. "They can hear you as well as I can. If you'd use your eyes, you'd see. Those are wolf tracks. He's not scaring it away. This feller is actually running after it. He's chasing it into those trees. That's no Injun."

"Gabe, that's nonsense."

"Just look at it. When that feller gets close, the wolf tries to weave away. The runner is right close to its tail. Now keep an eye out and shut the fook up."

The tracks continued through the stand of bush into an opening on the other side, where the trail ended in winding spirals. Gabe stared at the drag marks, which led back into the stand of bush. The hunter, when dragging the carcass back, angled away from the trail. Gabe checked behind, but didn't see Aaron.

"Aaron," he whispered. With no response, he yelled his name louder.

A black figure dropped from the trees. Gabe tried to race away, but his horse reared. As they fell, he screamed because it touched him.

—◦◦◎◦—

When London and Kerry returned to the farm, the other three were already sitting around a fireplace and eating. Their wet winter gear was hanging close to the fire.

"Find anything?" Joe asked. The two just sat down in chairs without removing their clothes.

"Did you lads even go out?" Kerry asked.

"Of course we did. We just got soaked, is all," Bradley said.

"Sure you did. I believe you," said Kerry and gave London a disbelieving look.

London smiled. "Me, not for a minute." He raised his cup, offering them a toast.

While Kerry was struggling to retie his boots, he said, "In town, we were told that a courier that was supposed to bring the mail went missing. We also met a nervous farmer who warned us not to go north because he heard that there's trouble up there. He believes that they might be rogue soldiers."

"He was convinced that we should go west across the strait and go north by way of Fort Montgomery," London added.

"Most of the farmers we saw didn't have anything to say," said Joe. "But there was a guy, like the one you talked to, who said the same thing. Cross at Fort Montgomery, he said."

"I don't like it," Bill said. "Gabe and Aaron should have been back by now."

"We've got a few hours of sunlight left, and by the sound of it, those boys need our help," said Kerry.

"You don't want to have a good meal and ride out in the morning?" asked Joe.

"If they're in trouble, don't you think that might be too late?" asked London. "What if it was you out there? You're right, though; we want something to eat. What you got?"

---◦◦◦---

The riders went north on the road from town until they found a pair of horse tracks veering off towards the forest. They were following someone who had been running with an unusually long stride. Kerry and his men tied their horses up at the treeline.

"While that fellow went across the field in front of the treeline, these men went straight into the trees."

"And they didn't come out," said Jim. "Kerry, are you sure you want to do this?"

"Well, for one, we don't know for sure these are our boys. We're just here to find out what we're up against. We're not here to get into a fight. Rogers?"

Bradley Rogers was refastening his pack to his saddle and wasn't listening.

Joe, without waiting, followed the tracks into the forest. The tracks led them into a forest that was mostly tall elm, white pine, and oak growing out of land that rolled slightly over an occasional outcrop of rock.

"Look at that," London said. "The fella they were chasing just disappeared."

Kerry waved them on to keep following the others' path. The men followed for about another quarter of a mile.

"Well, will you look at that," Joe said. "They got attacked here."

The tracks showed that the men had fallen and tried to fight off an attacker.

"There are no tracks where he came from."

"So he just appeared?" asked Joe.

"He climbed a tree, is my guess," Kerry said.

"So he jumped from a tree?" asked Joe.

"Or a demon creature, like Aaron said," said Bradley.

"If we had time, we could go looking around for his other tracks, but we're going to keep walking in single file on this track line. We don't want them to see any sign of us until we're gone. Understand, Bradley?"

"Why do you keep asking me?" he asked.

After walking for almost another hour, Kerry raised a fist, knelt down, and told them to hush. "Do you see someone?" Jim whispered.

Kerry pointed ahead. About a thousand feet away, he saw something moving. The others moved up to see. London peeked over Kerry's shoulder.

"But the trail winds left," Bradley said.

"And you don't think it goes there?" Joe says.

"You think there's any more of them?" asked Jim.

"Wait and see," Kerry replied.

"Looks like there's a hut behind him."

"Can't see nothing. Need to get closer," Bradley said as he snuck ahead.

"Fool, they're going to see you."

The trail wound to another trail, which was well-worn with footprints.

Bradley froze when he heard something coming from his right. He put up a fist, then waved for the rest behind him to quickly back up on the curved path. He had to step off the path to get out of sight.

Someone passed.

Long minutes later, Kerry asked Bradley what he'd seen.

"A man was walking with a deer. A pet, maybe?"

"Is that really what you saw?" asked London.

"The hands held strings."

"Is that really what you saw?" London repeated.

"I don't know what I saw. Damn it. Did I see gloves?"

"No. Those were hands, and no, they weren't holding a leash," London told him.

"No. It can't be right."

"They went into its neck, right? And what it was came from the fingers, right?"

Horrified, Bradley stared at London. "How do you know?"

"Because I saw one of them kill things. And it tried to kill me."

Bradley passed behind the others. "We got to go."

"But do we really know how many of them there are?" Kerry asked. "Do you see Aaron or Gabe?"

"And it only took one to get them both. And that tree didn't have leaves. He was a stealthy one, wasn't he?" said Joe.

"Maybe it brought them back like those deer," said Jim.

"The problem here is that there's little to hide behind. The stand of trees is not particularly thick, and the snow shows our tracks," said Joe. "If we get too close, they're going to see us."

"So, the answer is obvious," London said.

Everyone stared.

Kerry rolled his hand to tell him to get on with it.

"Get Joe here to climb the tallest evergreen."

"What if they see me?"

"Do you want to follow a path with no cover or climb a tree?"

Joe pointed to a tree behind them.

"No, I think you should climb the one ahead of us. It's closer and a lot taller," Kerry said. It was about sixty feet away.

Joe climbed quickly until he reached the height of the surrounding trees. He had slipped twice to climb the next six feet.

"What's he doing?" asked Kerry.

"Maybe he's stuck?" asked Bradley.

"You going to go up and get him?" asked London.

"If they see him, nothing will stop him, will it?" said Bradley.

As Joe started his descent, the men heard something approaching on the trail. The men waved at Joe, but he didn't acknowledge them. He slipped again on a branch and lost his footing. Dangling from a single branch, he looked down. He must have seen the man approaching because he froze. The figure rushed by on the trail. Joe pulled himself up, wrapped a leg on a branch higher up and moved to hide behind the thin trunk.

Joe didn't move for what seemed to take an extremely long time. When he decided to come down, he moved fast. He slipped off a branch. He fell from a dozen feet up. Joe tromped back with a limp. He showed Kerry three fingers. "We have got to go—now," Joe said and hurried past the others.

Bradley ran ahead. He wasn't acting stealthily. He was running.

When Joe stopped to catch a breath, Kerry asked, "So what is it?"

"There are lean-tos around a fire, for their campsite, and there's a pit at the back. It's filled with dead things. Most of the bodies were human. They looked like London said, and I recognized Aaron's jacket."

"God Almighty," Jim said. He and others moved past and kept running. They didn't slow their horses until they were miles away.

On the ride back, Kerry and London sauntered behind the others.

"You do know that they would have forced Aaron and Gabe to tell them where the farm is," London said.

"I was thinking about that," Kerry said. "If we had to, how could we possibly fight those things?"

"We have an advantage. They want something from me."

"The stone, you mean?" said Kerry.

London nodded.

Jim slowed to be in line with the pair.

"So, London, tell us again how you managed to kill one of them," Kerry asked.

"If you's going to fight them, don't face them up front, keep low, and try to keep them surprised, is what I gotta say," London said.

"If we're going back to the farmhouse, you know they're probably going to know about it," Gabe said.

"So, we lay out a trap," said Jim.

Kerry and London nodded.

They kept riding toward the farm, which was about an hour and a half ride from where they found the creature's encampment. Jim checked behind him to make sure he still had his axe.

After adding logs to the bonfire in front of the barn, London took some more spoons of mash from his bowl. His hand was shaking, but he wasn't cold.

From behind him, he heard something rushing through the snow. "You've got something that doesn't belong to you." London turned to see a man like Matantu dressed in leather-like clothes. This one's coat, hat, and mitts were a greyish fur that mimicked a wolf's coat.

"What could you possibly want from me? I'm just an ignorant feller and I's just doing my chores. Mean no trouble for nobody. Maybe you should talk to the owner. He knows lots. If he doesn't know, maybe he can tell you who does."

"I'd say you're London. Not too many coloureds in these parts."

"How would you know?"

"Your friends were very talkative."

"Aaron?"

"And his friend."

"Are they still alive?" London asked.

"You can ask them," he said.

Two others of his kind appeared behind him.

London took a last spoon of mash.

"So, if I give it to you, will you let me go?"

"If you give it to me, we'll treat you real fine."

"Just like Aaron?"

"Sure, just like Aaron."

"I don't have it, but I can find it."

"Well, don't just sit there, go get it."

London lit a torch and told them to follow him. He opened the front door of a small corn crib. The small building's length was equal to the height of three and a half men. The height was six feet shorter. The siding was made of wood planks and didn't have any windows. The loft on the floor above was accessible by a ladder.

The grey-furred figure asked him what he was doing.

"I left it in here. Didn't want no-one to steal it. You know it belonged to my Jane. It was a wedding gift. But you should know that already. Weren't you told that, and if not, how come?"

"Be cordial, London."

"What Missa? I's just telling you things. Did you know that Jack Wizak is looking for you?"

London heard them talking but didn't understand a word of it.

When he entered the barn, two followed. "I knows this, 'cause he spoke to me and told me things."

"Where is it?"

"Just a minute, I got to get it. I'm only giving it to yous, because I want no trouble. No trouble, Yes, siree."

As London climbed the ladder, he heard one of them ask, "Where are you going?"

"I told you, I've got to get it. Just give me a minute."

London looked back through the ceiling opening and tossed a stone down by the foot of the stairs. "There it is."

At that point, he heard the sound of a creature at the door being pushed into the crib. Screams from outside implied that his men were having difficulty closing the door. Using a flint, London lit a torch. He ignited a hay bale next to him and tossed the torch onto a pile of hay bales against the wooden wall on the floor below.

London jumped out of a hole in the siding they had smashed open earlier. The barn exploded in flames behind him. He landed in the snow, but the flaming hay bales surrounding the building that the others lit were nipping at his feet. After rolling away, he feverishly searched for the axe and knife he'd hidden before his visitors arrived.

He found Kerry by the front door. They obviously had a problem pushing the man who was blocking the door inside. A grey arm that was chopped off lay on the ground in front of the door. Joe Carver lay dead on the ground. A creature was still bashing against the front door that the men had attempted to hammer shut. Kerry was trying to light more bales piled against the door, but it wasn't working.

On the side of the barn, Jim was hammering the wood siding back as a creature struggled to pound its way out.

Bradley, with his axe, was taking swipes at another creature, who stepped out in front of him. There was a knife in its back.

A fifth creature approached. London and Kerry ran to stop it.

Jim ran to help Bradley, but the creature shot tendrils into Bradley's shoulder. Jim froze because he couldn't believe what he was seeing. The tendrils stretched through Bradley's neck and head. He attempted to chop off the creature's arm, but it was using its victim as a shield. As it drew strength from the body, the knife in its back got pushed out, and the wound started healing.

Jim knelt and kept slicing at its leg with his axe.

Kerry stepped in and managed to chop a hand off, but the creature's tentacles reached into his thigh, which made him drop his axe and freeze. Its truncated arm smashed Kerry in the head. London lunged, stuck a knife into its side, and from another side, swung his axe into its neck. He kept at it until something smashed into him, throwing him into the air.

The creature Jim was fighting fell over and managed to thrust tendrils into his stomach while Jim was trying to push his knife deep into its throat.

London's arm felt broken, but he managed to get to the grey body that had fallen on Jim. He removed the knife from the monster's neck and madly cut the tendrils that reached into Jim. He kept stabbing the beast until he believed it was dead. When he managed to roll it away, he saw another creature staring at him.

"Six is definitely not three," he mumbled. He looked carefully at the moving shadows, and he made out three more behind that one.

One behind all of them said, "You can stop now."

"You. I thought you were dead," London said.

"Matantu liked to exaggerate."

"Jack Wizak," said London as he recovered his stance. "You took your time, didn't you?"

"I didn't know I was expected. From what I heard, I would have thought you'd have more sense than to play with these folks. Should I come back later?"

"No. No, please don't."

The other creatures quickly backed away. Skins from the black marks on their neck and collar flared up threateningly. One ran behind Jack and reached for his back. Jack quickly spun and thrust a fist into its chest. Screaming, it pleaded, "No. No, please." Jack grabbed an arm and threw it ten feet into another grey-furred creature. Jack put a boot on its face and asked, "Are you coming peacefully—yes or no?"

"Yes. Yes!" it screamed.

"What about you two?"

They put up their hands in front of their faces in submission, and the threatening folds of skin disappeared.

The black boot mark on the face of the fallen creature was healing, but it moved very meekly.

As Kerry hobbled toward London, Jack pointed to the blazing flames coming from the barn and asked, "Why'd you do that?"

"What? Those demons deserve to go back to Hell. That's a god-awful question. They tried to kill us."

"And you tried to kill them," said Jack.

"It's not the same. What are you going to do with them?"

"He's going to take them back to get milked," said London.

"What?" asked Jack.

"To suck them of their healing," said London. "It might kill them, but your kind does it, anyway."

"Doesn't mean I agree with it."

"Don't debate it, just get rid of them," said Kerry. "People of Alburgh won't like to learn that we burnt this feller's barn, will they?"

"They'll still have a barn. For a corn crib, they could have done better," London said.

"You're right. Let's get out of here," said Kerry.

"Missa Wizak, thank you for helping my Poppa. There wasn't a day he didn't have something good to say about you helping him get his Nelle. I just wish you were there when Matantu took my Jane Ammon."

Jack just gave him a short nod.

"Hope you got your Wekatesk."

"You told your boy," Jack said. "Do you have it?"

"You gave it to my Poppa."

"But your parents are no longer here, and I do need it."

"I don't have it. Thomas Wright took it."

"Where?"

"Somewhere in Burlington. He's seeing a doctor. I don't know where."

"Where are you going?"

"The Grand River."

"The Kichi Sibi, you mean."

"What?" London asked.

"The people who live there call it that. Is it near the falls?"

"They told me that there's a lot of them. And there's a big one there. Matantu told me that the stone is a key. They want to use it to free more of their people. It cost my Jane her life. If you take it from him, use it wisely."

Jack left without saying goodbye. He attempted to touch one of the grey-furred creatures, but it raised a hand in defence and said, "Don't touch me. I can walk."

The rest proceeded in line, with Jack following.

London looked back at what was left of the burning corn crib and then at Kerry. "That doesn't look good," he said.

"Nothing compared to what we did to them."

"What are we going to do?"

"Damnation, right now, we're going to sit and have us a good cup of tea. Ain't that right? Then why don't you give the horses a nice bunch of carrots?"

"Damn right," London said as they stumbled back to the farmhouse.

London stopped the bleeding and washed the wound on Kerry's thigh. It looked like just a puncture. Kerry told him that he felt pretty good. "From what I've seen, they give the victim some healing before sucking out life. Maybe you'll get lucky, and it'll heal by itself."

"Do you know that for sure?"

"No, but it sounds good. Don't you think?"

While Kerry slept for a couple of hours, London collected provisions. He spent most of his downtime scouting for the farmer's whisky stash.

When Kerry woke up, he saw that London was still fully dressed. Bowls of porridge were set on the table.

"You're right, it's time to go," Kerry said. "We're lucky that none of the neighbours have shown up already. I don't want to be here when they ask why there are so many dead bodies around. And how do you explain why the fella that owns this place is still missing? We'll get hung if we stay."

"And don't forget the four that we lost," London said.

Kerry stood, picked up a bowl, and nudged London to pick up the other. "To the lads," he said as they clicked bowls.

"For seeing another day," replied London.

Kerry took a taste of the porridge and then waved his spoon. "I'll tell you what," he said. "I'll do what I can to put out the fires. You go see if there's a wagon. We'll just wheel them into a pen."

"No, I've got a better idea," London said. "We'll dump them in the crib with the others and light them up. Folks will believe that they all died in the fire."

Staring at the nauseated look on Kerry's face, London added, "Me neither. Lord Almighty, I don't want to touch any of them."

"It's almost time for some folks to do their milking. We've got to be quick," Kerry said.

Outside, the pair swung the bodies into the burning building and covered them with bales and more planking collected from the main barn.

With a blazing inferno behind them, in spite of their wounds and tiredness, both of them raced out of there as if banshees were chasing them. The riders didn't talk to one another until they were forced to slow march across the ice.

"You think we should have stayed longer?" London asked.

"You mean for the horses to get warmed up? Or us taking more food than we did. Not me. I was expecting one of those things to sit up and come back to life. So help me God, you mean—like seeing those gates of hell again; I'd rather not. No, definitely. Thank you very much."

"Jack Wizak, who was there—you know, there's no way he just dropped by when he did.

"You mean that he was just standing around?"

"Damn. He could have stopped the fire," said London.

"And all the people that died," Kerry added. "Lord Almighty."

"Easier taking back three than eight, isn't it?" London said. "And who knows where he's going? How long do you think he was here?"

"No idea, but he might have followed us. I hope he wasn't asking folks about us."

"London, no one is going to believe anything we saw. Nobody knows much anyways. We gotta cross the ice before the sun comes up.

"Yeah. The ice. Oh, Lord Almighty," London moaned. "Kerry, do you remember what we told the others?"

"Damnation."

"Do you know how to set lots of traps? And how do we get us some deer?"

En Route

Thomas stood on the ice of Lake Champlain, looking north. He started jumping on it. Mary caught up to him and said, "The sleighs are a lot heavier than that. If it cracks for you, then we're in trouble."

"It's getting warmer. I don't know if it will be safe on the Grand. The ice here looks solid enough."

"You're looking more like yourself."

"Whatever I had, I'm on the mend. The open air helped. You, on the other hand, look like you're at your wits' end."

"There's so many people in camp, and they are always there. Actually, it wasn't that much better at home, with London and his family. It's fine when Philemon comes for a visit. When he believes that he's at home, it can get to be a touch grinding.

"What are you going to do with that rock?"

Thomas pulled the necklace out from his collar and looked at the stone.

"I'll have someone look at it," he said. "In Montreal maybe, more likely when I return to Woburn. Those contractors need to be paid, don't they?"

"Don't you wonder how he came by it?" Mary asked.

"No way a slave could have gotten it honourably."

"If it turns out to be something of value?"

"I'm sure we can work out something that is amenable—a modest finder's fee, perhaps."

"I'll be glad when they can all move on, won't you?"

Both London and Kerry weren't sure if they would ever be able to sleep soundly again. It was like they were still walking with an army of the dead. Both were bursting to relieve their burden, but neither was willing to give their say. Light yellow topped a bright band of orange around a sinking sunset. The caravan tracks led up to large raging fires onshore.

London dismounted. His children came running. He gave Annie a hug.

"I didn't think you'd find us," Annie said.

"Of course you did," her father said, and then reached to give Rachael a hug, but she stepped away.

"You missed Poppa," he replied.

She crossed her arms and looked away.

"Rachael, I missed you too. You have no idea how much. Can I have a hug? Maybe a tickle?"

He stepped over, ready to tickle her, but she stepped forward and opened her arms. He went on his knees and embraced her. "Baby Rachael, you have no idea how I've missed my little girl. Every minute. Nothing matters more than both my girls."

He looked at Annie and Abner. "I had to leave. I had to make it so you were safe. That's all done."

"I knew you'd come back," Abner said.

"No, you didn't," Annie said.

"So there was more of them?" Joshua asked.

"There's no more, and we're moving on. That's all." London got up.

"I told Mr. Wright to wait, but he didn't," Joshua said.

From behind them, Bill Moorwood asked, "Is that all you brought back?"

"You moved on from Burlington, and we had to find you. What did you expect us to do? A deer and a bunch of birds is all we could carry. Sorry."

"Where are the others?"

"You best talk to Kerry. Those men worked with Matthew. He'd know better than me."

"Tomorrow, Mister Philemon wants you to drive his sleigh. He expects us to be off the lake and into Lower Canada by sundown tomorrow."

"Is he all right?" asked London.

"What's wrong with you?" asked Bill. "We've got to get going. The thaw is already setting in."

"If it were me, I would have kept going," said London. "You haven't even passed Alburgh yet."

"Where?"

"Yes, sir. Sooner the better. Gotta move."

Once the woodsman was out of earshot, Abner turned to London. "Did you really lose what you hunted, or was that all there was?"

"It was slim pickings," London said.

"You told us you was going after them."

London noticed Annie's wide-eyed stare.

"Nothing is going to bother anyone. Best to just forget about them."

"Your jacket is ripped, you're not wearing your hat, and it looks like your boots are burnt," Joshua said. "And you got a bump on the side of the head. Did birds do that?"

"And why did all those men run off?" Abner asked.

"Like I told Bill, Kerry is the best one to answer that. You could pester him if you like. In the meantime, I got to bring the horses to the cook. How about showing me the way?"

London led the horses while the children raced ahead. After the game was dropped off, London told Abner, "I did run into Jack. He asked about the stone. He knows that Thomas Wright has it."

"Am I going to get it back?" Abner asked.

"Don't know, but I'll do what I can."

"Missa Morewood let Joshua drive but wouldn't let me."

"You're getting bigger and growing. Fact is, the ox might pull you off, and the sleigh would ride right over you. Soon you'll be able to do so many things —maybe too many things."

"What's that mean?"

"You's growing up too fast."

"And why can't I?"

"I'm not saying no. I'm saying that I got to see what Missa Philemon wants from me."

Noticing Thomas's wife, who was minding her four youngest, London decided to bring her a bowl of soup.

"Why can't I?" whined seven-year-old Elizabeth.

"No one is going back on the ice," Missus Wright ordered.

"Maryanne is. Rug is."

"No, Ruggles is not. Dinner will come soon enough."

When London offered Missus Mary a bowl, she scowled. "And where were you? We thought you ran off."

"Hope you enjoy your taste of veal, ma'am," he said with a smile.

She tasted it. "The Lord has dearly tried our resolve on this road. There must be order. Can't have you scamping about whenever you feel like it, can we?" She took another sip of her soup. "My thanks to the kitchen, though. It is appreciated."

"Missus Mary, you might have noticed these boots. I was told they used to belong to your husband. Philemon had me throw my other ones away for these. They looked like they was as good as new. How come he didn't want them?"

"I don't know why Thomas would have kept them. I was told that they belonged to your brother," she said. "They didn't get used much because the head of the plantation took them from him before having him thrown in jail. Philemon came back with the boots and you."

I knew it, thought London. He felt like grabbing something and throwing it into the fire.

"Had something to do with the war," said Thomas's wife. "And that's all I know."

London froze.

"It's going to be hours before dinner. Get Polly and the boys to mind the children, please," she ordered. "I have several things I need to get done before then."

London unclenched his fists when he noticed that Polly and Maryanne were talking to young workmen again. *Maryanne wasn't wearing that bow of hers. Out of spite, maybe?* He wondered.

—⌒◎⌒—

At supper, London brought his girls a stew of venison, potatoes, and carrots.

"Annie was kicking Ruggles again," Rachael said.

"And?" asked London.

"They said that you left us," Annie said.

"It was Phil," said her sister. "He rides a horse."

"That sounds like something he would say," London said. "Annie, you know if Abner does something like that, Ruggles is going to kick you."

"No, he won't," Annie said. "Because he likes me."

"Best to treat your friends like friends, I'd say. Rachael, don't you agree?"

She nodded. "So there's more of them?"

"Like Matthew? Well, there was."

"So, there's no more stones?" Rachael asked.

"Like when James Savage and you was throwing at the tree? No, that's right. That's the end of that. We's free of them."

He checked to make sure Abner and Joshua weren't around to drop in on the conversation, and he quickly skipped away to get them some water.

⤛◎⤜

Abner and Joshua stood against trees near the contractor's campfire while eating supper. Abner had just finished relaying a story about why only Kerry and his father returned to camp.

"Can see why he didn't want you going," Joshua said.

"Why's that?"

"They never would have given you a horse."

"Move off," Abner replied, and Joshua snorted a laugh.

"So what you going to do when we get to where we're going?" Abner asked.

"Learn me how to cut with an axe. Be like James Savage. No way I want to do what they were asking us."

"No more poopers?"

"No more poopers," Joshua replied and raised a fist in the air.

"And you?"

"I'd like that," Abner said as he looked back at his father, who was talking with the crew chief.

"Your father?"

"We're not going to be far. Besides, we got to learn something different while we can, and from what I've heard, the woodsmen are all leaving next year. We gotta do, what we gotta do." Abner noticed that his sisters were with his father. As he moved to head back in their direction, Joshua said, "I lied."

Abner stopped. "About what?"

"Told you I couldn't remember things. Told you I couldn't remember my father. Remember?"

"Yeah."

"I couldn't remember him, like you know yours. That was cause he died when I was born. It was my mother I couldn't remember. Was jealous, is all."

"Of what?"

"You knew your parents, but for me, it was different. My mother was a Munroe," Joshua said. "Her folk didn't think my father was good enough and did everything to scare him off. His family didn't accept them because they were Irish; funny because Wyman's have Irish in 'em. Both families hated me because I was their bastard. My parents ran off to spite them and had a real hard time. My father died soon after they was married.

"Before running off again, my mother left me with her family. Like my father, I don't remember her at all. There was no stopping me, when I overheard that these folks were leaving for somewhere. Lavina, I've seen her give the others a good kick. She's got a real mouth on her. She's not like the rest."

As a grin started to form, Abner gave him a pretend jab to the gut.

"Hey, mud, put 'em up or I'll give you what for."

"Yeah, tard," Abner said as he balled his fist. As they both jabbed the air, the weights on their shoulders lightened, and they allowed themselves to laugh.

—◦◉◦—

The next morning, London drove Philemon's sleigh. The man was still weak. His two oldest sons rode ahead. The caravan left Lake Champlain and the border into Lower Canada without any new faces bothering them.

"Did you see a doctor, as I suggested?" London asked.

"Just a bad cough, that's all," Philemon said. "Something everyone gets. Good mustard plaster would fix it, but no one listens to me. Too much idle chatter. The fool wanted to bleed me. I took something to purge the system, and it just made me feel worse. I'm glad we're away from him.

"London, I heard you say that my brother is better. What promises has he been making?"

"I thought you were doing this together," London said.

"We have plans. He's often shortsighted and bullheaded. We need to keep an eye on him all the time. We don't expect that he'll want to stay long. Montreal or York might be more to his liking. Then again, being so provincial, he might even prefer Prescott."

"What would you have done if your brother didn't get better?"

"I'd make the most of God's good graces. Not much would change. I'd do what's best for everyone, of course. We're in changing times. We're going to change the world. There's more lumber, water power, and good land than anyone could want, and it's all ours. We live in marvellous times. And we got good Christian people with us. Good industrious farmers. There's as much land as anyone would want to sow. It's a new world. Just stay the course."

"My brother died behind bars, but you got those boots," London said.

"What?" asked Philemon. After a long moment, he said, "Oh. Zach."

"These boots."

Philemon stared at them without saying anything.

London broke the silence with a "Yes."

"A farm. I want a farm and a new world. Let's stay the course," London said.

Philemon coughed and struggled for words.

"Yes," is what he said, eventually. After another long moment, he added, "It will be marvellous. All we have to do is stay the course."

Ten minutes of silence passed before he muttered, "They wouldn't have sent him away if he had just waited a bit longer. Just another year was all."

London focused on the cold, damp, driving wind. What the sickly man beside him said wasn't enough.

—❦⊚—

After crossing a thin part of the St. Lawrence River, the sleighs set up camp across from the island of Montreal. Thomas directed London to prepare steeds for the male heads of households. Philemon told him earlier that they intended to inform the authorities that he had a deed that allowed them to settle. In turn, each of them would offer to swear allegiance to God and country.

London led a horse toward Thomas Wright.

"Is that for me?"

"Yours is over there," London said as he pointed to a line of saddled horses. "Whose boots were these?"

Thomas frowned. "My father gave us new boots for the war. I remember waiting in line and being real hungry. Philemon had his on, and mine was in his pack. Someone gave us some bread out of his pocket, and Philemon gave the boots to him because he didn't have anything on his feet. I didn't know until after we joined up that they were mine. I lit into him and never let him forget it. When you're going to battle, the one thing you need is a good, solid pair of boots. I heard that he eventually gave them to you." Laughing, he said, "That's so just like him. Father wasn't so forgiving. When he originally found out that he had given them away, Father forced my brother to go get them back."

"Just after he returned from the war?"

Thomas nodded and stared at the horses. "There were lots of arguments. I think it was his way of trying to toughen him up. Both of them were obstinate."

Looking at London's horse, he asked, "Where are you taking that?"

"I'm told that the heads of households are going into town. Philemon said that I should be there as well. They want us to swear allegiance, isn't that right?"

"Well, I didn't believe that's really necessary."

"My son tells me that you took my wife's necklace. It has been in our family for a very long time."

"I was told that it belonged to someone else. How could your people have gotten something like that, honestly?"

"It belonged to my father, and he came by it honestly."

"I doubt that the authorities in this country will believe you."

"I take it that you've decided to keep it."

Thomas remained silent.

"Philemon has promised farmland to all the heads of households, with real signed legal documents. He told me that I could if I wanted, and I do. I'm a freeman, and I'm told that this country recognizes freemen."

"I understand your point of view, but your Jane is not here."

"Ask my children. She is as alive as the forests and any of the creatures around us. She'll always be with us, even when she's not. Settlers would appreciate it if they knew that the people they were dealing with kept their promises. And like you said, it would be good for the authorities to know that the people moving in are good and faithful Christian folk. That's what it takes to get them to recognize your deed. Isn't that right?"

Thomas, without saying a word, mounted his horse. He waved to Samuel Choate and the rest of the men to follow. Ahead of London, John Allen asked, "But doesn't the businessman's club have rules?"

Philemon coughed and then said, "New land, a new time. I've even seen half-breeds there. We'll deal with it."

Samuel Choate, who rode alongside Philemon, said, "And I want to get me a good map. If Philemon's not being led by an ox, you can be sure he's lost." Everyone but Philemon laughed.

The Promised Land

September had not ended. Thanksgiving had not yet come, but flames of the maple's colours shone amongst the towering white pines throughout a countryside shaped by winding waters and tectonic forces. These hosts were preparing to permit themselves to be laid bare to feed and protect new growth and small earthbound creatures.

Philemon Wright, who stood with a gun next to London, was well aware that a killer cold was coming. He took a shot at a pheasant and missed again. They were hunting on slopes overlooking log cabins that were built near the water. London gave him another preloaded rifle. Philemon gave it back and asked him to take a shot.

London was caught off guard. *It's his brother,* he thought. *He would have asked Thomas.*

London saw another pheasant but shot high. "Clearly I'm not made out for this, but thanks for letting me try," he said. He reloaded it and gave it back to Philemon.

"London, you have provided loyal and faithful service to my father and my brother for a long time now. I don't see any reason for there to be a change. Continue as you have. I'll have my men build a small cabin for your family."

"Missa Wright, are you saying that house will be mine or for me to use?"

"Well, London, if you decide to move, what would you need a house for?"

"Missa Wright, what kind of cash money will I get?"

"Cash money? Well, we have always given you what you need. Isn't that right, London?"

"Missa Thomas paid me some cash money, and I saved to buy things."

"Well, I'm sure we can work things out. We have ideas for big things coming. You've managed farming work at the Woburn house and have admirable penmanship. We run a big operation. There's a discussion of new and interesting possibilities. We'll see London. I just thought you would appreciate my thoughts on this. Maybe we should focus on bringing back something bigger for dinner."

"Missa Wright, I've been thinking. This is a free place like Massachusetts was for coloureds. I've been thinking about visiting Montreal. There are no coloureds here, and my children would like to meet some of their own kind."

"Well, it's my understanding that slavery here is legal, just not enforceable. London, why don't we talk about that when they're older? Your Annie is only eight years old. Aren't you putting the cart before the horse?"

"Nine," corrected London.

"Now, let's not scare away the birds." Philemon walked on.

"So, Missa Wright, you wouldn't have a problem if we moved to Montreal?"

Philemon stopped. "London, I have a copy of a warrant for the arrest of an Oxford who stole some shoes from my brother."

"Missa Wright, you know that piece of paper was written for my brother and not for me. Your father sent a letter to ours to say it wasn't true. I know because I've read it."

"I'm sure that, in time, someone might do some research on the matter, but if I tell someone there was a theft and I showed a legal document that someone should be returned, it would take a long time to sort it all out. Trust me, London, it is better to be on my good side than have me set my heels in."

The men didn't talk anymore. They just followed a deer trail. The wind was strong, but the tracks were fresh.

Philemon took a shot at a flying goose and missed. He noticed that London wasn't following him. He was looking at the rough water in the Gatineau River.

"I can give you a lot on the other side, next to Thomas's. It will be all yours. With that axe, you and Abner can build a place of your own."

"And how's I going to get there?"

"A raft. Yes, make yourself a raft. There's lots of rivers. It will be good to have. Knowing how to help folks get across, that's a really good thing, don't you think?"

"If I cut lumber on my property, we could sell it, couldn't we? And there be a lot of cash money, wouldn't there?"

"Making yourself a solid raft is a start, isn't it?"

London knew that Philemon didn't own the land and that he was still trying to get the ownership authorized. When the time was right, he knew he had to get something in writing. Looking back at the Grand River below, London took a shot at a running rabbit and narrowly missed. He watched a strange, lone, black bird with a bulging stomach flap earnestly trying to climb higher. It arced east. *He's lost and alone, isn't he? Surely eats well, though,* he thought.

As Philemon took a shot at another bird, London watched another rabbit race away. Maybe I should suggest laying out some traps, he thought.

When London heard another wolf howl, he muttered. "Jane, I know you're listening. I met an Injun named Askuwheteau. Someday, I'll get him to teach me to hunt." He licked his lips. "And won't that be something?"

—❦—

The hunting expedition was just an excuse to bide time for the arrival of Philemon's brother. From the hill, they watched the canoes approach as they walked back to the Wright cottage. Philemon was returned reluctantly with the few rabbits and pheasants.

After leaving the game at the house, they went to the water's edge to stand next to Kerry Williams, Bill Moorwood, and another woodsman. The contractors had just finished dumping loads of cut hardwood planks next to a sawhorse and were watching Askuwheteau, who was a local Anishinaabe, paddle his canoe ashore. He stepped out into the water. Two Frenchmen, Michael and Francois, who were in the other canoe, paddled alongside.

Askuwheteau's long black braids dangled in front, over his deerskin pullover shirt. The long buckskin leggings were covered by his calf-length boots. A waist belt supported a small pouch and a breech cloth.

The men on shore helped to haul the canoes across the grass. In Askuwheteau's canoe lay Philemon's dead brother.

It had barely been a year and a half, and the head of their community died at the young age of forty-two. Thomas had gone on a scouting trip upriver. Askuwheteau had found the body and brought it back. It was pale, dried out, and emaciated.

Since the frost was going to set in soon, they arranged to bury him on his property as soon as a coffin could be made. Since a site for a church or a graveyard hadn't yet been agreed on, it was decided to put him in a temporary grave at least until spring before they considered moving him somewhere else.

"Monsieur Wright, the body is quite rancid, and Askuwheteau wants his canoe back," Michael said. "C'est une mauvaise idée."

Thomas's corpse was wrapped in blankets.

"Bill?" Philemon asked.

"Two days. Can't just throw him in a hole."

Philemon didn't respond.

"How about another blanket, or a goat, or a nice pot?" asked London.

Askuwheteau showed two fingers.

"Boys, you heard them. Hurry it up. We can't afford to give everything away, and we definitely need those canoes to get him across."

Kerry pulled London aside, away from the others, and asked, "So what killed him?"

"What do you think?"

"Hydrophobia? Don't let anyone touch him," said Bill Moorwood.

London walked Kerry away from the others. "From what Askuwheteau told us, it's like what Matthew did. I saw Thomas leave with the stone around his neck, and it wasn't there when he came back. Wekatesk—she's what got him killed."

"What in heaven's name are you talking about?" Kerry asked.

"Jack Wizak got the stone and made a deal with at least one of them to find what he was looking for. One of them got free and killed Thomas."

Philemon stepped over to where the two men were talking. "What are you two saying?" he asked.

"We shouldn't move Thomas's corpse around," London said. "Sounds like he had what you had. Are you feeling all right?"

"Don't be silly. It was just a stupid cough," Philemon said. "Are you saying I'm going to die? Don't be ridiculous. Besides, what I had was nothing. Others had it, and it went away. Now keep that nonsense to yourself. I won't have you disturbing the women and the hired help."

Philemon looked London up and down. "Make sure they do it right." He started to turn away but came about again and added, "London, you should consider throwing those boots away and getting yourself a new pair."

—⊚—

A blanket was wrapped around the corpse. The men hauled it into the finished coffin. After the box was nailed shut and the coffin was loaded into Askuwheteau's canoe.

Yes, siree, it's a time of change, thought London. He looked forward to walking across what was going to be his. *To touch the soil, dream of what was going to be planted, and imagine what could be given to his children and theirs.* He was so full of what he was going to do and what he could do.

"Les filles?" Francois, the Frenchman, asked London, as his finger drew from his girls to the canoe.

"Where's Abner?" London asked.

"Someone's got to dig out the stumps," Philemon said. "The land is not going to clear itself, is it? And if we don't get the harvest in, we'll starve. We all have to make sacrifices, don't we?"

"But maybe—" London said.

"It wasn't my choice. It was his. He and Joshua are working with the woodcutters. He's wanted to do that since he got here. Maybe you just don't listen. London, that's my brother lying there, and we're not going to leave him out in the sun. Now get on with it, please. When you get him to his property, you'll see flags that we laid out. That's where we want you to dig the grave. Best you head out real quick. If you give the women any more time, they'll follow you, and trust me, you'll never get it done. They'll keep changing their minds."

London gave a reluctant nod. "Annie, Rachael," he said. "Do you want to see where we're going to live? It's going to be ours."

"But we can't swim," Annie said.

"There'll be plenty of time to learn, but for now we'll trust these two strong men to get you there. I'll be right behind. Just hold on tight to the edge and don't stand up."

Francois and Michael, with the children, paddled away from Philemon's property on the Gatineau River toward the Grand River. Askuwheteau and London, with Thomas's coffin, followed behind. London stopped paddling near the mouth of the river. He focused on the water's blackness. *No signs of life here nor at the shores,* he thought. He palmed some more water and lifted his head back to feel the taste on his tongue, the light wind on his face, and the afternoon sun. Puffy clouds were shifting across the blue.

They're leaving us, he remembered.

The canoe was being dragged by the Gatineau's steady-moving current. Within the ripples, he thought he heard, *Where did she go?*

Again, he palmed some more water, lifted his head back to feel it on his tongue.

Again, he thought he heard a sound saying, *The shadow creatures—they came from the dark water.* The unreal memory was followed by the calls of crows.

Askuwheteau asked him something.

London turned around and saw that he was being ordered to paddle. He paddled to catch up, but as they entered the Grand River, he slowed to admire the long rapids and waterfalls that spilled into the river a couple of miles to their right. Again, he thought he heard something, and the water and the wind became unusually calm.

Askuwheteau tapped the canoe with his paddle, and London picked up the pace again. The others had veered left and were heading for shore.

London heard something. He looked back and saw only Askuwheteau's frown. When he looked ahead, he watched a dark black hand, from the water, reach for the gunnel of the canoe and pull hard.

"Les filles."

"No!" he screamed.

In the next year, Abner followed Joshua and worked with the woodcutters. They learned how to clear land and build with timber. Some of the men stayed, and in the years that followed, the boys continued to work their way north, clearing bush up the Gatineau. When those shores were cleared, the pair moved with the work upriver, west along the Grand.

London cleared lumber with other crews who cleared timber east along the Grand. To get to his property, he needed a raft. Once it was built, he used it for hauling lumber. To make cash money, he started hauling as far as a French place called Quebec City. The scale of the runs became a serious business. Huge rafts supplied cut timber for British ships.

In those days, London and the boys felt like they were going to the ends of the earth. To remain in places that they believed were untamed and wild, they had to travel farther and farther away.

London Oxford was seen walking them trees, felling two-hundred-foot white pines, marking, sorting, and uprooting. He drove full loads by winter sleigh and spring cricks with high water. They moved fiercely. Men and logs spilled forcefully through the froth. Timber sometimes got hung or bobbed back up and sometimes accompanied by the dead. The work was unforgiving and merciless.

London tied cage cribs, sized and ordered timbers, and rode the rafts through turbulent white waters like the mighty Sioux. Any danger, any new thing, he, like his son, was willing to confront so long as he didn't have to stay on the land that was promised to him.

Askuwheteau's hunting training refusals were unrelenting and were kept that way until the man returned in war paint and boasted at having acquired skills from another tribe.

London Oxford was seen and heard over many fires, ranting with a grip on a treasured jug on many haunted nights. Many witnessed his loud, maddening rants about the Wìsakedjàk, the water, fire, and revenge, but not always in that order.

The bird returned to the cove above the falls. For a lifetime of seasons, the two drifted along the Grand. The howls from the shadows of the wolf were incessant. As was their nature, they ignored her background calls and continued to follow the perpetual hunt of an ever-elusive muskellunge.

Afterword

London Oxford was given a large tract of land across the Gatineau River from the first Wright homestead. It was next to Thomas Wright's allotment in Templeton Township. Cash money enabled him to acquire hundreds of acres, dwarfing the size of Wright's hundred-acre homestead in Woburn.

Less than two lifetimes later, my father's people settled in that township. A church was built on London's lot, and that's where my great-grandparents Thomas and Allie Sullivan married.

According to a death record, Jane Ammon, the wife of London Oxford, did not go north. Before the caravan left (i.e. October 27, 1797), she "perished abroad, in a storm." Unfortunately, the two girls were with her and not her husband.

Appendix 1: People, Places, and Names

People

Matantu was known to the Lenape people. They associated their bats, stinging insects, and poisonous plants with him.

Wekatesk (i. e. Northern Lights) was a woman of Wìsakedjàk's kind that **Wìsakedjàk** was searching for.

Wìsakedjàk is pronounced as "wih-sah-kay-jock." Some have erroneously confused him with the nickname of Jack Wizak.

Places

Alburgh is a town in Vermont that was renamed Alburg.

Kìchì Sibi River today is known as the Ottawa River. The English referred to it as the Grand River.

Pasapkedjiwanong is a river "that passes between the rocks." The French referred to it as the Rideau River (i.e. the curtain).

Te Nagàdino Sìbi means "the river that stops (One's Journey)." The French referred to it as the Gatineau River.

Wright's settlement became the city of Hull which was later renamed to Gatineau. It is across the river from Ottawa—the capital of Canada, which initially was known as Bytown.

Names

Anishinaabe is a singular form referring to an Algonquin speaker.

Anishinaabeg is a plural form referring to Algonquin speakers.

Anishinaabemowin is the language of the Anishinaabe.

Haudenosaunee means "people of the longhouse". Others have referred to them as the Six Nations Confederacy and the Iroquois. The name Iroqu (Irinakhoiw) however was originally an insult label for them by the Algonquin meaning "rattlesnakes." The French referred to the name as Iroquois by adding an "-ois" suffix.

Kanien'kehá:ka is the name the Mohawk people identified themselves. They were known as the "People of the Flint Place". They were the most easterly tribe of the Haudenosaunee (Iroquois) Confederacy. They were known as the "Keepers of the Eastern Door." An Algonquian-speaking tribe (Mohicans) referred to them as Maw Unk Lin (Bear Place People). The Dutch transliterated this to "Mohawk."

Terms

Gunnel is a strip along the top of the sides of a canoe.

Hydrophobia which means "fear of water." It is an old term for rabies.

Appendix 2: Settler Families and Immediate Relations

Characters & Ages in 1800

London Oxford   32
Abner Oxford   12
Annie Oxford   7
Rachael Oxford   5

Thomas Jr Wright 41
Mary Sprague Wright 41
Tom   16
John   14
Polly   12
Elizabeth   7
Lucy   5
Not directly referenced: Abigail (3), Benjamin (2)

Philemon Wright 40
Abigail Wyman   Wright 40
Phil   17
Bearie (Tiberius) 12
Maryanne (Mary) 9
Ruggles (Rug)   7
Christopher   2
Abigail (Jr2)   4

Lavina Wyman Allen   30 (Abigail Wyman Wright's sister)
John Allen   27

Margaret Wyman Choate 34 (Abigail Wright's sister)
Samuel Choate   30

Joshua   Wyman Jr.   12
Joshua   Wyman Sr.   32 (Joshua's father)

Lydia Wyman Brooks   30 (Abigail Wright's sister) Died 1800
Caleb Brooks   24

Elizabeth Wright Symmes 43 (The oldest Wright's sibling)
Capt. John Symmes   45

Eleanor Wright   (Thomas Jr. Wright's sister); Born 1762

Characters referenced before 1800

Coffey Oxford   (London's father)   N/A
Nelle Donnahue   (London's mother)   N/A
Zach (i.e. Zeruiah [sic]) (London's brother), 8 yrs. older
Patte   (London's sister),   7 yrs. older

Thomas Wright Sr. (Wright Patriarch); Died 1795; 86 yrs
Patience Richardson (First Wife); Died 1748
Sarah Wright, (Daughter), <Born> 1748; Died N/A

Elizabeth Chandler (Second Wife); Born 1721; Died N/A
Abigail Wright, (Philemon's daughter); Died 1796; 6 yrs

Jane Ammon Oxford, (London's Wife); Died 1797; 27 yrs

Appendix 3: Site Map

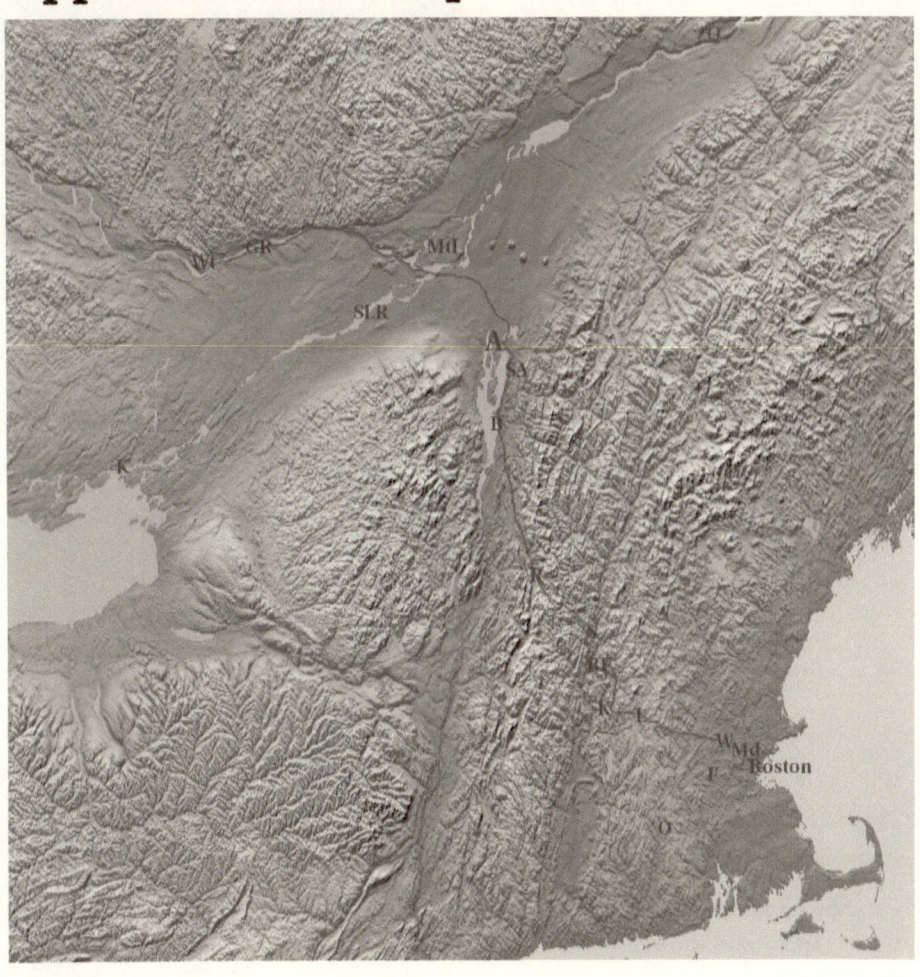

Locations:

O: Oxford, Mass.

F: Framingham, Mass.

B: Boston, Mass.

Md: Madison, Mass.

W: Woburn, Mass.

L: Lunenburg, Mass.

K: Keene, NH.

BF: Belle Falls, NH.

S: Springfield, NH.

R: Rutland, Vt.

B: Burlington, Vt.

SA: St Albans, Vt.

A: Auburgh, Vt.

Mtl: Montreal

Wt: Wright's town

GR: Grand River

SLR: St. Lawrence River

K: Kingston

Q: Quebec

News And Behind the Scenes Look at Stories:
https://www.lawrenceobrien.ca//newsletter/

Thank you for you curiosity and perseverance.

And please leave a review. I would appreciate to see what you have taken away from your read of **SWALLOWING THE MUSKELLUNGE.**